"Look how it changes shape, Fessran," she said.

"Don't play with it," Fessran snarled, her ears back. "Kill it."

Ratha raised one paw, dipped it into the ash, stared at the fire curling around the branch. "No." She put the paw down.

"Ratha, kill it!" Thakur cried. Fessran showed her teeth and crept toward the fire. Ratha blocked her. She tried to push past, but Ratha shoved her back. Fessran skidded in the ash and fell on her side. Ratha stood between her and the Red Tongue, her hackles up, her tail fluffed. Two pairs of slitted eyes met.

"This is my creature."

"The Red Tongue is no one's creature. Kill it." Fessran scrambled in the ash, pulling her paws underneath her. Ratha tensed, feeling her eyes burn. "I will kill it or I will let it live, but it is my creature."

CLARE BELL, a native of Britain, has worked in television production, welding, and design. A manufacturing test engineer for a major computer company, she now lives in Palo Alto, California. Ms. Bell is also the author of *Clan Ground*, which is available in a Dell Laurel-Leaf edition.

Ratha's
Creature

C L A R E　　B E L L

LAUREL-LEAF BOOKS bring together under a single imprint outstanding works of fiction and nonfiction particularly suitable for young adult readers, both in and out of the classroom. Charles F. Reasoner, Professor Emeritus of Children's Literature and Reading, New York University, is consultant to this series.

Published by
Dell Publishing Co., Inc.
1 Dag Hammarskjold Plaza
New York, New York 10017

Laurel-Leaf Library ® TM 766734, Dell Publishing Co., Inc.

ISBN: 0-440-97298-1

RL: 6.6

Reprinted by arrangement with Atheneum Publishers, a division of Macmillan Publishing Company

Printed in the United States of America

November 1987

10 9 8 7 6 5 4 3 2 1

WFH

Ratha's Creature

CHAPTER 1

RATHA LEAPED over a fern thicket and dug her paws into the spongy ground as she dodged sharp horns. One prong sifted through her fur and she skittered away from the beast. She turned and stood her ground with hunched shoulders and twitching tail. Her quarry advanced. A two-pronged horn on the stag's nose joined the crown of points on the head and it lowered the entire array, charging at Ratha. She launched herself at the deer, both front paws spread. She landed on her rear paws and bounced sideways as the multi-horn pivoted heavily, trying to catch her on its spikes and pin her to the ground.

Each time the horns came near her, Ratha jumped sideways, forcing the stag to turn in a tight circle, unable to build up any speed or momentum. After several such circles, the beast's knees were trembling and Ratha smelled the sweat that was darkening the coarse, gray-tipped coat. At last the animal stopped and lifted its head. Wary brown eyes studied Ratha from behind the forked nose horn as she planted all four feet in the mossy soil beneath the trees, still but tensed, ready to spring if the deer lunged again.

The beast danced uneasily on its slender legs, sweating

and snorting, turning one eye and then the other on Ratha. She knew that it had no experience with those of the clan. Most meat-eaters the three-horn encountered would tuck their tails between their legs when that fierce spiked crown turned their way. The fanged ones would run, not bounce around in circles. The stag's eyes were angry and the beast lowered its crown and pawed the soil, but the rage in its eyes was dulled by fear.

Ratha fixed her eyes on those of the deer. Slowly, deliberately, she walked toward it. Still tossing its head, the stag backed away from her. Ratha felt the intensity of her stare as she watched the beast retreat, and a feeling of triumph began to grow as she placed one paw after another on the multi-horn's reversed tracks and smelled the creature's bewilderment. She moved from one side to the other, blocking any attempts it might make to get past her. At last, she told herself, she had mastered the skill. At last the weeks of practice would yield results. Thakur's whiskers would bristle with pride.

A dragonfly buzzed across Ratha's nose, its iridescence stealing her attention from her quarry. The stag bellowed. Ratha jerked her head around, but she had barely time to realize she had lost control before the beast was on top of her, striking out with sharp hooves and goring the dirt with its horns.

Ratha fled, tucking her tail and squalling. The stag chased her and they ran a frantic race through the trees. Ratha glanced back as her paws slipped and skidded on pine needles and saw the points just behind her tail.

"Up a tree, yearling!" a voice yowled on her left, and with one bound, Ratha was halfway up a young pine, beyond reach of the tossing horns. She climbed higher, showering her opponent with bark and stinging wood ants. "Thakur!" she wailed.

A copper-brown head appeared through a clump of curled ferns. Thakur looked up at Ratha and down at the stag. He gathered himself and sprang onto the animal's back. He flung his powerful forelegs around the three-horn's neck and dug his rear claws into its back as it plunged and screamed. As Ratha watched from above, he twisted his head sideways and drove his fangs into the stag's nape behind the head. Ratha saw his jaw muscles bunch in his cheeks and temples as blood streamed down the stag's neck, and she heard the sound of teeth grinding on bone. His jaws strained and closed. The stag toppled over, its neck broken.

Thakur paced around his prey as it kicked and twitched. Then he stopped, his sides still heaving, and looked up at Ratha.

"Are you any better at climbing down from trees than you are at stalking three-horns?"

Ratha felt her hackles rising. "*Yarrr!* That buzz-fly flew in front of my nose! Didn't you see?" She turned herself around and started to back down the tree.

"The last time, you were startled by a mud-croaker. If you can't keep your mind on what you are doing, yearling, go back to Fessran and her dapplebacks."

The cub dropped the rest of the way and landed beside him. She turned her head and nosed along her back. That prong had come close to her skin.

"Never mind a few tufts of fur," Thakur said crossly.

"I don't mind losing cub fur." Ratha smoothed her coat, now turning fawn but still faintly spotted. She lifted her head and stared defiantly at Thakur. "I was close, wasn't I? If I hadn't looked away, he would have been on his way to the herd."

"Yes, you were close," Thakur admitted. "Your stare is good; I see you have worked on it. Now you must learn to let nothing distract you. Once you have the animal's eye, don't lose it. Make them fear you and make that fear paralyze them until they cannot disobey you." He looked at the fallen stag, lying still in a patch of sunlight. His whiskers twitched with what Ratha knew was annoyance. "I didn't want to kill that one. He would have given the does many strong young."

"Why did you kill him? The clan has meat."

"It wasn't for meat." Thakur stared at Ratha and she noticed a slight acrid tang in his smell, telling her he was irritated. "Nor was it to spare you. I could have chased him to the herd. He broke your stare, Ratha. He learned that he did not need to fear you and that you feared him. Beasts that know that kill herders."

"Why must we have three-horns in the herd?" Ratha grumbled. "They're hard to manage. They fight among themselves and bully the other animals."

"They are larger and yield more meat. They have more young. And," Thakur added, "they are harder for the raiders to kill and drag away."

Ratha trotted over and sniffed the stag, filling her nose with its musky aroma. Her belly growled. She felt a firm paw pushing her away. "No, yearling. Meoran will be displeased enough that I killed the beast. He will be further angered if any fangs touch it before his."

Ratha helped Thakur drag the carcass out of the sun and brushed away the flies. Her belly rumbled again. Thakur heard it and grinned at her. "Patience, yearling. You'll eat tonight."

"If Meoran and the others leave anything but hide and bones," Ratha complained. "There is never enough meat at the clan kill, and I have to wait until those even younger than I have filled their bellies."

"How do you know they are younger?" Thakur said as Ratha took one last hungry look at the kill. "Cherfan's spots are no darker than yours."

"*Arr.* Cherfan ate before I did last night and I know his litter came after mine, Thakur Torn-Claw. I am older, yet he eats first."

Thakur soothed her. "Your spots are just taking a long time to fade. You are too impatient, yearling. Two seasons ago, I ate last and often went hungry. It was hard for me then and I know it is hard for you now, but it will change."

Ratha twitched one ear. "Shall I try the three-horn again? Maybe a doe would be easier than a stag."

Thakur squinted up through the trees. "The sun is starting to fall. By the time we find one, Yaran will be looking for you."

Her whiskers went back. "*Arr,* the old roarer. Hasn't he enough cubs to look after that he must worry about me?" She snorted, thinking about her lair-father. Yaran had a harsh, gravelly voice and no inhibitions about speaking his mind. She knew that had his brother Meoran not been the firstborn, Yaran would have been clan leader and, she admitted, perhaps a better one than Meoran. He was kind to her in his rough way, but he would stand no nonsense from cubs.

"We have time left for some practice, Ratha," Thakur said, regaining her attention. "I noticed that your spring was too high and that midair twist needs improving."

He started her practicing dodges, turns and springs. After watching and commenting on her technique, he assumed the part of a wayward herdbeast while Ratha used her training to capture him and force him to the herd.

As Thakur watched the lithe muscled form darting and turning in front of him, he remembered how hard he had argued with her lair-father about training her in the art of herding.

"She is quick, she is strong, she can outsmart most of the cubs born before her," he'd told Yaran as the two stood together in almost the same place as he was now, watching Yaran's small daughter chase a young dappleback. "Look how she runs that little animal and has no fear of it. Not to train her, Yaran, would be a waste and the clan can't waste ability like hers."

"True, three-year-old," Yaran rumbled, swishing his gray tail. "She is strong and she is strong of mind. It is already difficult to make her obey, and I fear that training her as you suggest would make her less tractable than she is now. And less easy for me to find her a mate."

Thakur remembered arguing until his tongue was tired and then going to old Baire, who was then leader, taking Ratha along. Baire saw the cub's talent and overruled Yaran. Thakur was allowed to teach her his skill. He and Yaran exchanged few words these days, but that loss was small in comparison to Ratha's gain.

The cub sprinted back and forth in the grass, the afternoon sun turning her fawn coat to gold. Soon her spots would be gone and she would no longer be a cub. Her spirit challenged him and sometimes frustrated him, but he never tried to break it as he knew Yaran had. And, although he would scarcely admit it to himself, in the back of his mind was the hope that when she grew old enough for a mate, she might take him, even though his family and age placed him low in comparison to the clan status of other males Yaran might choose for her.

Thakur raised his chin and scratched at a flea behind his ear. "Despite what I say sometimes, yearling, I have no regrets about choosing you to train. You are good, Ratha, in spite of your mistakes. When I have finished training you, you will be the best herder in the clan." He paused. "I don't often praise you, yearling. Perhaps I should." He routed the flea and lay down again. "Here is something that will please you more than words. I want you to stand guard with me and the other herders tonight."

Ratha sat up, her whiskers quivering. "Can I? Will Meoran let me? He needs the best herders of the clan."

"I told him that you are good enough. Meoran may think little of me in other ways, but when I speak about herding, he listens. Do you want to come?"

Ratha swallowed. "Will there be fighting?"

"If there is, you will keep out of it. Do you want to come with me tonight?"

"Yes!"

"Good." Thakur got up and stretched, spreading his pads against the ground. "Help me drag this kill to the dens and I will see that you get enough to eat this evening. The clan cannot let those who guard the herds against the Un-Named grow weak from hunger."

"Will the raid come tonight?" Ratha asked, pacing alongside her teacher.

"Meoran thinks it will. He has scouts watching the Un-Named."

"I've seen them a few times. They hide behind trees or crouch in the shadows. They watch us just as we watch them." Ratha trotted to match Thakur's longer stride. "I've often wondered who they are and why they are without names."

"Perhaps you will learn tonight, yearling," he answered.

They reached the stag's carcass. Thakur pushed one stiff foreleg aside and seized the neck while Ratha grabbed the rear leg by the hock. Together they lifted the kill and carried it away through the trees.

CHAPTER 2

RATHA FOLLOWED the white spot bobbing in the darkness ahead of her. She smelled resin, heard needles rustle and ducked beneath a branch that overhung the trail. She had seen the moon through the trees as she left her den, but here the dense forest hid its light. The white spot grew smaller and Thakur's footsteps fainter. She hurried to catch up. She didn't need to follow Thakur's tail tip; she could guide herself well enough at night even though she was used to living by day. But the white spot drew her on and she followed without thinking, as she had followed the white of her mother's tail through the tall grass of the meadow. Ratha remembered the one time she had dared to disobey. Panic had tightened her belly and sent her scampering back to Narir. She was beyond her cubhood now, but the night to her was a very large and awesome creature and the flickering spot ahead promised protection.

She followed, looking about as she ran, and wondered at how her vision changed at night. She had run night trails before, but they were short paths from one den to another, short enough that the thoughts filling her head as her feet trod the path never let her notice what she was seeing. Now the trail was longer and she was beginning to shed her cub-thoughts with her spotted fur. Now, as if it knew she was using her mind with her eyes, night crept out of its murky den and showed itself to her. The crystal light of the moon cut through the trees and gave every knobbled root, scaled patch of bark or curled fern a harsh presence, a clarity that was too sharp. She looked at night-lit trees and stones and felt she could cut her paw pads on their edges.

Ratha smelled mossy stone and damp fur. She heard Thakur's pads slap on mud as he paced the streambank. He hunched himself, a compact shadow against the moon-lit stream, and leaped across. On the other side she saw him wave his tail.

"Cross, yearling," he said. "You have jumped it before."

She crouched on a flat stone at the water's edge, trying to judge the distance to the other shore. The beating in her throat made her thirsty and she lowered her muzzle to drink. In the faint light she saw her own face. Her eyes, green in daylight, were now swallowed up in black. She had seen her own reflection many times before and, when young, had drenched herself trying to swat it. Ratha looked at her night face, the broad nose, small fangs and strange expanded eyes. She turned away from it and jumped over the stream.

Thakur's tail was flicking back and forth and he smelled uneasy. There was another smell in his scent, one Ratha didn't know. She trotted toward him, shaking the mud from her paws.

"Hurry, yearling. The others have gone ahead and I don't want them to wait for us." His eyes reflected moonlight as he turned once more to the trail.

He set a faster pace than before. Ratha had to gallop to keep up and she felt the weight of her dinner drag at her belly as she ran. She lifted her head, gulping the coolness of the night air to soothe the pulsing in her throat. Smells of the meadow were mixed with the smells of the forest, telling her they would soon be there. The forest began to open. A few stars and then the half-disk of the moon appeared through the canopy.

A branch cracked. The sound was close and sharp, making Ratha start. Thakur, ahead, glanced back but didn't slow down. The trail ran up a small rise and veered around at the crest. Here the canopy opened and the moon lit the trail. The light silvered Thakur's coat as he galloped around the curve toward the hollow beyond. Ratha panted up the grade after him, wishing her legs were longer and she had eaten less. As she approached the top, there was a dry scratchy sound. Bark fell from a tree trunk. She looked toward a gnarled oak near the top of the rise. One of its large lower branches paralleled the trail for some distance, making it a short alternate route. As Thakur disappeared over the crest of the little hill, a form dropped from the oak's branches and ran along the lower limb. For an instant the stranger paused, crouched, one forepaw lifted, staring back at Ratha. Then he was gone.

She leaped off the trail, cutting through the brush. Tucking her tail between her legs, she fled down into the hollow.

Thakur was nowhere to be seen and Ratha stopped, when she regained the trail, her heart pounding. "Ssss, yearling," came a voice close by. "Here." Thakur lifted his head from a clump of ferns. "Has Narir taught you no better trail-running than that? I thought a shambleclaw was coming through the bushes."

"I saw him, Thakur," Ratha interrupted, her whiskers quivering with excitement.

"What did you see?"

"The Un-Named One. He was there on the branch after you passed. He looked back at me."

"*Yarrr.* The Un-Named never allow themselves to be seen. You saw some clan litterling who imagines himself to be a night hunter." Thakur snorted.

Ratha's jaw dropped in dismay, then her ears flattened. "No. I saw him. He was there on the branch as if he wanted me to see him. And I have seen him before."

"When?" Thakur asked.

"Many clan kills ago. I had a fight with Cherfan and he chased me into a thicket at the end of the meadow. He was in there asleep and I ran right over him. He snarled at me."

Thakur left the ferns and came to her. His steps were quick, his eyes sudden and intense. Ratha smelled the same odor about him she had noticed before.

"Did you tell anyone else?"

"Only Cherfan," Ratha said hesitantly, "and he never listens to me."

"Why didn't you tell me?" His voice had a harshness to it Ratha seldom heard, even when he was scolding her during training.

"I didn't know enough then. Why, Thakur? Are you afraid of the Un-Named One?"

"No."

Ratha turned toward the trail again, but he nudged her and she stopped.

"Wait, Ratha. The Un-Named One . . . did he say anything to you?"

She blinked. "You mean, did he . . . speak?"

The strange smell about Thakur was stronger and suddenly frightening. She sensed he wanted something that he also feared and that he wanted it very much. Ratha felt her tail creeping between her legs and her hackles rise.

"Yes, cub. Did he use words?"

She felt her eyes grow wide as she crouched and he stood over her. Was it the night's touch that made him seem almost menacing?

"Ratha."

She backed away from him. A hanging frond touched her back and she jumped. She whined miserably. "Thakur, I don't understand. Everyone knows that the Un-Named Ones don't speak. They can't. They aren't clever enough."

Thakur drew back his whiskers and Ratha heard him snarl to himself, "Yes, Meoran. You believe the clanless ones are witless as well. Teach it to the cubs and see how the clan fares."

"Thakur, the Un-Named can't speak any more than a herdbeast can," Ratha said hunching her shoulders stubbornly.

He sighed. His voice grew calm, changing him back into her teacher again. He paced beside her, licking her behind the ears. "I'm sorry, small one. I did not mean to frighten you. Perhaps I should take you back to Narir's den." He lifted his head. "This night is strange. I smell things that make me uneasy. This night is not for a cub."

Ratha sat up and groomed some of the dried leaves out of her fur. Then they went on.

At first, Ratha could think only of the stranger whose eyes had glowed at her from the old oak. Was he one of the Un-Named? And why had Thakur asked her such strange things? There were no answers to her questions. Not yet.

Things moved abruptly at night, making Ratha turn her head and flatten her ears. She was much more aware of motion at night than during the day. Movement she seldom noticed in daylight, such as a grass blade swaying or a leaf falling, brought her head around and made her whiskers bristle. It was not fear, although night was fearsome. The pulse in her throat was excitement. She felt alive this night. All her senses were extended and her skin tingled as if the sensitive whiskers on her face were growing all over her body.

There was a rustle in the bushes ahead on the trail. Thakur skidded to a stop and Ratha nearly ran into him. Over his back, she could see a dark form fleet away.

"There he is again," she whispered. "I did see him!"

"*Arr!* Fool, to show yourself!" Thakur hissed into the darkness.

"He is a bad hunter, Thakur," Ratha said. "He is noisy, like me. He is stupid," she added, wagging her tail arrogantly. "All of the Un-Named are stupid and I am not afraid of any of them. *Ptahh.*" She spat.

"Hurry then, yearling," Thakur said dryly. "We will need your courage in the meadow tonight."

He took up the trail again and she followed.

Teeth ground together, a drawn-out groaning sound. The herdbeast belched and made wet mushy noises as it began chewing its cud. Ratha crept near, shaking her paws every few steps. The air was moist and the grass dewy. A light mist made the moonlight hazy and muffled the crickets' song. The animal shifted on its belly. It snuffled and grunted as it watched her with small suspicious eyes set forward in a long block-shaped skull. It flicked large ears, like those of a three-horn, and swallowed the food it was chewing.

Ratha drew her whiskers back. The idea of eating grass disgusted her and the idea of bringing it up again and rechewing it was even worse. Meat was much better, she thought. It was chewed once and when it went down, it stayed down, unless it had been eaten too fast.

The animal clamped its jaws together and eyed the cub ill-temperedly. Although it lacked horns, the creature used its big head like a battering ram. The barrel body and short legs made it look vulnerable and clumsy. Several of the herders had earned broken ribs by assuming it was.

The animal belched again. Ratha wrinkled her nose and padded away.

She glanced up and down the meadow at other herders

who stood in a ring around the flock, their faces to the forest. She yawned and stretched until her tail quivered and saw an answering gape from another shadow in the mist. Nothing was going to happen tonight, she thought. The fright on the trail was all the excitement she was going to get. And perhaps Thakur was right and her Un-Named apparition was just a clan-cub.

She ambled past a fern thicket and heard a pair of dapplebacks snorting and pushing at each other in the dark. Dapplebacks usually climbed on top of each other in the spring season, but these two were starting early. Ratha smelled the rich lure-scent of the mare, the sweat and rut of the little stallion. The odor repelled her and fascinated her, making her think of the scents on trees that clan males had sprayed.

The odor also made her think of Thakur and the way he had licked her behind the ears on the trail. She listened to the dapplebacks bumping together and the little stallion's rhythmic grunts, her tail twitching. These thoughts were new, not cub-thoughts at all, and she approached them as warily in her mind as she had approached the belching herdbeast.

Her feet were getting damp from standing in one place. She shook them. The mist was growing thicker. She decided to find Thakur.

His scent was mixed in with herdbeast smells, forest smells and the smells of other herders. Ratha separated it from all the others and followed it to him. He was crouched on top of the sunning stone, his tail curled across his feet, speaking to Fessran who stood nearby.

Ratha trotted quickly toward them and skidded to a

stop, feeling the wet grass pull between her pads. Thakur cocked his head at her. She walked to Fessran and touched noses.

"Clan herder, two of your dapplebacks are hiding in the fern thicket," she said. "I can chase them back to the herd for you."

"No, Ratha. Leave them be. I'll look after them," Fessran answered in her soft voice.

"That little stallion doesn't stop, does he? You'll have enough dappleback colts to feed the clan well."

"*Yarrr.* Thakur, you think only of your belly." Fessran launched a disgusted swipe in his direction and Thakur ducked.

"I am pleased that she has done so well," Fessran said seriously, looking at Ratha.

"Yes, I am also pleased. There are not many of the female cubs who have the ability, but she does and she has worked hard."

Ratha was startled to see Fessran bristle.

"Have you grown as short-whiskered as Meoran?" she snarled. "The female cubs have no lack of ability. Our fleabag of a clan leader won't let me train them! Drani's daughter, Singra, has the same talent as Ratha. But her father forbade it and Meoran said he would chew my ears if I taught my art to any cubs except the ones he selected." Fessran lowered her head and lashed her tail. "And Singra was not among the ones chosen last season or this season. Now it is too late and she grows soft and fat. *Yarrr!*"

"Gently, Fessran," Thakur soothed. "You know how hard I fought for Ratha."

"You only succeeded because Baire still lived. Now Meoran stands as clan leader and no she-cubs train as herders. *Ptahh!* He would mate me to a gray-coat and put one of his whelps in my place. How I hate him, Thakur!"

"*Ssss,* there are other ears in the meadow tonight. Be wary of your words, Fessran."

"Wise Thakur. You always were more cautious than I." Fessran smoothed her fur. "Those two dapplebacks should be finished. I'll run them back to the herd."

"Fessran." She stopped and looked back at Thakur. "I'll do my best for Ratha. You are the one I can't protect. Choose your words with care and you may be safe."

"My temper often chooses my words for me." Fessran's whiskers twitched ruefully and she trotted away.

Thakur sighed and settled himself on the damp stone, fluffing his fur. Ratha lifted a hind foot and scratched herself.

Across the meadow a herdbeast bawled. Thakur sat up. Another animal bellowed. Hooves beat, rushing through the grass. A harsh yowl began. It rose to a shriek and another answered. Ratha jumped up, her fur on end. Thakur leaped off his perch.

"That wasn't a clan voice," he said grimly as Ratha bounded to join him. She saw other herders running; heard wailing calls and snapping branches.

"Yearling, stay here," Thakur said sharply.

A form appeared in the mist and galloped toward them. It was Fessran again.

"Thakur, the raiders have broken in at the end of the meadow. They've already pulled down two deer. Hurry!"

Thakur turned to Ratha. "Watch the dapplebacks, yearling. Keep them together."

"What if the raiders come?"

"They won't." Fessran showed her teeth. "Not this far."

"If anyone attacks my herd, I'll fight." Ratha lashed her tail eagerly.

"You will not." Thakur glared at her. "You will climb the nearest tree and stay there until I call you. The clan can lose a few dapplebacks. Not you."

"*Arrr.* I want to go with you, Thakur."

"This is not cub-tussling, Ratha. I told you that before we left. You are not to fight. Is that understood?"

"Yes-s-s." Ratha sighed.

A herdbeast cried out and then choked as it fell. Muffled yowling came through the ground mist.

"Hurry, Thakur," Fessran hissed and the two sprang up and galloped away, leaving Ratha alone.

She shivered and looked up at the sky. The moon was a hazy smear of white, the stars were gone. She jogged toward the scattered herd of dapplebacks and began circling it, driving the little horses into a tighter bunch. They sensed the danger and were restive, squealing and milling. The little stallion shepherded his flock of mares together and tried to separate them from the other dapplebacks. Ratha drove them all back, nipping at their flanks. Once she had the herd packed together, she kept circling it, staying far enough away not to panic the animals, but close enough to catch any strays.

She stopped, panting, flicking dewdrops off her whiskers. She listened to drumming hooves and shrill cries from the other end of the meadow. A body fell. Another herdbeast down, she thought. She flattened her ears. None of the Un-Named dung-eaters would touch Fessran's dapplebacks, she promised herself. The little horses stood together, their heads raised, their stiff manes quivering. Ratha gained her breath and began circling the herd again. Running kept her from thinking; kept her from being frightened.

On the opposite side of the herd, she caught a glimpse of something moving in the fog. A low, slender form; not a herdbeast. Ratha bared her teeth and dashed around the outside of the flock. She stopped and sniffed. She knew that smell. She nosed the ground. The smell was fading in the dampness, but footprints were there. Her tail began to flick as she peered through the mist in all directions. Where had he gone?

A sudden shrill scream told her. Ratha plunged into the middle of the herd, sending animals scattering in every direction. The killer was there, dragging his thrashing prey through the grass. Ratha opened her jaws in a full-throated roar as she charged at him. The raider jerked his head up, pulling his teeth from the dappleback's neck before Ratha barreled into him, knocking him sprawling.

She scrambled to her feet. She had barely time to see his hate-filled yellow eyes before he leaped at her.

Ratha flipped onto her back and pedaled furiously, raking her adversary's belly with her hind claws. She felt her front paw strike his chin as he snapped at her flailing feet. He missed, but his head continued down and before she could knock him away, his teeth raked the skin over her breastbone. She seized his ear and felt her teeth meet through the skin. As he dragged her along, she twisted her head and tasted oily fur when she scored his cheek with her small fangs. He dived for her belly and got a mouthful of her claws. His rough tongue rasped her pads; his teeth sliced the top of her foot. One claw caught and then tore free.

He seized her ruff. Her head snapped back as he threw

her to one side. Her chest burned and throbbed. Warm blood crawled like fleas through her fur. Ratha writhed and wriggled, but she only felt the teeth sink deeper into her ruff as he lifted her and threw her down again. One heavy paw crushed her ribs and a triumphant growl rumbled above her. The teeth loosened from her ruff and the paw turned her over. When everything stopped spinning, she saw two glittering eyes and fangs bared for a last strike at her throat.

In one motion, Ratha curled over and lunged. Her teeth clashed against his and she felt something break. She grabbed his lower jaw and bit hard until her cheek muscles ached. His saliva wet her whiskers and was sour in her mouth. Blood welled around her teeth, tasting rich and salty as bone marrow.

He screamed and shook her off.

Ratha rolled away, staggered to her feet, spitting blood. He was crouched opposite her. She felt her chest burning and her ribs heaved. If he caught her again, he would kill her. Why hadn't she listened to Thakur?

He pounced. She jumped aside. He whirled, lunged, and again she dodged him, making her shaking legs obey her. An idea began to form in her mind as she sprang away from him again. Thakur had trained her to trick the herdbeasts. The three-horn stag had been as intent on killing her as this Un-Named enemy. The Un-Named, Meoran had said to all the cubs, were no smarter than herdbeasts. Could she use her training to trick this killer?

She watched him carefully as he gathered for another attack. She waited until he was almost on top of her and jumped straight up, coming down behind him. She spun around and watched him shake his head in confusion until he sniffed, looked back over his shoulder, whirled and pounced. Ratha saw him land on empty grass, a tail-length away from her. She grinned at him, her tongue lolling.

The Un-Named One snarled, showing a broken lower fang. Ratha waggled her whiskers at him from a safe distance. He rushed her again and she bounced away. She started to lead him in circles until she had him almost chasing his own tail. She danced around exuberantly, taunting him.

"Dung-eater! Scavenger!" she hissed as he staggered dizzily. He glared at her, his eyes burning. "Cub-catcher! Bone-chewer!" Ratha paused and caught her breath. "Poor stupid bone-chewer," she hissed. "You can't even understand what I'm saying, can you?" The Un-Named One stood panting as Ratha danced around him. "*Yarrr,* you couldn't pounce on your mother's tail," she said, showing her teeth at him. "When Thakur gets back, he'll chew your other ear off, you eater of mud-croakers and chewer of bones!"

"Clan cub, you have lots of words. Say them now before I tear out your throat."

Ratha froze. Her eyes went wide.

"What are you staring at?" the other said.

"Y . . . you." she faltered. "I never thought. . . ."

"That the clanless ones could speak?"

Ratha stared at him, her mouth open.

" 'Poor bone-chewer,' " he mimicked, " 'you can't even understand what I'm saying, can you?' " Before she had time to answer, he leaped at her. She saw his paw coming and ducked, but she wasn't quick enough. He clouted her on the side of the head, knocking her down into the wet grass. By the time she staggered to her feet and her vision cleared, he was dragging his prey toward the forest. She lurched after him, tripped over her paws and fell on her face.

"I don't care if you can speak," she yelled after him, "you are still a scavenger and bone-chewer!" The only answer was the muffled sound of a body being dragged across soggy ground. Ratha tried to get up, but her paws wouldn't stay underneath her. She sprawled miserably on her front. The dapplebacks were scattered all over the meadow, easy prey for other raiders. There was no way she could get them rounded up before Fessran and Thakur got back. She put her chin down on her front paws, wondering if Fessran was going to leave enough of her in one piece for Thakur to punish.

CHAPTER 3

RATHA WOKE shivering. The heavy moisture on her coat was soaking through to her skin. Droplets from her brow whiskers dripped onto her nose. She blinked and shook her head. Fearing that she had dozed away the rest of the night, she peered into the mist for signs of dawn or of Thakur's return. She saw neither. The sky was still murky overhead and the half-moon a faint wash of light above the dark mass of the trees.

Ratha drew her front paws underneath her and pushed herself up. Pain lanced across her chest and into her forelegs. She felt one of the bite-wounds on her neck pull open as she bent her head down to lick her front. She coaxed her hindquarters up and stood, hanging her head. Everything ached, from her teeth to her tail. Neither Thakur nor Fessran had returned.

The wind blew past her ears with a hollow early-morning wail. It had no effect on the mist, which only grew thicker. Ratha could barely see the grass a tail-length ahead. She tried a step and winced as the motion jarred the pain from her jaws into her head, where it sat throbbing behind her eyes. Why hadn't she listened to Thakur and climbed a tree when the raider came?

Ratha felt something wedged in her teeth, behind one upper fang. With her tongue, she worked it loose and felt it. A scrap of skin with slimy fur on one side and bitter-tasting wax on the other. A piece of the raider's ear. She grimaced, spat the ear-scrap out and pawed it aside, feeling a certain grim pleasure.

She tried a few more limping steps, clamping her jaws together to keep her head from ringing. As she walked, the burning knot in her chest loosened, freeing her stride. She spotted something solid in the fog and broke into a shaky trot toward it, hoping it was one of her escaped dapplebacks. She drew her whiskers back in disgust when she realized that she'd been stalking the sunning rock. Well, at least she knew where she was. She hopped on top of the stone and sniffed, knowing that the moist, still air captured and held scent-trails. There. A faint trace, but growing stronger. She inhaled the musky odor of the little horses and climbed down off the sunning rock after them.

Ratha found the dappleback stallion and his mares huddled together, the mist swirling around their legs, their stiff manes and coats flecked with sweat and dew. The faint trace of moonlight made the dapplebacks' eyes phosphorescent as they watched her. The stallion reared and whinnied, showing his short, pointed canine teeth. Carefully she cut in behind the herd and, as the horses retreated from her, guided them to the sunning rock. She circled the flock, driving the dapplebacks together into a tight bunch. Some of the stragglers returned to the herd, but Ratha knew from the individual scents missing from the herd-smell that many more of the animals were lost or slain.

Ratha stopped her nervous pacing. She stood still and listened, but she could only hear the dapplebacks shuffling behind her. The fog muffled all sounds except those close by. She could neither see nor hear anything from the other end of the meadow. Only smells reached her and they made her fur stand on end. The tang of sweat was acrid in her nose; the odor of blood rich and metallic. The strongest smell was fear, and it seemed to spread over the meadow mixed in with the mist, paralyzing everything it touched.

Another shadow, dim, then definite. A familiar smell, then a familiar figure.

"Ratha?" Thakur's voice was cautious.

"Here, Thakur," she answered.

Ratha touched noses with Thakur. He was panting; she felt his warm breath and wet whiskers on her face. "Yearling, this is much worse than I thought it would be. Meoran has badly underestimated the raiders this time."

Ratha felt fear shoot through her like the pain in her chest. "Have we lost the herd?"

"No, by our teeth and claws we've held the raiders back, and if we can hold them until dawn, the fight will be over, for the Un-Named Ones do not attack by day." Thakur paused and sniffed at her ruff. "You bleed, yearling."

"I fought, Thakur. I know you told me to climb a tree, but when he killed one of Fessran's dapplebacks, I ran at him."

Thakur sighed. "I have trained you too well. Your lair-mother is going to chew my ears for bringing you back wounded."

"I chewed his ears, Thakur," Ratha said fiercely. "He got the dappleback, but he left some skin between my teeth."

"*Huh*," Thakur grunted, circling her and nosing her. He licked the bites on her throat, rasping away the fragile clots. He squeezed the wounds with his jaws, forcing the blood to run freely. Ratha squirmed and whimpered.

"Quiet, yearling. Do you want to get an abscess? You will if these heal too quickly. There. I'm finished."

"Thakur," Ratha said quickly. "I know who that raider is."

He blinked and stared at her, an odd stare that made her feel uncomfortable.

"The one on the trail."

"Yearling, that was—" Thakur began.

"No, he wasn't a clan whelp! Would a clan-cub have

killed one of Fessran's dapplebacks? Thakur, I saw him and I fought with him." Ratha paused, watching him carefully. "You asked me, on the trail, if he had spoken to me when I ran over him that time in the thicket, when I was a cub. It frightened me. I saw him again tonight and I think you are going to ask me the same thing again."

"No! I wish you would forget what I said on the trail. I didn't mean to frighten you."

"But I'm not frightened any more. I want to know why! Why did you ask me if the Un-Named One spoke?"

"Ratha, I can't . . ." Thakur began. A muffled swish of grass interrupted him and Fessran limped out of the fog. She sniffed once and glared at Ratha.

"*Ptah!* I fight raiders and she can't even keep a mangy herd of dapplebacks together without losing half of them. Has it been so long since I trained you, cub?"

Ratha opened her mouth to retort, but a glance from Thakur stopped her.

"I'll help you find the rest of them, Fessran, when I've taken Ratha back to Narir," he said soothingly.

"If the Un-Named will let you through," Fessran snarled. "They are thicker in the forest tonight than the fleas on Meoran's belly."

"Can you take care of the horses by yourself until I get back?"

"Yes. Take the cub and go, Thakur. She'll be safer in Narir's den." Fessran limped away, leaving Thakur and Ratha alone.

"I fought raiders too!" Ratha hissed angrily. "Why didn't you let me tell her?"

"There wasn't time. Yearling, we've got to hurry. I don't want you here if the raiders break through."

"Do I have to go back to the den?" Ratha asked, padding shakily alongside him.

"Yearling, haven't you had enough for tonight? You're barely able to stand up and you think you're ready for another scrap with the Un-Named? No, I think I'd better take you back."

She yawned. "All right, Thakur. I am tired."

They had not gone far when several forms emerged out of the mist and jogged toward them. Ratha's heart jumped, then she recognized them as clan herdfolk.

"Thakur Torn-Claw," said the first one.

"Srass of Salarfang Den," Thakur answered. "How is the trail tonight?"

Srass lowered his head and Ratha saw his whiskers twitch. "The Un-Named grow bolder. They attacked another party of herders who were trying to join us. Our people made it through, but two were badly bitten." The herder turned his eyes on Ratha. "I would not run this trail tonight, young one."

"She would be safer in a den," Thakur argued.

"Then dig one here in the meadow." Srass shrugged as Thakur glared at him. "Do as you wish, Torn-Claw, but if you take the trail before dawn, neither of you will reach clan ground."

"I thought the Un-Named only killed herdbeasts." Ratha's voice was thin.

"They kill anyone who is of the clan. They hate us."

"*Yarr*, Srass," snarled one of the herder's companions, an older male with scars and broken teeth. "You speak as if the Un-Named had wit enough to hate us. Has Meoran not said that those who are Un-Named and clanless are beasts no less so than the ones we herd?"

"Beasts can also hate," Srass muttered, but his tail was low and Ratha smelt the sudden change in his scent. He was afraid. "All right, Tevran," he said hastily, not looking at the other. "I am not questioning our leader's words, so you need not listen so closely."

"You had better stay in the meadow, Torn-Claw," said Gare. "I hear the cub is a promising herder and the clan should not lose her."

Thakur turned away, his whiskers quivering. Ratha cocked her head at him. "May you eat of the haunch and sleep in the driest den, clan herders," she said politely to Srass and Tevran.

As Thakur passed her, she heard him growl under his breath, "May your tail be chewed off and all your fur fall out, Tevran."

With one last glance at the two herders, Ratha lowered her head and padded after him.

"Are we going back?" she asked, catching up.

"No, Srass is right. The trail is too dangerous."

"Now I want to go home. My underfur is wet." Her voice was petulant.

"We can't, yearling. Not until dawn."

"What if the raiders break through?"

"Then both of us go up the nearest tree."

Ratha shivered and shook herself, sending dewdrops flying. She sneezed.

"Come back with me to the sunning rock," Thakur suggested. "You can curl up beside me and Fessran. We'll warm you up."

"Fessran is angry with me," Ratha grumbled.

"I'll tell her to sharpen her claws on someone else.

Come on, yearling," he said as Ratha yawned, a gape that stretched her mouth and made her jaw muscles ache again. Thakur waved his tail imperiously, but Ratha was in no mood to follow. She flattened her ears and turned away from him.

"Ratha!"

She ignored Thakur's call as she trotted away into the fog.

There was a drumming of feet behind her and the sound of wet grass swishing. She stopped and glared back at Thakur.

"You idiot cub, you can't go back by yourself!" Ratha turned her head aside and trotted off in a different direction. Again Thakur blocked her.

"Go away. I don't want you as teacher any more," she snarled. "Fessran may be hard, but she listens to me and answers my questions. And I am not a cub. You wouldn't have brought me here with you if you thought I was."

"The way you are acting tells me I may have made a mistake. *Yarr!* Yearling, come back here!" he called as Ratha galloped away. She ran as hard as she could, twisting and turning so that Thakur would lose her trail. Soon the fog muffled his footsteps and they died away behind her. She ran on, aching and shivering, not sure where she was going and not really caring. There was a feeling in her throat as if a piece of meat were stuck there, and swallow as she might, she couldn't get it down.

At last Ratha jogged into a patch of frosty grass and stopped to rest. The cold was pulling the fog out of the air, laying it on the ground in crystals of ice. She fluffed her fur. Running had warmed her, but as she stood, the chill began to creep back again. She lifted her nose. Some stars were showing through the mist overhead. Everything was quiet now.

Ratha peered between two white-covered stalks and ducked back. She didn't want to be found by anyone, whether it was her teacher or the Un-Named raider. Her whiskers trembled. She whimpered softly and closed her eyes.

She was afraid of the night, of the raiders, of Thakur, but what frightened her most was the change in herself. A cub wasn't supposed to get angry with her teacher. A cub wasn't supposed to question, to doubt, or to sense that things were wrong. When had the awareness come?

She hung her head miserably. Had she imagined that the Un-Named One had spoken during the fight? It was easy to believe that she hadn't heard his words and less frightening to believe so. Less frightening for her and Thakur. But why? Why should Thakur even care whether the scavenger had talked?

Because he knows they can, something in her mind answered, and, for a moment, she was startled by the realization.

Everyone thinks the clanless ones are stupid, Ratha thought. Meoran tells us to think that way. But if Thakur thinks they can talk, as we do, perhaps he thinks they aren't stupid, either.

"The Un-Named One spoke to me," Ratha said aloud to herself. "I know he did."

She sat down and stared at nothing for a long time. None of it made any sense.

"Thakur is wrong," she muttered. "I am not a cub any-more."

She stared at the faint form on the grass beside her for a long time before she realized that it was the first trace of her shadow. As the milky light began to spread over the horizon behind the trees, Ratha blinked and shook her head, not sure whether she had been awake.

The sun rose, chasing the fog away into the trees. The hoarfrost melted back into dew and the drops hung from grassblades and the leaves glittered. Sounds reached Ratha's ears and she turned her head.

She had run so far across the meadow that she couldn't see the sunning rock and she wasn't quite sure where she was. As the fog slid away, it uncovered the carnage of the night's battle. Bodies of slain herdbeasts, both three-horns and dapplebacks, lay still and stiff. Nearby were smaller forms, the torn remains of both the herd's defenders and attackers. From where she hid, Ratha couldn't tell whether the slain were clan folk or raiders. The clan believed the Un-Named Ones were different, yet they all looked alike in death, Ratha thought, as she crept from her hiding place.

She shook her head, trying to get rid of such thoughts. It was day. There were tasks to be done: herdbeasts to graze and water, cubs to teach and feed. The clan would gather itself together, bury its dead and go on. There was no other way. Things didn't change. After all, day still came. Ratha grinned sourly to herself. Thakur would probably even expect her for a lesson, once she had taken a nap and had her wounds attended to. Thakur would treat her as if this night hadn't happened and expect her to be the same cub he had led out on the trail one evening very long ago.

But I am not the same, Ratha thought as she wandered back across the meadow. *I have changed in a way I don't understand.*

CHAPTER 4

BLUE WINGS fluttered in the boughs above the trail. A volley of squawks broke lose and the two quarreling jays chased each other in and out among the branches. Startled, Ratha glanced up, catching only the flash of white tail feathers as the two combatants disappeared. She had forgotten that birds could be so noisy. The owls and nightjars she saw floating over the meadow at night were utterly silent.

The warm tongue of sunlight washed her back as she emerged from beneath the trees. She felt the heat sink through her fur to her skin and she yawned, feeling lazy. How long had it been since she had seen the full sun of day and heard birds singing? Ever since the first raid, it seemed. Other clan herdfolk had also learned to live by night, guarding their animals from sudden attacks by raiders.

Even their best efforts could only slow the loss of herdbeasts to the enemy. This season was the first time that the number of animals killed exceeded the number of young born, and the clan knew that unbalance could not continue for long. The need for more herders was so great that cubs who had only partially completed their training were taken to guard the herds. Among them was Ratha. She was eager to leave Thakur's tutelage, for ever since the night of the first raid, she had made little progress and knew that it was because she no longer trusted him. He had refused to answer her questions about the clanless ones and denied that the Un-Named could speak. Later he said he had never hinted that they could. Ratha knew this lie was intended for Meoran's ears and did not fault Thakur for that. Even when they were alone, he refused her the truth, even as his eyes betrayed his words.

She sensed that there was another fear keeping him silent. When she pressed him to explain, he lost his temper and mocked her. What she had heard, he said, was her own imagination or the sound of the wind in the grass. Only a cub could believe that the Un-Named One spoke. Only a cub.

She knew it was Thakur who had encouraged her, fought for her and had even stood up against her father and the clan leader so that he could train her. At times, her resentment weakened in the face of this knowledge, but she was a clan herder now, with many responsibilities and little time, and Thakur had many new cubs to train. They seldom saw or spoke to each other.

Ratha ambled along the path, her tail swinging, enjoying the morning.

She had already worked the previous night, but when one of the herders who took the day watch fell ill, she had asked to take his place for the sake of a ramble in the sunshine. And, although she wouldn't admit it to herself, for the chance of seeing Thakur.

She hopped over the stream at the meadow's edge. The dapplebacks grazed in the shade on the far side. Fessran was there too, showing three fat spotted cubs how to dodge kicks from the feisty little horses. Ratha waved her tail at Fessran and the other herder paused in her lesson.

"Ho, Fessran? Where's your randy little stallion? I don't see him."

"In the thicket, with a mare, as usual," Fessran answered. "If it weren't for him, the Un-Named would have eaten all of my flock long ago."

"What's he doing?" one of the cubs piped up.

"Making more dapplebacks," said Fessran.

"Oh." The youngster looked thoughtful. "Will we see them when he comes out?"

The cub's teacher grimaced. Ratha gave Fessran a wide-mouthed grin and lolled her tongue out.

"That isn't the way it happens, Mondir," said a voice next to the question-asker. Stung, Mondir shoved his muzzle against the other's nose. "Since you know everything, Bira, you tell me how it happens."

"I don't know everything," the female cub said, wrinkling her nose and sitting down on her tail. "But my lair-mother did tell me it's something I will do when I am big. And you will too."

"What? Make dapplebacks?" Mondir protested loudly and then wilted when he saw four tongues lolling at him.

"*Yarr!* Don't the lair-mothers teach you litterlings anything?" Fessran grumbled. "Away with you, Ratha!" she growled. "I have cubs to train."

Ratha grinned at her and jogged away. As she left, she heard Fessran soothing Mondir, who had begun to whimper.

"No, litterling. You won't make dapplebacks when you grow up. I'll explain it to you when the lesson is over. . . ."

Ratha trotted toward a flock of three-horned deer and cud-chewers, her charges for the day. It was going to be a lazy morning and an even lazier afternoon. None of the raiders would show their whiskers before dusk. Perhaps she could even cajole one of Fessran's students into watching the herd while she took a short nap in the sun.

Ratha found the group she had been assigned, circled them once and flopped down on her side, her eyes half-closed, listening to the three-horns tearing up grass. The sounds of grazing were punctuated every once in a while by a rumble or a belch from one of the cud-chewers. Ratha's whiskers twitched. Those animals were disgusting, but they were also very tasty. One always had to make compromises.

The day's warmth faded briefly and she opened one eye to see the sun slip behind a cloud. She waited for the cloud to pass and soon felt the warm rays on her coat again. She flicked an ear and glanced up at the shadowed cloudbank gathering on the opposite side of the sky. The rainy season had ended early and spring had been dry. The forest floor had lost its dampness and dried sticks cracked underfoot wherever one went. A little rain might be welcome, if rain was all these clouds would bring, Ratha thought, not particularly liking the look of them.

The clouds began to mass and march across the sky. The air grew still and tense. Ratha stood up. The herdbeasts smelled the oncoming storm and crowded together, jostling each other.

Across the meadow, Ratha could see other herders raising their muzzles to the sky as they stood among the beasts they guarded. Even Fessran had stopped teaching and was shooing her young students back to their mothers' dens.

The day darkened as the low clouds scudded over the sun. Heat lightning cracked the sky. Thunder grumbled.

Ratha trotted around her charges, glancing from time to time at the other herders and their animals. The herd-beasts milled together, their trotting legs and barrel bodies eclipsing the low, slender forms of their guardians.

Several more clan herders appeared at the trail head and galloped into the meadow. With a twinge of pain, Ratha recognized a familiar coppery coat. She had little time to think about Thakur. The deer and cud-chewers broke into short, nervous runs, and Ratha galloped back and forth, trying to keep the herd together. She loped around with her tongue hanging out, flattening her ears and flinching whenever lightning flashed and thunder boomed above the animals' bawling.

An old pine had poked its top through the forest canopy near the meadow. Ratha caught a glimpse of the tree before she was blinded by a burst of light; deafened and knocked over by the shock. Ratha rolled to her feet. Nearby, several three-horns had fallen and were staggering up, their eyes wild. Ratha's gaze swept the meadow. Beasts were running in front of her. Above the thunder came another sound, the sharp crackle of flames. The old pine was burning.

The herders stood with raised hackles as their animals ran past them.

The old tree shot sparks and dropped burning branches, setting the forest alight. The flames rushed and roared, leaping from tree to tree until the fire reached the meadow and the grass began to burn.

"To the creek!" a voice cried, jarring Ratha out of her stupor. Thakur galloped past her, snarling and snapping at the panicked three-horns. "Keep them together, Ratha! Drive them to the creek!"

Other herders bounded to join them. With their help, Ratha and Thakur turned the flock and drove the deer toward the stream at the trail head.

"It isn't deep enough, Thakur!" Ratha panted, alongside him as they raced after the deer.

"I know, but we can follow it to the river. String them out!" he called to the other herders as the lead animals splashed into the creek. "Keep them in the water!" Herders on both sides of the stream forced the three-horns to wade at the center. Soon there was a line of deer bounding and splashing down the creek. Thakur braked to a stop, balancing himself with his tail. "Next, the dapplebacks," he said to Ratha. "Come on."

Together they galloped back to Fessran. The herder was hissing at the horses. Ratha could see that she was terrified by the fire and enraged by her charges' stupidity.

"They don't have the sense to run away," Fessran gasped, coughing. "They run toward it!"

The fire reached into the meadow. It swept after the fleeing creatures, driven and fed by a fitful wind. It blinded them with smoke, choked them with ash and threw cinders on their coats. Ratha joined Fessran and Thakur, helping to drive the dapplebacks into the stream after the deer. The little stallion, maddened by the flames, fought the herders for control of his mares.

Ratha leaped over a low swath of orange fire, nearly singeing her belly. The dappleback stallion broke away from the herd and raced around her. She darted after him, then skidded to a stop, afraid that the rest of the herd would scatter.

"Get him!" Fessran appeared, her eyes watering, her cheek fur smoke-blackened. "I'll keep the rest of them moving."

Ratha bounded after the dappleback, now visible only as a shadow in the acrid haze hanging over the grass. A gust of wind cleared the air for a moment and she sighted her quarry. The little stallion reared, squealing and striking out with its four-toed feet. Ratha saw Thakur duck and spring, catching the dappleback's foreleg in his jaws. He hung on as the horse jerked and wiggled, raking its leg to ribbons against his teeth. Ratha saw him plant his paws in the smoldering ash and drag the crying stallion forward. Thakur's fur was bristling and his eyes large and wild, but his jaws were locked around the dappleback's foreleg and he wouldn't let go. The horse jumped and bucked, pawing at him with its free foot. Behind them, the fire surged, boiling black smoke.

The wind shifted, turning Thakur and the dappleback into shadows in the smoke. Ratha grabbed a breath of clear air and plunged through the haze. The stallion backed, pulling its leg through Thakur's teeth until its foot was in his mouth. Tongues of flame leaped out. Ratha's sight blurred, her eyes watering. She heard a high ringing scream from the dappleback's throat. The horse broke free and toppled backwards into the flames. Ratha saw it rear up again, its back covered with fire. It shrieked once more and fell writhing on its side. Again Thakur darted at it, seized a foreleg and dragged the burning animal through the grass.

"Thakur, leave him!" Ratha called, the hot air searing her throat so that she could barely croak out the words. She galloped after him. He had abandoned the carcass; it lay, its skin curling beneath the flames. She looked for Thakur again, but she couldn't see anything through the haze. The fire sounded close. Dancing orange surrounded her in all directions and the roar deafened her.

"Cub! This way."

Ratha wheeled and leaped at the voice, almost landing on top of Fessran. The other herder butted Ratha ahead. The ground dropped away beneath her paws. Water rushed against her chest and dragged at her legs as she floundered in the stream. A splash and Fessran landed beside her.

"Where's Thakur?"

"I don't know."

Ratha's feet touched the bottom as the downstream current pulled at her sides. The water reflected flame colors from the fire dancing on the shoreline. Cinders shot into the water and died with a hiss.

Ratha slid over a little fall into a pool, bruising her flank on a stone. Fessran slithered down after her and they began to swim, holding their heads above the water. Ahead was the flock of dapplebacks, their wet coats gleaming as they waded in the graveled shallows. A burning twig fell into the stream near Fessran and she veered to one side as it sputtered and sank.

Ratha swam ahead of Fessran, paddling fiercely to keep her head above the water. Her toes scraped gravel and she grounded in the shallows. She pulled herself out, caught up with the wading dapplebacks and wove her way through them. Fessran stayed with the horses and Ratha saw the other herder lift a dripping tail in farewell as she left her behind.

Past the shallows, the stream narrowed and coursed over rocks and boulders. Ratha clambered across the water-worn stones, her pads slipping on algae and moss. As she worked her way downstream, she passed other clan members who hadn't been in the meadow when the lightning struck. Gray patriarchs, frightened yearlings and mothers with squalling cubs in their jaws swam and waded beside the grim herdfolk as the fire devoured the forest behind them. Rags of flame fluttered on the pines that lined the stream bank and crawled along branches overhead.

Soot filled the air and the fire's wind seared throats already raw from running. Ratha drew her paws up to her body and submerged herself except for the top half of her head. She tasted muddy water running past her lips and dragging at her whiskers. She let the current carry her, only using her aching legs to pull herself over stones or to claw at the muddy bottom as the stream spilled through rapids.

The creek deepened and quickened, carrying the weary swimmers and their beasts beyond the fire. The air grew cooler above the water and Ratha sucked it into her burning lungs. She could no longer see the herd of three-horns ahead. Some of the forms that drifted past her were moving limply wherever the current pushed them. Frightened, Ratha struck out for shore, but the current was strong and the banks had become muddy cliffs.

The sun glowed red through the gray pall that hung among the trees, staining the stream with blood-color. Ratha felt herself sinking. Water filled her mouth. She strained her head upright, coughing and spitting. The current swept her over a rocky weir and plunged her into a cauldron that spun her around. A new and stronger flow snatched her away from the stream current. Dimly she felt teeth seize her tail and then her ruff, dragging her back against the river's pull. She floated weakly on her side, her tongue trailing and river water filling her mouth. Her flank bumped something and she felt her wet coat grate on sand as she was hauled onto the beach. Paws and noses nudged her onto her stomach. Her whole body convulsed as she vomited muddy water. She sank back onto her side again, feeling her senses slip away into the darkness.

CHAPTER 5

SAND GRAINS tickled Ratha's nose. She woke up sneezing, blowing up a small sandstorm in the den, which made her sneeze some more. She bumped her head on the low ceiling and peered up to the entrance.

Framed in the opening, with a background of clear sky and hanging fronds, was a four-toed foot. A dappleback foot. The hoofed toes shifted, dislodging more sand into the hole. It landed on Ratha's face. She blinked and grimaced. A narrow muzzle dipped into the picture and one black eye regarded Ratha. The eye blinked and its owner snorted.

Outside, Ratha heard running and yowling. Thakur's voice rose above the others. "Fessran, get your dapplebacks off the beach! They're walking all over the dens!" The dappleback's muzzle disappeared, and the foot vanished with a last spray of dirt.

She crawled out of her burrow and shook her head, her ears flapping. The sand felt warm and gritty on her pads as she blinked in the morning sunlight. Birds made a cheerful racket overhead and the river sang with them as it ran past the beach. She nosed her back and licked her coat. Her tongue scraped coarse matted fur. She dug with her fangs at filth caked in her undercoat, moving her tongue quickly to avoid the sour tang of old dirt. She drew back her lips fastidiously and tried to use only the points of her fangs, but she couldn't help tasting herself and wished that someone had dragged her out of the den and given her a bath.

She attacked the hair mats until they yielded and her tongue probed deeper into her fur, feeling the arch of each rib beneath her skin. She paused in her grooming, took a breath and coughed. Her chest still ached a little, deep inside. She decided to leave the rest of the grooming task until later. She ambled down the narrow beach, feeling the loose sand grow firm beneath her paws as she approached the water's edge. She stood there, listening to the wavelets lapping, and watching fish dart through the shadows on the bottom.

Ratha squinted across the river to the opposite shore. Most of the trees were still standing, although shorn of their leaves and needles. The ground beneath them lay bare and ashy, stripped of brush and forest litter. At first, the scene across the river looked bare and desolate, but as Ratha stared harder, she saw that it was not. New patches of pale green showed amid the fire-scarred trunks.

Ratha's whiskers twitched. How long, she wondered, had she lain in the burrow dug for her in the sand? Long enough for her to stink like an unwashed litterling. Long enough for the burning thing to pass and new foliage to show. The thought frightened her and she shivered despite the sun's warmth on her back. Her stomach felt hollow and there was grit between her teeth. She peered at her rippled reflection and saw that she looked as thin and bedraggled as she felt. Her tongue ached at the thought of more grooming. She yawned and stretched: stiffly, cautiously. She crouched, curling her tail around her feet, letting the sound of the river lull her.

Her eyes were almost closed when she heard pads grinding on sand behind her.

"So this is the cub," said a heavy voice, not Thakur's.

Ratha turned, squinting against the glare.

"Come here, Ratha, and give proper greeting to our clan leader," Thakur called.

She spun around, sliding in the loose sand. She gulped, blinked and stared at Thakur's companion. What had she done, she wondered frantically, that she was being singled out for Meoran's attention? He never spoke to any of those low in the clan unless they had displeased him or broken clan law. Her heart beat fast. *Is it because I heard the clanless one speak? Did Thakur tell Meoran what happened that night?*

Thakur stamped silently on the sand, warning Ratha not to delay. She loped clumsily up the beach, halted and walked up to Meoran. She lifted her chin and bared her throat to him as she stood in his shadow. Meoran lowered his heavy head and nosed her at the vulnerable point beneath her ruff, where the pulse lay just under the skin. She stood still, knowing that if he wished, he could take her life, without need or explanation. Even those high in the clan bared their throats to him, and there were whispers among the clan folk that his teeth had been bloodied in what was supposed to be only a gesture. Ratha remembered others saying that old Baire had never abused this ritual right.

Ratha felt her ears starting to flatten and pricked them forward until the ear muscles ached.

"May you eat of the haunch and sleep in the driest den, clan leader," she said.

Meoran's ruff slid past Ratha's nose as he withdrew his muzzle from beneath her chin. His odor was like his voice, dull and heavy, with a threatening undertone. His ruff was coarse and thick—almost a mane. He stepped back from her, leaving large pawprints in the sand. Ratha stared at his tracks, knowing that her whole foot wouldn't fill the imprint made by his center pad.

"Will she be able to swim the river and drive the herd tomorrow?" Meoran turned to Thakur.

"She almost drowned. When Yaran and I pulled her out of the river, he thought she was dead."

"I lead the clan back across the river, Torn-Claw. Either she swims or she stays here." Meoran looked at Ratha, his eyes glinting yellow in his wide face. His jaws looked massive enough to crush a three-horn's skull with one bite. "Old Baire thought you were strong enough to be a herder, cub. I might not have made that choice, but Thakur tells me your training hasn't been wasted."

Ratha glanced at Thakur and saw that the muscles at the base of both ears were quivering as he tried to keep his ears erect.

"Will one day make such a difference, clan leader?"

"The longer we leave our dens and our land, the less we shall have when we return."

"To what? Look across the river. The Red Tongue has eaten the grass and the leaves. Where will our beasts graze?"

"There is new growth." Meoran yawned, snapping his jaws shut.

"Not enough to feed an entire herd."

Meoran's eyes darkened to cold amber and he showed his fangs as he spoke. "Torn-Claw, if you are wise, you will not mention this to me again. I let you speak once before the clan gathering. I even restrained myself from excusing you for your cowardice. Is that not enough?"

Thakur flinched and glared down at the ground so that Meoran couldn't see his eyes.

"If you have no stomach to walk amid the Red Tongue's leavings," Meoran added, "stay here with the she-cub until the forest grows again."

"I will swim, clan leader," Ratha blurted, stung at being thought a weakling. "I will help drive the herd."

"See, Torn-Claw?" Meoran grinned, showing most of his teeth. "The small one is not afraid. She shames you, herder." Thakur kicked at a log of driftwood, half-buried in the sand. His eyes met Meoran's. "We will both be ready."

"Good. I want no delays." Meoran turned and left.

Ratha sat down and began digging at her coat again as Thakur stared after Meoran and drove his front claws into the sand. Ratha stole a glance at him as he shook both feet free of sand and cleaned them, biting fiercely between the pads.

"Fessran's dapplebacks woke you," he said. "I may go and chew her ears."

"You're angry at Meoran, not Fessran," Ratha said cautiously, her nose in her fur. Thakur gave a low growl. "Why? What did he mean, saying you weren't brave? I saw you catch the dappleback. You would have saved him."

His tail twitched, making snake-patterns in the sand. He lowered his head and started to pad away.

"Thakur."

"Yearling, more words will do me no good and may do me harm. Wait here. I'll be back soon." He wheeled and galloped away down the beach.

When Thakur returned, he was carrying several odd objects in his jaws. He dipped his head and dropped them in front of Ratha. Their legs waved. She sniffed, wrinkled her nose. "I don't eat bugs."

"They aren't bugs. Try one. I'll show you how to bite the shell off."

Thakur selected one of the crayfish, held it down with one paw and bit the head off. He worked it to the side of his mouth, got his jaws around the arched carapace and cracked it. He pried it open with his claws, peeled the shell away and stripped out the meat with his front teeth. He dangled the morsel in front of Ratha. The aroma teased her nose. Delicately she licked and then nibbled at it. The meat was chewy but light and sweet. She snapped, gulped and waited eagerly for another. When Thakur had fed her twice, he nosed the rest of the crayfish toward Ratha.

"I thought I'd better feed you up if you're going to swim tomorrow," he said, choosing another multi-legged morsel from the pile. It tried to scuttle away from him but he seized it by the tail and dragged it back. The flailing legs and antennae threw sand grains. This one was smaller and Thakur didn't even bother to peel the shell off. He took the crayfish into his mouth, crunched it and sorted out bits of meat and shell with his tongue.

Ratha spat out a shell and eyed Thakur. "Why is Meoran so impatient to return to clan ground?"

"I don't know, yearling. Perhaps he dislikes the thought of any other animal in his den."

"Or the Un-Named Ones on clan territory."

Thakur drew back his whiskers. "I doubt it. He thinks so little of them that ground squirrels in his den would bother him more. Even the recent raids haven't taught him that they are more dangerous than he thinks."

"You know a lot about the clanless ones, don't you, Thakur?" Ratha said cautiously. She watched his eyes. Thakur lowered his muzzle, ostensibly searching for another crayfish.

"Yes, yearling, I do."

"Why don't you tell Meoran what you know?"

"He would listen to me as well as he did today. Yearling, don't ask me any more."

Ratha bit down on a stubborn carapace and felt it bend in her mouth.

"Forget about the Un-Named, Ratha. The Red Tongue has driven them far away. They won't come back for a while."

There was silence, broken only by the sound of the river flowing and Thakur's crunching shells.

"I know why you don't want to go back," Ratha teased.

Thakur stared at her, eyes narrowed, whiskers back. "You do?"

"You're so fond of these river-crawlers you can't give them up."

Thakur relaxed. His sigh of relief puzzled Ratha, his odor told her she wouldn't get an answer if she asked him why.

"You are clever, yearling. I see I can't fool you. Yes, I have grown fond of the river-crawlers and I'll take some with me on the way back."

Ratha watched him as he ate. His odor, his eyes and everything else about him told her that the reason he didn't want to return to clan ground had nothing to do with river-crawlers.

Ratha trotted over the beach, her pads obliterating for a moment the maze of tracks in the sand. She stepped in a pile of dung and hopped on three legs, shaking her foot in disgust, while the dapplebacks covered her tracks with sharp-edged toe prints. The beach wasn't big enough for this many animals at once, she thought, wiping her pad clean in a patch of scrubby dune grass.

The three-horned deer stood together in a tight bunch eyeing the clan herders. The stags pawed and thrust their spikes into the sand, their musky scent sharp with ill temper. Herdfolk rushed at them, singly and together, trying to shy the males away and split the herd in half. Ratha, knowing she was still too weak for this task, watched as Thakur and Fessran sparred with two big males guarding the center of the herd. Skillfully the two herders drew the stags aside and Meoran led a drive into the center of the herd. The mass of animals shuddered and then broke apart. Herders on both sides of the split kept the milling animals separated.

Ratha jumped up. Her task was to join with the other herdfolk in driving the dapplebacks, cud-chewers and other animals between the three-horns.

"Keep the deer on the outside!"

Ratha glanced back and saw Meoran yowling orders down the beach. Herdfolk snarled and nipped at the deer, driving them into the river. Over the backs and heads of the little horses, Ratha saw the deer plunging and tossing their heads, throwing spray from hooves and antlers. The sound of the river was lost in the clamor of splashing and bawling. The water boiled and darkened with mud, churned up from the bottom. Ratha saw flashes of white in the water, as silt-blinded fish thrashed and jumped to escape the animals' hooves. The dapplebacks followed the deer into the river and the herders followed them.

Ratha ran down the beach, leaped and bellyflopped into the water. She opened her eyes, gasped at the cold and started paddling. Ahead of her, the short-legged dapple-backs swam beside the wading deer, bouncing in the brown current that swirled past the three-horns' legs. Ratha's feet left the bottom and she began to swim after the little horses, feeling the water pull through her pads at each stroke. She angled up against the current, which buffeted her chest.

Now the deer were swimming, only their necks above water, their crowns forming a moving thorny forest around the dapplebacks. Ratha felt the water churn beside her and saw Thakur's slick head and dripping whiskers. She grinned at him over her shoulder and got a mouthful of muddy water as a wave slapped her in the face.

"Can you swim it, yearling?" he called as she sneezed and spluttered.

"I'll swim it, Thakur," she answered, water running out of the corners of her mouth. "Don't stay beside me," she protested as he bobbed alongside, his tail dragging downstream in the current.

Ratha settled down to the business of swimming, keeping her paws going in a steady rhythm and her nose above water. She fixed her eyes on the herd, moving in the water ahead of her. The three-horn deer formed an open ring around the dapplebacks and other animals, breaking the force of the current so that the smaller animals didn't have to fight it. Even so, the flow was sweeping the little horses to one side of the ring, piling them up, flank to flank, against the deer. The three-horns kicked and poked the dapplebacks away, but the current pushed them back again. Trapped against their irritated neighbors, the dapplebacks squealed and bit.

Ratha swam in their wake, tasting blood in the water. Her stroke was slowing, her paws so heavy she could hardly move them. The ache in her lungs had begun before she had swum a few tail-lengths, but now it was a grinding pain, radiating from her breastbone into her chest. Her wet fur dragged her down. The water lapped along her cheek and the base of her ears. The shore seemed no closer and the herd farther away.

Thakur was swimming alongside her on the upstream side, staying close enough to grab her if she went under, but otherwise offering no help except an encouraging "Halfway, yearling."

"Halfway, Thakur," she bubbled and kept on stroking.

Ratha's breastbone felt as though it would split and she was sobbing from exhaustion by the time her claws scraped bottom on the other side.

There was a tug at her ruff and the wet warmth of a body at her side. Thakur steadied her, while she found footing on the loose gravel. Slowly she waded to shore beside him and hauled herself out.

Weary as she was, she lifted her head and squinted up and down the beach. The tracks were there, but the herd had gone. The beach was quiet except for wavelets lapping along shore and her soaked pelt still draining onto the sand. Ratha ground her teeth together, crunching gritty sand between them. Meoran hadn't bothered to wait. Yaran might have, but he was too afraid to cross Meoran. For all they knew, she had drowned in the crossing. She felt a nudge; a voice in her ear.

"It doesn't matter, yearling. Lie down and rest."

She turned and flattened her ears. "Meoran thinks he

is rid of me, the weakling, the she-cub. When he sees me it will be like rubbing his face in dung." She grinned, still panting. She turned and staggered up the beach, knowing Thakur could do nothing except follow.

He did. She heard his paws crunch on the sand as she made her way over the rippling dunes on the high part of the beach. She saw that he looked at the ground as he walked and not ahead to the forest, whose fire-scarred trees spoke of the Red Tongue's passing. The burn smell hung in the air, and though it was mixed with the fresh scent of new growth, the odor brought with it the memory of the fire. Thakur began to lag and the ends of his whiskers trembled.

Ratha had gone several paces beyond him before she knew he'd stopped.

"Thakur?" She looked back. His shaking was worse than hers. "Thakur, are you sick?"

He stood, frozen, staring at the sand a few tail-lengths ahead of him. His fear-smell wafted to Ratha. Hesitantly, she came to him and nosed him.

"Now you see why Meoran called me coward," he said, hanging his head.

"Why? What are you afraid of? The Red Tongue is gone."

"For me it hasn't gone." Thakur said in a low voice. "Ratha, I can't walk across there now. Stay here with me for a few days. We can eat river-crawlers."

Ratha glared at him. "I want to make Meoran eat dung. The longer we wait the further away he gets." She turned away.

"Idiot cub!" she heard Thakur yell at her back. "Ratha,

you can't go back by yourself. You couldn't fight off a weanling cub let alone a pack of Un-Named raiders."

"Then come with me." Ratha stopped and looked back at him, flicking her tail.

"I can't."

"Why?"

"I saw that dappleback die, yearling. You weren't close enough to see it, but I did."

"Thakur, the smell isn't that bad. The ash will be soft beneath our feet. We'll travel fast."

He hung his head. "I can't."

Ratha yawned in frustration. She felt a sudden fury rising like acid in her throat.

"I don't care about your burned dappleback! I want to go back to the clan. Maybe Meoran was right when he said your father was an Un-Named bone-eater!"

She was down in the sand before the last word was out of her mouth. Thakur stood over her, almost on top of her while her head rang from his blow. She shrank into a miserable ball and wished she could melt between the sand grains. She could feel his shadow on her, feel his pain, feel him waiting. . . .

"I thought Meoran was just spreading lies about you," she faltered.

Thakur gave her a smoldering look. "No. He was spreading the truth about me, which, it seems, is far worse. Where did you hear it?"

"At the clan kill. I overheard Meoran talking to Yaran. I was busy eating, but I heard enough."

Thakur took a breath. "All right, yearling. Yes, what you heard is true. The one who sired me had no name, even though he was more worthy of it than many in the clan. My mother Reshara chose unwisely."

"I thought our law said that both the lair-mother and lair-father must be named in order for the cubs to be named," Ratha said.

"So why do I bear a name?" Thakur grinned ruefully. "Old Baire took pity on Reshara even though she sought outside the clan for a mate. He let her stay until her two cubs were born and then she was driven out. He let me live and gave me my name. He had that much mercy."

Ratha lifted her nose from the sand. "Cubs? You have no littermates in the clan."

Thakur looked uncomfortable and she knew he had not meant to say as much as he had. At last he sighed. "My brother runs with the Un-Named. Reshara took him with her when she left the clan."

"Why didn't she take you?"

"Old Baire asked that she leave both of us with the clan. Although our father was Un-Named, Baire knew we were far from being witless."

"Then why did she take your brother?"

"She disobeyed Baire. She took my brother and fled. My father came to get me, but Baire's son, Meoran, was lying in wait for him."

"Meoran caught you," Ratha breathed.

"Meoran killed my father and caught me. I fought, but I was only a litterling. He put a paw on me and tore out some of my front claws with his teeth."

Ratha looked down at Thakur's right front foot and shivered. She had once asked him how he lost his claws, but he had distracted her with something else. The foot did not look very different from the other but Ratha guessed that scars lay beneath the fur.

"Did you ever see Reshara or your brother again?" she asked.

"Reshara is dead now, Ratha," he said, in a tone that discouraged her from asking anything more.

She tested her legs and clambered to her feet. Thakur looked beyond her to the burn.

"Go, yearling. I'll follow," he said.

Ratha went ahead until she reached the border of the beach where the sand was streaked with charcoal.

Beyond the upper beach the forest floor was ash and charred stubble, with a few green blades poking through. Ratha sniffed, grimaced at the smell and passed onto the burn. She walked carefully, for the ground was still dew-damp and the ash slippery beneath her pads. Once or twice she looked back. Thakur was following. His tail bristled and his whiskers trembled and she could see the fear in his eyes, yet he said nothing as he walked behind her across the burn.

The farther they traveled, the harsher the landscape grew and the more acrid the burn smell. Here the fire had burned recently and more intensely. Saplings stood, charred forlorn sticks that would never put forth another leaf. Trunks of gutted pines lay in their path, blocking the way. Ratha leaped over them easily, but coaxing Thakur across them was another matter and more than once she had to force him up and over a still-smoking log.

Thakur followed Ratha across the burn until they were blocked by a tangle of downed trees and brush. In among the charred twigs was one still burning. The flame flickered against the pale sky and danced between blackened twists of bark.

To Ratha, the Red Tongue was an animal and its life should end with its death. To find the Red Tongue alive here, even this faint and flickering part of it, was contrary to all she knew of life or death. Behind her, Thakur whimpered, the sounds escaping from his throat despite his wish to hold them back. She butted him, trying to make him go forward, but he balked, unwilling to pass the Red Tongue in the downed tree.

Ratha stared at the flame. To go around the fallen trees meant a weary trek out of the way. But she knew she couldn't get Thakur through the tangle, even though there was room to crawl beneath the interwoven branches. He stood frozen behind her, eyes closed, panting, unable now to overcome the terror that held him prisoner.

Ratha grew angry and spat at the fire-animal. Lashing her tail, she walked toward the burning twig. A sharp gust made the flame flutter back as she approached, and she grew bolder. Around the Red Tongue, the air shimmered as if it were flowing water. The smoke was thick and resinous.

Anger and a growing fascination drew Ratha to the Red Tongue, and she stared into the blue-gold heart of the flame. It was, she thought, a thing that danced, ate and grew like a creature, but unlike a creature, once killed it wouldn't stay dead.

With flattened ears and streaming eyes, Ratha lunged at the Red Tongue's black throat. Her teeth sank into charred wood and she twisted her head sharply. The branch broke off. She held it in her mouth for several seconds, watching the flame curl and hiss near the end of her nose. The charcoal tasted bitter and Ratha flung the branch away. It rolled over and over in the dirt. The fire flickered, hissed and went out.

Ratha pawed the branch. She scratched the burned bark, trying to find the elusive fire-creature, but the wood was cold. When she lifted her head from the branch, Thakur's eyes were on her. Carefully he padded forward and sniffed at the branch where the Red Tongue had been. Ratha stood to one side, panting a little from excitement.

"Can you crawl through the thicket now, Thakur?" she asked.

"Yes, yearling, I can," he said quietly. "Lead the way."

There were other places where the Red Tongue still guttered weakly on twigs or bark and Ratha broke the branches off and smothered the flame. Each time Thakur would sniff the charred wood to convince himself that the Red Tongue had vanished. Ratha offered to teach him her newly acquired skill, but Thakur hastily declined.

The sun stood at midpoint in the hazy sky and Thakur and Ratha were approaching another stand of gutted pines when they heard the sound of approaching feet.

Thakur lifted his muzzle and pricked his ears.

"Fessran?" he called.

"Ho, herder." Fessran jogged around the far end of the smoking brush, keeping her distance from it.

"How far is the clan?" asked Ratha, coming alongside Thakur.

"Less than half a day's run, if one could go straight through. Having to go around all the brush tangles and fallen trees makes the journey longer." Fessran sat down and licked soot from her coat. "I'm surprised that you have come this far."

"We went through," Thakur said. "Ask Ratha."

"You can crawl through, yes," Fessran said doubtfully, "if you don't mind the Red Tongue's cubs licking at your coat."

"I don't worry about the Red Tongue's cubs." Ratha grinned. "Watch."

Fessran came alongside Thakur and stood. Ratha trotted past them to the pile of downed trees, hopped up on a log and seized a branch with fire dancing at the tip. She bounced down with the twig in her mouth, threw it on the ground and kicked dirt on it. She grabbed the end and rubbed the glowing coals in the ash, which billowed up around her, making her sneeze. When the cloud settled, Ratha swaggered toward Fessran and Thakur, the burned stick still in her mouth. Fessran hunched her shoulders and retreated. Ratha stopped where she was.

"Come and sniff it, Fessran," she coaxed. With a glance at Thakur, who hadn't moved, Fessran approached Ratha, extended her neck and brushed the charcoaled bark with her whiskers. She grimaced at the smell and shied away as if she expected the fire-creature to revive and leap off the branch at her. Eyes fixed on the spot where the Red Tongue had been, Fessran crouched. Thakur nosed the branch.

"*Yarr!*" Fessran's tail swept back and forth in the ash. "It is gone. You killed it!"

"I can only kill little ones," Ratha said, still grinning around the branch end in her mouth.

"No one can do that," Fessran said, straightening

from her crouch, her belly smeared with ash. "Not even Meoran."

Ratha strutted, her ruff and whiskers bristling. "Clan leader, *ptah!* Who is he compared to the slayer of the Red Tongue?"

"One who would rip you from throat to belly if he heard your words," Thakur said, stopping her swagger with a penetrating look. Ratha wrinkled her nose at him, tossed the stick away and began scrambling across the fallen trees.

The three of them didn't see the Red Tongue again until the sun had fallen halfway down the sky. Two saplings had fallen together, their sparse crowns interwoven. The Red Tongue crouched inside a nest of branches that sheltered it from the wind. Ratha stopped, shook the soot from between her pads and stared.

"That one isn't in our way," she heard Thakur say. "You don't need to kill it."

Ratha took a step forward. Thakur was right. She should go on and let the creature be. She lifted her muzzle and smelled. The odor was acrid, stinging her nose, burning her throat. The hated smell.

"Leave it, Ratha."

She glanced at Thakur. He and Fessran were turning away. Another step toward the trees. Another. The fire's rush and crackle filled her ears. The flames' mocking dance drew her to the base of the trees and she stared up, awe and hatred mingling in a strange hunger.

She climbed onto one leaning tree, which shook and threatened to break under her weight. She balanced herself and crawled up the slender trunk, digging her claws into fire-brittled wood. She crept up until she reached the Red Tongue's nest and began to snap away the dry twigs that guarded the flame. The creature seemed to shrink back as Ratha destroyed its nest. It withdrew to a single limb and clung there, as if daring her to reach in and pull it out. She shifted her weight and glanced down.

Fessran and Thakur stood near the tree, alternately staring up at her then at each other, brows wrinkled in dismay.

She cleared an opening large enough for her head, gulped a breath of air, tensed and lunged at the Red Tongue's branch. Her teeth ground on wood. A branch broke beneath one of her paws, and she flailed wildly, bouncing in the treetop. The branch in her mouth splintered, with a crack that jarred her teeth. Her claws hooked, held, tore loose, and she slid. Her ears were bombarded by a volley of snapping limbs, and everything blurred, as the tree's crown disintegrated. Black twigs, blue sky and the fire's mocking orange tumbled together, whirled madly and crashed to a stop.

Ratha lay in the ash, her body one large ache. She opened one eye. Things were still moving. She sighed and shut it again.

Voices. Thakur's. Fessran's. A scuffing sound, someone kicking dirt. Ratha jumped up, shaking her ringing head. She staggered, squinting. Something moved. She planted all four paws and forced her eyes to focus on Thakur's image, still blurred. Something was flickering between his legs as he jumped back and forth. Smoke boiled up behind him. Ratha heard the scuffing sound again and a thin, frightened yowl.

She pitched toward him, barely supporting herself on wobbly legs.

"Grab the end!" she heard Fessran call as Thakur made short useless rushes at the burning branch. "Take the end and rub it in the dirt as she did!"

But Thakur was too timid. Ratha saw him shy away again, his eyes wild with fright. Fessran blocked Ratha's view as she charged the fire and frantically pawed dirt and ash into it. The Red Tongue paled under the gray cloud. It sputtered, choking. Ratha saw the muscles bunch in Fessran's shoulders. The fire grew smaller; started to fade under her frenzied strokes.

Yet the fire-creature still lived and Ratha didn't know what it might be able to do. Fessran was too close to the hail of sparks leaping from the flame.

"Fessran!" Ratha called and the other female paused in her stroking and glanced over her shoulder as Ratha stumbled toward her.

"So you live, young one. I thought you'd killed yourself with your foolishness."

"Fessran, get away! You're too close to it!"

Another shower of sparks went up and Fessran coughed in the thick smoke swirling around her. She sneezed and backed away. "Slay the creature, Ratha!" she hissed, squeezing her eyes shut.

Ratha jumped at the guttering fire and seized the end of the branch in her jaws. She threw it down, but the Red Tongue was stubborn and clung to the wood. She pawed the branch, rolling it over, yet still the creature peeked from between patches of curling bark. She crouched, watching, growing too fascinated with the creature to kill it. The fire crept out of its hiding place, as if it sensed that the initial assault was over. It burned cautiously along the top of the log. Ratha circled it.

"Look how it changes shape, Fessran," she said.

"Don't play with it," Fessran snarled, her ears back. "Kill it."

"Why? If we stay far enough away, it won't hurt us. It is only a cub, Fessran."

"It grows fast. Kill it."

Ratha raised one paw, dipped it into the ash, stared at the fire curling around the branch. "No." She put the paw down.

"Ratha, kill it!" Thakur cried. Fessran showed her teeth and crept toward the fire. Ratha blocked her. She tried to push past, but Ratha shoved her back. Fessran skidded in the ash and fell on her side. Ratha stood between her and the Red Tongue, her hackles up, her tail fluffed. Two pairs of slitted eyes met.

"This is my creature."

"The Red Tongue is no one's creature. Kill it." Fessran scrambled in the ash, pulling her paws underneath her. Ratha tensed, feeling her eyes burn. "I will kill it or I will let it live, but it is my creature." She leaned toward Fessran. The other's eyes widened in dismay. She got up, shook the flaky ash from her coat.

"You don't want to fight me," Ratha said as Fessran sidestepped around her. The other female glared at her one more time and lowered her head. "The Named do not bare fangs against the Named," she said harshly, "and I do not bare fangs against one I trained. Very well. The creature is yours. Keep it or kill it as you wish."

There was the sound of feet padding away. Fessran

turned her head. "Thakur has gone," she said and took a step after him.

"Are you going with him?" Ratha asked. Her anger was gone. A hollow, empty feeling crept into her belly as she watched Fessran turn, her eyes following Thakur's pawprints in the ash.

"I should. He is my herd-brother. You don't need either one of us. You have your creature."

Ratha felt herself start to tremble. "Fessran . . ."

The other female stood, her tail twitching, something shifting around in the depths of her eyes. Ratha's tongue felt numb and heavy in her mouth.

"Find Thakur, then," she said. "Tell him I didn't mean to frighten him. After you have found him, come back to me."

"I doubt he will come back here, Ratha."

"Then send him on ahead and come back by yourself." Ratha tried to keep her voice steady, but she knew her eyes were pleading. Fessran stared beyond her to the fire. Ratha followed her gaze and said, "The creature is dying. It does not matter whether I kill it or not; when you return it will be dead."

Fessran snorted. "You were ready to fight me to protect a creature already dying? You make no sense, Ratha."

Ratha opened her mouth to speak, found no words and hung her head. She didn't know why she had tried to protect the Red Tongue; why her sudden anger had made her threaten Fessran and scorn Thakur.

Ratha saw Fessran's eyes soften. "Wait here while I track Thakur. I will return for you then." She padded away, leaving her footprints on top of Thakur's. Ratha watched her for a while before turning back to the fire.

The flame had shrunk to a pale orange fringe that huddled on the branch.

Ratha crouched beside it, curled her tail around her feet and watched it.

What are you? she asked it silently.

The flame crackled back.

Do you speak like me, or do you only growl like the Un-Named Ones? Ratha crept closer, laying her chin on the ground. *You are so tiny now that you couldn't hurt me. Whose cub are you, little Red Tongue?* Her breath teased up small clouds of ashes and made the fire flutter. *Don't die, little Red Tongue,* she thought.

The flame jumped, doubled its size for a moment, then shrank again.

Ratha lifted her chin, stared at the creature, extended her neck and breathed gently on it. Again the fire gained strength as it fed on her breath. Ratha jerked her whiskers back, opened her mouth and exhaled.

After a while, however, the flame began to flicker and die down into glowing coals. Ratha had to blow hard to coax the creature up again and it wouldn't stay. Her breath wasn't enough. It was dying. It needed something else. Ratha watched it, feeling helpless.

The charred branch broke; crumbled. Embers glowed orange and the warmth beat on Ratha's face as she leaned over the fire. Again, she blew, raising a fountain of sparks. One landed on some dry needles and flashed into flame. For several moments, the second fire outdid the first one; then as it consumed the needles, it fell and died.

Ratha trotted to the scorched spot, sniffed it; turned back to her creature. She felt she was on the edge of an answer.

It needs . . . it needs . . . I know what it needs!

Ratha almost stumbled over her own paws as she ran to seize a twig covered with brown needles. She dropped it on the embers and jumped back as the fire spurted up again.

My creature needs to eat, she thought, whisking her tail about in her excitement. *It won't die if I feed it.*

She scurried about, collecting food. She found that the fire wouldn't eat rocks or dirt and balked when fed green stems, but would leap and crackle happily over dry needles and twigs. It also displayed a disconcerting relish for fur and whiskers. Ratha was careful to keep hers well out of its reach.

The fire burned fast and grew large. The waves of heat made Ratha's eyes water. She stopped feeding it and soon it grew small again.

The song of a bird far across the burn made Ratha lift her head. She saw that it was evening. The sun's edge was slipping below the horizon and the red-streaked sky was fading to violet. A single cricket began chirping; then the chorus joined in. Ratha listened to the noises, muted by the night and the soft hiss of the dying Red Tongue.

The burn lay open beneath the star-filled sky. With no trees to hold the day's heat and break the wind, the air grew cold. Ratha, prowling in the shadows beyond the firelight, fluffed her fur and shivered, despite the summer stars overhead.

When she came back and lay down by the flame, it spread its warmth over her; her shivering stopped. She yawned and stretched her pads toward the flame. She hadn't felt so warm and comfortable since she was a nursling curled up in the den with her mother. She rolled onto her front, tucked her forepaws under her breast and fell into a light doze, waking now and then to feed her fire.

The night grew colder. A harsh wind hissed in the trees. Ratha crept closer to the fire. She gathered a bundle of twigs and moved it nearby so that she need not leave her creature's warmth to search for the food it needed. The fire's sound became friendlier to her ears and she thought, sleepily, that her creature was purring. The sound lulled her and she dozed.

Ratha woke, not knowing what had disturbed her. She lay still, peering through half-closed eyes, her chin on the ground, trying not to sneeze despite the flaky ash that stung and teased her nose. A slight tremor in the ground beneath her chin told her someone was coming.

Thakur? Fessran? The intruder moved downwind of her and she could catch no scent.

She heard two sets of footsteps; one in counterpoint to the other. Two pairs of eyes glinted, green stars in the dark. She saw two forms; one hung back; the other approached. Firelight painted the newcomer's coat with dancing shadows as it crept out of the night into the Red Tongue's circle. The intruder raised a wary head, squinting into the flame, and Ratha saw that it was Fessran.

She crouched, limbs tensed, muscles bunched, her belly fur brushing the ground. She took a few quick steps and stopped, her flanks quivering. Ratha watched her pupils dwindle to points as she looked past the flame.

"You are still strong, wretched creature," Ratha heard her hiss. "Did you kill the one who tamed you and eat her to gain your strength?"

Ratha sat up. Fessran's head turned sharply, her neck fur bristling in spikes. "Ratha?"

"Here, Fessran. Behind the Red Tongue."

"So the thing hasn't eaten you even though it is stronger than before. You told me it was dying."

"It was." Ratha skirted the fire, came to Fessran, extended her neck to touch noses, but there was no answering nudge. Ratha drew her head back, wary of the other's raised hackles and narrowed eyes. "It needed to eat," she said, feeling awkward, yet slightly proud. "I found what it wanted. I fed it and kept it alive."

"*Ptah!* Thakur and I have journeyed here for nothing. Keep your creature. Feed it and play with it all night if you want. My summer coat isn't thick enough for this wind. I go."

"Fessran." Ratha pawed her flank.

Fessran said, her ears back, "I have run far in the cold this night. You begged me to return. You told me the Red Tongue would be dead by then. *Ptah!*"

Ratha retreated as Fessran spat. The two eyed each other. Fessran lowered her head and turned away. "Are you cold now?" Ratha asked.

"*Yarr?*" Fessran halted and looked back.

"You are cross because you were cold," Ratha said patiently. "Are you cold now?"

"What a question! How can I not be with the wind blowing through. . . ."

Ratha waited. Fessran stopped, blinked and fluffed her fur. "Your creature warms us," she said in surprise. "I remember now; when we ran from the Red Tongue, I felt its hot breath on me and I ran faster."

"There is no need to run from it now. My creature is only bad when it grows too large. I know how to keep it small," Ratha said, a touch of pride in her voice. Fessran's hackles smoothed, but she gave no indication of staying. She padded out past the rim of the firelit circle and melded with the darkness until only her eyes and teeth showed. Ratha followed to the brown-shadowed edge and shook herself as a sharp gust tore through her thin summer coat. She heard Fessran shiver.

"Come back to me and my creature," Ratha called. She waited, then turned around in disgust and walked back to her Red Tongue. Something made her look into the dark. The eyes hadn't gone. They still stared out at her.

Ratha ignored them. She flopped down, her belly to the fire, spreading her pads and feeling the heat flow around them. She heard hesitant footsteps behind her and began to grin.

"Be a good cub, my little Red Tongue," she said softly to the dancing flame. "She may soon be your friend if she sees no reason to fear you."

The footsteps grew quicker then and stopped. There was the soft brush of a tail being curled across feet. Ratha rolled her head back. Fessran sat behind her as if she were a wall protecting Fessran from the Red Tongue's capricious play.

"You like it, don't you?" Ratha said.

Fessran's whiskers twitched. Her expression was still guarded, but her eyes, as she stared at the flame, were full of wonder rather than fear.

Ratha lifted her chin for a nuzzle and this time received an answering touch.

"Was I such a foolish cub to keep the creature alive?" Fessran's face softened. "Perhaps not, Ratha."

Ratha yawned, arched her back and stretched until her toes and tail quivered. "Thakur told me once that the clan-folk thought old Baire was foolish when he tried to tame three-horns and add them to our herds," she said.

"Those who spoke so had reason to be afraid," Fessran answered. "I saw many herders die on those horns. We learned much and now we can keep the creatures, but we lost many clan folk."

"Three-horns are good for the clan," Ratha argued. "Baire wasn't foolish to herd them. Maybe I'm not foolish to herd the Red Tongue. I already know much about it, and I can teach. Clan folk won't have to die to learn."

"May it be so, Ratha," Fessran said cautiously. "You speak of Thakur. I have left him waiting in the cold." She got up, shaking ash from her hindquarters.

"Call him here to warm himself beside my creature," Ratha said.

"I'll try, but don't forget that he fears the Red Tongue."

Fessran turned her back to the fire and called into the darkness where Thakur was still waiting.

Ratha saw him slink to the edge of the light where orange turned to brown and shadows grew long and wavering. There he crouched and would come no further despite Fessran's coaxing. He wrinkled his brows and squinted away from the fire with frightened, watery eyes.

"Herd-brother, Ratha's creature won't harm us. Come and lie down with me. The Red Tongue makes the night as warm as your den."

"My fur is warm enough," Thakur growled. "The Red

Tongue's light bites my eyes. I would rather see by starlight." He fluffed his fur against the wind. "The herdbeasts fear this thing and their fear is wise. Not to fear it is foolish." He looked at Ratha.

"I know about it. I don't have to fear it." She flattened her ears.

"I know about it too." Thakur's lips drew back and his fangs gleamed as he spoke. "Have you forgotten how it ate the forest? Have you forgotten the dappleback I dragged away? Fessran, that was your little stallion I tried to save. I dragged the beast away from the Red Tongue, but like the snake's tongue it struck." He huddled, trembling, terror shimmering with the firelight in his eyes. "The Red Tongue licked at the stallion until the skin was black and falling off. It licked until the entrails burst and the bones showed white beneath. *Aayowrr!*"

Ratha glared at Thakur, hating him for making her remember the time when the thing she now called her creature had run wild, destroying the forests. The ashy stubble she stood on was reminder enough. She grew angrier as her own fear, the fear she had subdued to tame the Red Tongue, now rose again.

"Meoran must think you drowned in the river crossing since you haven't yet returned to clan ground. If you don't return soon, he'll find a young male to take your place as herder."

"Don't taunt her, Thakur," Fessran warned as Ratha felt her nape start to bristle.

"I don't care what Meoran thinks!" Ratha snarled. Her belly churned as she remembered the clan leader's cold eyes and scornful voice. Meoran thought her a weakling, unfit for the task of clan herder. Despite her words to Thakur, the thought stabbed into her, driving as deep as fangs into her flesh.

She quivered, wishing she could blaze out like the Red Tongue, to engulf Thakur, Meoran and all those who doubted her, to burn until nothing was left.

Thakur lifted his muzzle. "You cared what Meoran thought when you swam the river. And if you didn't why, why, by the Law that named you, did you have to drag me across this place?" He scuffed a foot in the charred stubble. "The smell sickens me. The ash stings my feet. And you, Fessran," he said, turning to her, "why do you encourage this foolish cub? Would you lead one of your dapplebacks onto a cliff and hope it didn't fall off? I thought you had some sense."

"I do," Fessran said quietly, "and fear doesn't keep me from using it."

Thakur's eyes went back to Ratha. The green in them was pale. She hated him for his weakness and she saw him flinch as he felt the depth of her hatred.

His next words were measured and careful. He stared right at Ratha as he said, "I made a mistake when I chose you to train. I should have obeyed Meoran. Teaching you to herd was a waste. I will think hard before I accept another female to train."

"Go then!" Ratha spat, every hair on her body on end. "I'm tired of hearing you whine and tired of smelling your fear-scent. Go lie in the dark and cold, frightened one!"

Fessran's jaw opened, but before she could say anything, Ratha sprang at Thakur.

"If what Meoran said about me was true, then what he

said about you was even more so; your lair-father was an Un-Named chewer of bones, and you are unworthy of the name Baire gave you!"

She landed in front of him. He didn't flinch or strike out. He looked at her steadily. Ratha lifted one paw to claw him, found she couldn't and stamped in frustration, more furious at herself than at him. Thakur kept his eyes on her and the pain in them made her throat burn with shame. She wished she could dig a hole and bury her words deeper than she ever buried her dung.

"I will see you on clan ground," he said very softly and was gone.

For a moment, Ratha stood staring at his pawprints in the flickering light and smelling the sour traces of his smell. Behind her she could hear Fessran licking her coat. She listened to the tongue strokes and the muted guttural sounds as Fessran routed fleas and combed out snarls and mats. At last her voice came from behind Ratha's back. "He is a good herder. You did wrong to shame him."

Ratha spun around, all patience gone. "Go with him then. I can herd the Red Tongue by myself."

"You would do better, Ratha, if you herded your own tongue behind your teeth and kept it there for a while." Fessran finished grooming herself, shook her pelt and got up. "Now show me how you feed this creature of yours so I may keep it alive while you sleep."

Ratha swallowed the rest of her anger. Fessran was going to stay. That was enough. She showed Fessran her bundle of twigs and how to poke them one at a time into the Red Tongue's lair. When Fessran had mastered the task to her satisfaction, Ratha curled up in the ash, buried her nose in her tail and slept. The last sound she heard before she fell asleep was the soft crackle-purr of the fire burning.

CHAPTER 6

WHEN RATHA WOKE in her nest in the ash, morning had cleared the haze from the sky and deep blue arched over the burn. Slivers of green dotted the grounds; new shoots had come up overnight from fire-ripened seeds; each one so fragile that it bent beneath the weight of a single drop of dew.

Ratha sat up, yawned and brushed ash from her fur. She looked for Thakur before she remembered why he wasn't there. Half the night spent tending the Red Tongue had made her peevish, and the hungry rumbles in her belly didn't help her temper. A haunch of dappleback or some of those river-crawlers might be nice, she thought, feeling warm saliva filling her mouth. She swallowed and tried to turn her mind away from food. There was nothing to eat here. She would have to wait until she returned to clan ground.

"This place has food only for the Red Tongue." Fessran's voice came from behind her and the tang of smoke stung her nose. "And not enough, either. Your creature is a greedy thing; I grow weary of feeding it."

Ratha stretched one leg at a time and arched her back to get the stiffness out of it. She groomed her belly, glancing now and then at Fessran, who was poking the last few sticks into the Red Tongue's nest.

The morning breeze shifted, sending smoke into Fessran's face and she shook her head, blinking, her eyes tearing. She backed away, grimacing. "*Arr,* you ungrateful creature!" she growled. "I feed you and feed you and then you make my eyes sting!"

"Stand on the other side." Ratha yawned. "And you're feeding it too much. Keep it small."

"I will feed it no more; there is nothing left to feed it." Fessran rubbed her face on the inside of her foreleg, leaving the fur damp and spiky. She squeezed her eyes shut and opened them again. "There. I can see again."

"I can get food for it." Ratha pointed her nose at the tree. "Up there."

"Unless you can knock down the whole tree, you won't get very much," Fessran said, eyeing the stunted saplings dubiously. "Even if you can feed your creature for a while, we can't stay here."

"And if we go, what happens to my creature?"

"We'll have to leave it, Ratha."

"No!" Ratha planted her paws in the ash. "It kept me warm last night. It kept you warm too. It is a cub; it must be looked after and fed. If we go, it will die."

"We can't stay here," Fessran repeated.

"Why did you keep it alive last night if now you say it must die?" Ratha wailed.

"I was cold last night and I'm not now. I don't want

your creature to die either, Ratha, but staying here isn't going to fill our bellies."

Ratha circled the fire, pacing frantically. An idea struck her. "I want the clan herders to see my creature," she said, turning to Fessran who stood waiting, flicking her tail from side to side. "I can stay here with the Red Tongue while you bring them. Can you bring them, Fessran? I can stay."

"And be meat for the first hungry beast that comes along?" Fessran snorted. "If I left you here, I'd find only your bones when I got back, even if the clan herders would believe my words. *Arr!* What are you doing?" she cried in alarm as Ratha tried to snap at the flame and was driven back by heat and pain.

"I can't catch it. There is nothing to catch. I see it, but my teeth can't feel it."

"Do you think you can carry the Red Tongue by the scruff?" Fessran wrinkled her nose. "I may not know much about it, but I know it is not *that* kind of creature."

Ratha glared at Fessran, winced and licked smarting jowls. She turned once again to the enigmatic thing still dancing over its breakfast of twigs. Fessran had placed several small branches awkwardly, leaving broken ends sticking out. Gingerly, Ratha took one of these into her mouth and drew the branch from the fire. It was shorter than she expected and she shifted it in her jaws, fighting the urge to fling the thing away as it burned close to her face. Out of the corner of one eye she saw Fessran raise a paw to bat the branch out of her mouth. Ratha held her torch as long as she could before having to drop it back in the fire.

"There!" she panted. "I can carry my creature."

Fessran lowered her foot. "You wouldn't go very far before you dropped it. The sun is high, Ratha. We don't need the Red Tongue."

"No! You are just like Thakur, telling me to leave my creature. I found it, I fed it, and I'm going to take it back with me." Ratha flopped on her belly and stared into the fire.

There must be a way . . . there must . . . yes, there is.

Ratha caught Fessran peering into her face. She sat up abruptly, almost bumping the other's chin. "I know, Fessran! Look at the Red Tongue. See how the creature crawls along the branch? Do you see how the Red Tongue's passing turns the wood gray and feathery?" Ratha leaned over Fessran's shoulder as she snagged a charred stick with one claw and pulled it out of the fire. "Once the wood turns to feathers, the Red Tongue won't eat it. If I pick my branch up by this end," she said, tapping the blackened bark, impatient for it to cool, "I can carry it."

When the wood stopped glowing and smoking, Ratha got her jaws around it and lifted the branch out of the fire. She raised her head, holding the torch triumphantly. An instant later, the charcoaled end collapsed between her teeth and the lighted end fell on the ground. It flickered out. Ratha spat out a mouthful of embers, gagged and drooled on the ground, trying to cool the burning bitterness with saliva. Through pain-blurred eyes she glared at the Red Tongue, retching as fluid ran down her chin.

She panted rapidly and stuck her sore tongue out into the morning wind.

"*Arr!* I thought it would work," she said when she could speak.

"You did better the first time," Fessran answered. "Perhaps a longer branch not yet touched by the Red Tongue would serve you. Wait. I'll climb up and break one off."

Ratha stared, open-mouthed, as Fessran hitched herself up the sapling's slanted trunk. "You're helping me?"

"I prefer that to leaving you here." Fessran's head appeared in a crotch between two limbs. The tree's crown swayed as she balanced herself. She seized a nearby branch in her jaws, cracked it loose and tossed it down to Ratha. Several more followed, the dry wood snapping cleanly away from the trunk.

"My teeth weren't made for that." Fessran landed beside Ratha, sending up a cloud of flaky ash.

"Why did you knock down all those?" Ratha asked. "I can carry only one with the Red Tongue at the end."

"Yes, but *I* can carry the others. And when the Red Tongue creeps to the end of your branch, I will coax it into one of mine and give that one to you."

"Ah, but you are clever, Fessran," Ratha said.

"Not clever. Just hungry. Take the large branch for your creature." Fessran waited as Ratha lit the stick. "What about the rest of your creature?" she asked, her voice indistinct through the stick she had picked up.

"We will leave it and it will die," Ratha said. "But my creature has given birth and its nursling dances at the end of my branch. So will it always be with the Red Tongue." She paused. "Are you ready, Fessran?"

The other flicked her tail in answer and the two set off across the burn, Fessran in the lead, Ratha following, bearing the torch.

As the two traveled, the grass grew thicker underfoot, hiding the burn beneath a new carpet of green. Wild wheat stems stroked their bellies and flanks as they passed through, and Ratha had to hold her torch aloft to avoid setting the new growth alight. A sea of waving grasses covered what had been forest floor, swirling around the fire-blighted stands of pine and fir. Only the great redwoods still shaded the land, their heartwood still living, their fibrous bark only scarred by the Red Tongue's passing. The wild grasses grew thin in their shadow and the torch seemed to burn brighter in the cool, still air beneath their boughs.

But the trees were few and the grass triumphant as it spread far in the open sunlight. Ratha walked behind Fessran, watching her tail swing back and forth in time to her pace, listening to the fire snap and hiss. The only other sounds were of grass swishing past legs and the muted hammer of a woodpecker from its faraway perch.

The sun reached its zenith and began to fall again. Fessran had replaced Ratha's torch as many times as there were blackened stubs left along the trail. Ratha could hear Fessran's stomach growl and her own, she was sure, would meet her backbone by the time they arrived on clan ground.

Ratha slowly became aware that the continuous low gurgle in the background was not coming from her stomach or Fessran's. It was the sound of running water. She tried to scent the stream, but the acrid tang of torch smoke made her nose useless. She could only follow Fessran's lead.

Soon they were walking along a grassy stream bank. Fessran found a ford where the stream ran shallow over gravel. They began to wade across, Fessran still leading, Ratha behind.

Fessran reached the other side and scrambled up the steep bank, shaking mud and pebbles from her feet. "Here is where we swam with the deer away from the Red Tongue," she called back to Ratha, who still stood in midstream.

Ratha remained where she was, letting the water flow over her paws. The creek looked different in the open sun with grass instead of trees on its banks. But there, upstream, were the potholes she'd swum across and above them the waterfall she'd tumbled down. Her flank ached momentarily at the memory.

"I know your feet are weary, Ratha"—Fessran's voice cut into her thoughts—"but we have only a little farther to go."

Ratha's jaws loosened in dismay and she almost dropped the torch in the water. Only at little farther to go? She wished that she was back on the burn, still traveling; the goal of her journey too far ahead to have to worry or think about. Now, suddenly, she had arrived. Ratha looked up the bank to where her companion was standing. Clan ground. And she wasn't ready.

"Are you going to let your tail drag in the water all day?" Fessran sounded annoyed.

Ratha glanced down at her reflection. *Herder of the Red Tongue,* she thought wryly. A thin forlorn face stared back at her, holding the torch in its jaws. An echo of her own voice rang in her ears. *Clan leader, hah! Who is he compared to. . . .*

"Ratha, hurry." Fessran leaned down the bank. Ratha jerked her head up and sprang, dripping, onto the slope. Her paws slid on the muddy bank but Fessran seized her ruff and hauled her up.

Ratha paced back and forth on the stream bank while Fessran shook herself off. This was home ground, but very much changed. The forest no longer reached the stream and the meadow had altered shape and grown larger. The grass felt new and crisp underfoot. Ratha looked across the open land and remembered the cool dimness of the old forest.

The meadow stood empty. No beasts grazed; no herd-folk stood guard. Ratha shivered. *Where are they . . .?*

"Fessran, could the clan have gone somewhere else?" she asked, turning to her companion and speaking awkwardly around the branch.

"The meadow grass is not thick enough for beasts to graze," Fessran said. "And the dapplebacks like to browse in thickets. Our folk may have taken the animals further away to graze, but I am sure they will return to the dens at sunfall."

Fessran found the overgrown trail that led to the clan dens.

"The grass is bent here," she said, nosing about, "and here are the marks of large pads. Meoran and the others came this way not long before."

Ratha stood on the stream bank, her soggy coat still dripping. She stared across the meadow. She thought it was empty, but what had caused that patch of weeds to wave when the rest was still? The motion died out and though Ratha searched intently she could see nothing else. Her wet coat made her shiver again.

"Someone is stalking us," she muttered in response to Fessran's questioning look.

"Some clan cub out hunting grasshoppers." Fessran

wrinkled her nose. "Come out of the weeds, weanling, and give greeting to your betters," she called. The meadow remained still.

"That isn't a cub," Ratha said.

"How do you know? I thought you couldn't smell anything with the Red Tongue's breath in your face."

"My nose isn't telling me. I just know," she growled.

Fessran lifted her tail and waved the white spot at the end of it. No cub in the clan, Ratha knew, would disobey that signal. No one came, however, and Fessran lowered her tail. "Shake yourself dry," she said irritably to Ratha, "and leave whoever it is to their games."

Ratha shook her pelt and followed Fessran onto the trail. It wound among the few trees that had been spared by the Red Tongue and forest giants that had fallen across the path. Fessran seemed unsettled, even though this was a trail she had once known well.

She stopped, one paw lifted. Ratha halted behind her.

"They watch," Fessran hissed. "All along the trail they watch and they hide themselves. If you be of the clan, come forward and give greeting!" she called, but again no one came out, although Ratha sensed motion between the trees and caught the phosphorescent gleam of eyes.

"Are they the Un-Named?" Ratha asked, shivering again although her coat was almost dry.

"No." Fessran's muzzle was lifted. "I smell scents I know well."

"Then why do they not come out and offer greeting?"

"I don't know." Fessran walked ahead a short distance and called again. "I am Fessran of Salarfang Den, a herder of the clan. I walk by right on this ground. Do you hear me, those of you out there? Srass, that rank odor can only belong to you. And, Cherfan, I smell you along with Peshur and Mondir. Come and show yourselves!"

Her roar rang in the air, but once it died, the afternoon continued to slip into twilight in silence. Her ears and whiskers drooped. She crouched and picked up the branch she had dropped.

"Wait, Fessran," Ratha said. "My creature grows weak. It wants food. Give it the branch you carry."

Fessran laid her stick across Ratha's until it caught. She held it while Ratha kicked dirt on the dying old one and then gave the new torch to Ratha. The fire snapped and roared, gaining hold in the wood. Ratha carried it high as she trotted down the trail after Fessran.

Again there were rustling sounds in the forest near the path and again sudden glimmers of eyes in the growing darkness. Faraway calls told Ratha and Fessran that the news of their coming was spreading far ahead of them. Fessran paced on, her head lowered, her tail stiff.

"I smell a kill," she hissed back to Ratha. "The clan will meet us before we reach it; of that I am sure."

Ratha felt her saliva dampen the wood between her teeth. The hunger had become a dull pain in her belly, drawing the strength from her limbs so that she trembled as she walked and she could see that her companion too was betraying her hunger. Only the Red Tongue was strong.

They went up the grassy rise and over the knoll, past the ancient oak with limbs low to the ground, where, Ratha remembered, she had first seen the Un-Named raider.

Fessran's gait slowed. Her footsteps became quieter, then ceased. Ratha crept alongside her. "There. Up ahead." Fessran's whiskers brushed her face. "Do you see? There they are." Ratha felt the whiskers twitch and slide away. "Stay here, Ratha," Fessran said. "I will have words with them."

Ratha dug her claws into the ground to anchor her shaky legs. She stared back at the eyes watching her. They had come out of hiding and were assembled together in mute challenge. Ratha smelled the scents drifting to her on the night breeze. She searched for the remembered scent of the clan, of kinfolk, of herdfolk who had taught her their skills and those she had run beside in the meadow when the Un-Named, their enemy, were attacking. The scents were there, but not as she remembered them. The smell of the clan had become the smell of the pack.

As soon as Fessran had taken a few steps downtrail, a single hoarse voice rose from the front of the group. "Come no further unless you wish to feel our teeth in your unworthy throats!"

"Are you growing blind with age, Srass?" Ratha heard Fessran yowl. "You know me and you know Ratha, who stands behind me. Let us pass and eat at the kill."

There was only silence and burning eyes.

"The clan knows you, Fessran," said a deeper voice, and Ratha's hackles rose, for she knew that voice and hated it. "But the one who follows we do not know. Turn that one away and you may come and eat."

"The one behind me, clan herder, is one you know and know well," Fessran said. Her voice was strained and Ratha knew she was trying not to anger Meoran. "The smell that is mingled with mine is of the herder Ratha, the she-cub that Thakur and I taught."

"She-cub? We smell no she-cub," Srass howled, and Ratha could imagine that Meoran stood next to Srass muttering the words into the old herder's tattered ear. "We smell no she-cub. We smell only that which burns, that which we hate."

"Yaran!" Fessran called, startling Ratha by naming her lair-father. "If you stand among these mangy fleabags, answer me! Do you turn away your own, the she-cub that you and Narir bore?"

"I smell no she-cub," Yaran's gravely voice answered, and Ratha's belly twisted in a sharper pain than hunger.

"Have you all got dung up your noses? Ratha, come forward and show yourself so we may end this nursling's play."

Shaking, Ratha crept forward, her torch casting orange light on the path. As the torchlight fell on the pack, they cowered. Ratha saw Meoran blink and narrow his eyes to agate slits in his broad face.

"We smell no she-cub!" Srass's cry rose again. "We smell only the thing we hate. Drive it away! Drive it from clan ground." He showed his broken teeth at Ratha.

She tried to speak above the pack's howling, but the torch in her mouth kept her mute. "Let her speak!" Fessran cried, lashing her tail. "She is Named. Let her speak."

"Fessran, take my creature," Ratha hissed through her teeth. As soon as her jaws were free she faced the pack.

"Look! Fessran holds it. She doesn't fear it," Ratha said as Fessran stood beside her, the torch between her jaws. "This is my creature. I have brought it to the clan.

I am Ratha, who once herded three-horn deer. Now I herd the Red Tongue."

Ratha heard a muffled cry and Meoran shouldered Srass aside and came to the front.

Ratha felt the ground grow damp with sweat from her paw pads. Meoran's odor surrounded her and seemed to crush her as he would with his great weight. His eyes were enough to still a challenge in any throat. If the eyes failed, the massive jaws would succeed. Ratha caught the glint of teeth like tusks behind his lips and remembered a time when the scent of freshly drawn blood mingled with his odor and those in the clan went about with lowered heads and eyes dull with fright.

"There will be no herder of the Red Tongue on ground I rule," Meoran said, his gaze steady on Ratha.

"I have not come to offer challenge, clan leader. I bring my creature to serve you, to keep you warm while you guard the animals at night."

"We do not know you, clanless and nameless one. Take the hateful thing and go."

Cold seeped through Ratha and horror crawled across her skin like a flea seeking somewhere to bite. In those few words he had stripped her of her name, her kin and all that she knew and valued. Only one thing remained now and it blazed in the jaws of the one who stood beside her.

"Give me my creature," she said to Fessran, who gave her a startled look at the change in her voice. Ratha took the torch from her companion.

She turned, playing the firelight across the front of the

pack. They all squinted in pain and ducked their heads. Even Meoran lowered his jowled muzzle.

"Kill it!" someone screamed and the rest took up the cry. "Kill her and the thing she bears!" The pack glared at her with hateful eyes, but not one of them approached her as she swung the flame in a sweeping arc.

"Yes, kill it," Ratha snarled through her teeth. "Come then. Tear out its throat. Spring and break its back. Here it is. What? You shy away?" She grinned around the branch. "You don't know how to kill it, do you? Hah! Such sharp teeth the clan has. Surely you can kill a little creature like this? Or am I the only one who knows?"

"Sss, Ratha!" Fessran's whiskers were in her ears. "You run too fast on a trail you don't know. Thakur is in the pack. I smell him."

"What do I care for . . ." Ratha growled back.

"You will care very much if he speaks what he knows," Fessran hissed, stamping her foot near Ratha's.

"Kill the Red Tongue!" Meoran roared.

"How? We don't know how," the pack wailed.

"None of you know!" Ratha brandished the torch, swinging it viciously. "The Red Tongue is my creature. It can't be killed."

The howls died down into a low moaning. Some of those in the front were lifting their chins and baring their throats. Baring their throats to her and the Red Tongue, Ratha realized with a shock. Not to Meoran. Again she met the clan leader's eyes and saw kindling in them a rage that would never burn out as long as her blood ran warm and the Red Tongue danced on the end of her branch. There was no returning along the trail she had chosen to take.

Meoran glared at the nearest herder whose chin was lifted. He raised a heavy paw and struck the supplicant, driving the lifted muzzle into the dirt. Other heads turned in fear of him, but Ratha could see that their terror of the fire was greater and the sudden fear in his eyes told her he also knew.

Ratha lifted the torch, casting its light further across the huddled bodies, seeking Thakur. She heard his voice before she saw him.

"Hear me, you of the clan. The Red Tongue *can* be killed. I saw her do it."

Beside her, Ratha felt Fessran start. She saw Meoran spring over the backs of the crouching pack and land among them again, ignoring the squalls of those crushed by his bulk. He seized Thakur by the scruff and dragged him out of the crowd. He flipped Thakur on his back and spread a massive paw on his chest.

"You would speak, herder. Tell what you know." Meoran seized and shook him.

Thakur twisted his head to look at Ratha. "He will kill you, yearling," he said calmly, bright blood running down his neck. "Take your creature and run away now."

Ratha's lower jaw was trembling so that her teeth vibrated against the torch shaft and she could barely hold it aloft.

"Speak, herder!" said Meoran between his teeth. Ratha swung the torch at him, but Thakur was closer and in the way. However much Ratha hated Thakur for betraying her, she could not use the fire against him. She knew Meoran sensed her reluctance, for as he moved, he thrust Thakur in front of him, a shield between himself and the vengeful thing that fluttered on Ratha's branch. He clawed at Ratha from behind Thakur's head and over Thakur's shoulder. Fessran danced around them, trying to distract Meoran enough so that she could snatch Thakur from the clan leader's jaws.

Ratha caught glimpses of the pack, standing together behind Meoran. None of them moved to help him. They watched and waited to see who would be the victor.

"Run, Ratha!" Thakur called as Meoran threw him from side to side.

"Let him go, Meoran!" she snarled and lunged with the torch. Meoran jerked Thakur up so that he hung like a cub from the leader's jaws, rear legs dragging on the ground, front legs stiff and splayed apart. Ratha skittered to a stop before she drove the torch into Thakur's chest. She recoiled and staggered back. Thakur averted his face, shut his eyes and went rigid, his body tight and trembling.

"Why, Thakur?" Ratha cried and felt her insides churning in agony. "Why did you tell them?"

"It was not hatred, Ratha," Thakur answered as he sagged in Meoran's jaws. He grunted in pain as the clan leader gave him another savage jerk.

"If I run, he will kill you," Ratha said. "If I free you, will you come with me?"

Slowly Thakur opened his eyes. "I can't go with you. He won't kill me. He needs what I know."

Ratha stood paralyzed, staring at him, trying to find an answer in his eyes. Once he had been a teacher, a friend— and even something more. What had he become now?

She raised her head and met Meoran's slitted gaze. Beyond him, the pack eyed her. Her power was waning as the Red Tongue crept down its branch. There was still enough to hold them from her throat, but soon they would sweep forward and engulf her.

"Go, yearling," Thakur said again, his voice thin.

She felt Fessran give her a quick nudge. She turned, starting in fright at the shadows that seemed to jump from the trees as the flame's light passed across them. She broke into a trot and heard Fessran following.

Several paces down the trail she stopped, lifted the torch aloft and looked back. Meoran and the pack were still there, black forms against the night. Ratha turned and galloped away, the fire lighting the trail before her. They weren't following . . . yet.

She plunged ahead, ignoring her shaking legs and the gnawing aching pain in her belly. The worst pain she could not ignore. It came from her own words that hammered in her brain as her heart hammered behind her breastbone.

Thakur . . . why?

Ratha sprinted uphill toward the knoll and the old oak. Orange light gleamed on its leaves and an owl, startled from its perch, hooted mournfully and floated away.

"They come, Ratha," Fessran panted beside her. "I hear branches breaking on the trail behind us."

Ratha glanced to the side and saw a spare fire-lit form running alongside. Her breath hissed between teeth tightly clamped on the torch shaft. "Thakur . . . Fessran, what will happen to Thakur?"

"What he knows about the Red Tongue may save him from Meoran's teeth. It will not save him from mine if you are caught and killed."

"No!" Ratha nearly stumbled. She lost ground, falling behind Fessran. "He did not do it out of hate. Take no revenge on him; promise me that."

Fessran slowed, letting Ratha catch up. "My promise means nothing. Meoran will have my blood too, if he catches us. We will talk later, across the creek. Run!"

Ratha's torch still flamed, but half of the wood was charred. The brand was nearly exhausted, although the wind whipped it and forced it to burn brightly, devouring the branch.

We can break branches from the trees on the far side of the creek, Ratha thought. *If we reach them. If Meoran catches us before then, my creature will have no strength left to keep him from our throats.*

Ratha and Fessran topped the hill and ran down the other side. Ratha gained speed from the long downslope and the Red Tongue burned fiercely near her whiskers. Somewhere ahead was the creek. Beyond that, clan ground ended.

Shadowed grass flew by beneath Ratha's feet, and she stretched her body into the run. She saw only the swath of light the torch threw ahead of her, letting everything else slip by in a blur. She passed Fessran and left her far behind. Her speed and the rush of the Red Tongue gave her a wild exhilaration, as if she, not the clan, had been the victor.

She was too far ahead of Fessran to hear the other's warning cry.

The grass beneath her paws changed to mud and she was skidding, unable to stop. Whirling her tail, she back-pedalled, trying to keep her hindquarters beneath her. Mud piled up between her toes. Pebbles raked her pads.

The bank became steeper and dropped away. She gave one despairing kick that shot her out over the water. She lost control and tumbled. The torch sailed out into the darkness. For an instant, she saw two fires flash; one above the surface; one below. They met and died as the torch fell and sank.

Ratha hit the water and came up flailing wildly. She dug her feet into the stream bed and reared up, beating at the water with her paws. The fire was gone.

The stream rippled in cold moonlight as she searched for her creature. She splashed in the stream; sweeping her forepaw through the water; clawing at the bottom; even plunging her head beneath the water to search with her whiskers. Nothing.

She felt something bump her flank. She whirled and seized it. A familiar taste and charred smell told her it was her torch, but now, with the Red Tongue gone, worthless as any other stick. She let it drift away.

Ratha threw back her head and screamed in rage and terror. Now nothing could hold Meoran from her throat. And it had all been for nothing. The Red Tongue was gone.

She reared up again, slashing and tearing at the stream, as if it had flesh and could yield some retribution for killing her creature. She heard footsteps on the bank above her. A splash beside her nearly knocked her over. Sharp teeth fastened in her nape.

"Ratha!" Fessran's voice hissed behind her head. Fessran's breath was hot and moist on her skin beneath the fur.

"My creature! My creature is dead!" Ratha howled, her throat raw from her cry.

"The clan comes," Fessran said between her fangs. "Your noise will guide them to us. Be still!"

"They seek me. Run, Fessran. If they find me, they won't follow you."

"Speak again and I'll push your nose beneath the water. I too held the Red Tongue between my jaws and Meoran will not forget that."

The teeth fastened on Ratha's nape again and she was hauled through the water, dragged out and pushed ashore. She shook so badly she could hardly stay on her feet and the wind on her wet pelt made her feel as though she had no fur at all.

Fessran's slick coat gleamed faintly as she passed Ratha and moved up the far bank.

"Wait."

Fessran looked back, her eyes phosphorescent. "Clan ground ends here," she said, "but the clan's wrath doesn't."

"We can't outrun them. It has been too long since we've eaten," Ratha said.

Fessran lowered her muzzle and hunched her shoulders.

"Fessran, there is no hope they will spare me. But you may be able to turn their hatred away from you."

"How?" The eyes narrowed.

"The Red Tongue is dead. Meoran need not know that it was my foolishness that killed it. It was you, Fessran. You killed it and drove me off. He must have heard my cry."

"*Yarr* . . . and I hear him," Fessran muttered. "Quickly, Ratha."

"He'll believe it. Here," Ratha said, swiping at her belly and extending her fur-covered claws to Fessran. "A tuft of fur. Put it between your teeth." She lifted a paw and smeared Fessran's coat with the blood and dirt from her cut pads before Fessran could stop her. "There. I turned on you with the Red Tongue, but you struck it down and killed it. Can he doubt my blood on your fur? And the stick has come ashore downstream. Show him that when he arrives."

"Enough!" Fessran hissed. "He will never. . . ."

"You don't have time to wash yourself off before he gets here." Ratha pawed Fessran's face, leaving a smear along her jaw. She jumped back at Fessran's strike. The eyes were blazing.

"Get away from here before I make it real!" Fessran snarled.

Ratha ducked her head and scuttled away. She paused, lifted her head and looked back. "May you eat of the haunch and sleep in the driest den, Fessran," she said softly. "You are of the clan. You cannot leave them. I am the one whose way lies apart from the rest."

The other's eyes cooled. The tail gave one last twitch. "May the trail you run lead you back to us."

"See to Thakur," Ratha said.

"I will. Go now." Fessran's whiskers drew back. "I don't want you to see me fawning on Meoran."

Ratha leaped up the bank, leaving her behind. The howls of the clan sounded not far across the creek. Ratha trotted downstream for a short distance and angled off into the brush. Making sure that she was downwind from the stream bank, Ratha crouched in a thicket, listening. Her heartbeat threatened to choke her. Would her plan work? Would the clan leader believe Fessran's story and spare her? They needed good herders too badly to kill one needlessly.

If Fessran dies, Ratha thought, kneading the earth beneath her forepaws, *I will go and bare my throat to Meoran.*

The howling swelled, then fell silent. Voices spoke. Ratha was too far away to hear the words, but she caught tones. Meoran's deep growl, Srass's whine. Fessran's voice, rising and falling. Then, silence. Ratha tensed, grinding her teeth together, waiting for the outcry from the pack that would signal Fessran's death. Nothing.

She lifted her chin, swiveling her ears all the way forward, hardly daring to think that such a simple trick had saved her companion. She peered through the interwoven branches. The moon was silver on the stream bank. Forms paced up and down on the far side. Fessran was seated, speaking to Meoran. She extended a paw. Meoran leaned forward to sniff it while the clan gathered about them. Fessran got up, joined the others, and Ratha lost her among them.

She dropped down behind her thicket, dizzy with relief and weariness. She laid her chin on the damp ground and felt her heart gradually slow. The ache in her belly came back and the cuts on her pads began to throb. There was mud in the wounds, but she didn't have time to clean them. The wind might soon shift, carrying her scent to the clan and revealing her hiding place. Exhausted and hungry as she was, she had far to run before she would be beyond the clan's reach.

She yawned. *This would be a good place to sleep,* she thought, pushing herself up on her front paws. *If I did, Meoran would soon be standing over me, ready to give the killing bite.* She coaxed her reluctant hindquarters up and peered out of the thicket. The voices were silent. The clan folk had gone. Fessran was probably sending them on all sorts of false trails, looking for her.

She stepped out of the thicket and looked up at the stars. The trees here were fewer and she could see a greater stretch of sky. So many stars, she thought. Each seemed to burn like a tiny piece of her lost creature. The night wind touched her wet coat, making her prickle and shiver.

She was clanless; outcast and outlaw. Her training as a herder was worthless now, for she had no beasts to keep. There would be no more gatherings; no sharing of the clan kill. From now on she would have to provide for herself, and that no one had taught her.

Miserably, she crept away. She stayed in shadow beneath brush and trees, avoiding open ground where newly sprouting grass was bathed in moonlight beside the charred lengths of fallen pines. For a while, she chose stealth over speed, but at last her desperation drove her from cover. She ran from an enemy neither seen nor smelled, whose dark presence loomed up in every tree shadow, sending her fleeing from the path. She ran like a cub on her first night trail, fearful of anything that moved.

The wind grew bitter, hissing and rattling branches. The new ache in Ratha's chest did not distract her from the old ache in her belly, and she endured them both, until the hunger pain became a weakness that seeped into her legs. She stumbled from tree to tree, resting against them until she gained breath to go on. The trail faded away, or she lost it, for now she fought her way through thorns and ropy vines. She panted harder. Her pads grew slippery with sweat, stinging the gravel cuts. She was almost grateful for the pain; it kept her alive and angry when she was tempted to fall and lie amid the brambles that snared her. It was the anger that made her tear loose from them and stagger on, leaving tufts of fur behind.

The earth itself seemed to betray her, for it grew mushy underfoot and she sank at every step. The soft ground sucked at her feet, dragging her down, while the tangle thorns chewed at her ruff and flanks. She was caught and held by spikes growing from the vines, and struggle as she would, she could not break free. For a while she was still, regaining her strength. With a final effort, she wrenched herself loose, the thorns scoring her sides.

She overbalanced, toppled and started to roll down a steep grade. Limp and exhausted, she let herself go, dragging a claw now and then to slow her descent. She landed against something, heard a soft crunch and smelled the odor of woody decay. She tried to rise, but could only lift her head; the rest of her body was too weary to obey.

Ratha let her head loll, feeling damp moss against her cheek. Was this to be her deathplace? Would the clan find her here, a rotting lump of fur beside an equally rotten log?

No! She ground her teeth; she would not lie still, not yet. If Meoran and the others came she would meet them on her feet, with fangs bared.

If only she could have a little time to rest. That would be all she needed. Just time enough for the strength to flow back into her limbs and the ache in her chest to lessen. Then she would be able to fight if she had to, or to journey on, seeking water to soothe her throat and something to fill her belly.

The ground seemed to rock beneath her when she closed her eyes, letting her rise and fall as though she were a cub crawling on her mother's ribs. She opened one eye at the shadowed ferns hanging above her. The leaves were still, and she knew that it was not the ground that rocked her, but the depths of her own weariness. She let the imagined motion lull her into a daze, then into sleep.

Ratha woke abruptly, itching all over. Had all her fleas gone mad? They were all dancing beneath her coat, tickling her skin until the urge to be rid of them overcame her exhaustion. She twitched a paw and saw something white and wriggling fall on the ground. Whatever was crawling through her fur, it wasn't fleas.

With one bound she was on her feet, shaking hard until she thought she would jerk her pelt loose. Some of the invaders fell on the ground beneath her, but others remained as moving lumps in her underfur. Her tail bristled with horror. Was she so close to death that worms were seeking her body? She remembered seeing the carcass of a dappleback mare felled by sickness. The clan would not touch the tainted meat and the body was left for other scavengers. She remembered the sound that welled up from the carcass; a soft humming and whispering. It was the song of the death-eaters; the sound of dissolution. It was the sound of millions of tiny jaws chewing through cold flesh. Ratha remembered the song and shuddered. She shook herself again. She saw pale carapaces and waving legs on the moonlit ground beside her paws. Some of her horror faded into curiosity. These weren't worms, she thought, pawing at one scuttling insect.

She looked back to where she had lain against the fallen

log. The leathery wood was crushed inward, revealing a channeled interior. More pale termites swarmed and milled within the hollow, spilling out like a thick liquid around the edges.

She had landed right in a nest of them. No wonder she had awakened with the creatures in her fur! She nosed her back and trapped one moving lump between her fangs. She pulled it loose from her coat, feeling the hair thread between her teeth. The flailing legs touched her tongue and made her gag. She bit down on the insect and felt the carapace break.

She spat the mangled thing out, but not before a trace of its flavor escaped onto her tongue. She had been prepared for a bitter or nauseating taste, but instead found it bland and sweet, reminding her of the river-crawlers she had eaten with Thakur. Her hunger came back in a rush. She let saliva wash over her tongue, testing the flavor again. Not as good as river-crawlers, but definitely palatable.

She licked up several termites that were crawling by her feet, crunched and swallowed them.

Ha, eaters of death, she thought. *I will eat you!*

She cleaned up the others that had fallen from her fur and began grooming herself, eating the ones she found in her pelt. Not satisfied with those, she pawed at the nest, breaking more of the rotten wood. A seething mass poured out on the ground. She stepped on them and then ate them.

By dawn she was almost full. Daylight chased the termites into the depths of their battered nest, but Ratha no longer cared. With the cramp in her belly eased, she was ready to journey on.

For several days, Ratha traveled through thick woods of broadleaf and pine. Here the fire's touch had not been felt and the air beneath the trees was cool and dim, reminding her of her own forest before the Red Tongue's coming. She thought, as she prowled on needles, that she could make a new home among these silent trees. There were plenty of rotting logs that would yield their inhabitants to her claws, at least until she found some other source of food. Even as she thought about staying, her feet carried her on until the forest thinned and gave way to scrub and tangle. Only when she was clear of the trees did she stop to look back. The forest beckoned to her from within its gray-green depths, promising her quiet and safety. The horizon also beckoned, promising her nothing except challenge.

She turned from the forest and galloped toward the horizon.

CHAPTER 7

RATHA SNIFFED at the trail of tiny prints that ran over the flat and into the rushes. The stink of marsh mud rose to her nostrils, overwhelming the smell of her quarry. Her hindquarters trembled and she sat down. A wave of nausea swept through her, and her stomach threatened to disgorge the lake water she'd drunk early that morning, trying to still the hunger cramps in her belly.

The tracks led on further into the marsh. She coaxed herself up and followed them. The marsh shrew had run before her only a short time ago; the tracks cut sharply into the black mud. Ratha knew about tracks. Thakur had taught her to find straying three-horns and dapplebacks by their prints and how to tell if a trail was worth following.

She stopped and studied the ground. Here, the prey had been running. The tracks were deeper and farther apart. Tiny bits of caked mud, a lighter gray than the ooze, littered the trail as if flung from scurrying paws. Ratha's excitement rose as she padded alongside the trail. Saliva filled her mouth. Soon her teeth would crunch on bone and she would suck warm salty blood. The gnawing pain in her belly would cease. . . .

Ratha stopped. The tracks ended. One last footprint in the mud and beyond, nothing. She whined in dismay, nosing about around the trail. Could the shrew have leaped away onto a log or branch? She looked around, frantically. Nothing but mud on either side. Where had the prey vanished?

Again, she circled, trying to find the track. She stepped on something smooth and slender that bent underneath her pad. She drew back her foot and looked. Embedded in her pawprint was a feather; a long slim quill. Shrill cries overhead made her look up. Several birds wheeled high above her. From the shape of their wings she knew that they also ate flesh. Her whiskers drooped. Her prey was probably squirming in their talons or being torn apart by hooked beaks. This hunt was ended. She would have to begin again.

Ratha caught motion at the edge of her vision. She whirled around. A heavy beak clamped shut in the air where the nape of her neck had been.

For an instant, she flattened on the ground, staring up at her opponent.

The great bird cawed and raised its crest, staring at her with unblinking lizard eyes. Its weight sunk its talons deep into the ooze. Massive legs with scaled horny skin supported a body that was all bulk and neck, the tiny wings buried in hairy feathers. This one had not dropped from the skies. Atop the serpentine neck, the great head swayed and the beak gaped once again. A talon lifted. The inside of the beak was yellow; the narrow tongue a glistening pink.

For another instant, Ratha crouched, paralyzed, watching the talon and the open maw descend. Then she remembered her legs. The beak stabbed into black ooze. Terrified, she scurried away through the rushes as the hunter's hoarse cry of rage echoed over the marshland. She fled, turning and twisting, to throw her pursuer off the trail. She ran until her legs would no longer carry her and then she fell and slept in exhaustion until her belly woke her with the reminder that it had yet to be filled.

Afternoon found her tracking again. The prey was wounded or ill; she could tell by the irregular footsteps and wandering trail. Sometimes the prints were smudged by the impression of a dragging tail. Again, she followed, but this time she did not let the intensity of her hunt make her forget that she too might be prey.

The trail grew fresher and the smell stronger. She

crouched as she approached a fallen log in her path. On the far side of it she could hear soft rustling sounds, and the crack and crunch of seeds being eaten. Again she trembled and her belly grew tight. She slunk along the side of the rotting timber and looked around the edge. There it was. A little marsh-shrew with a dull striped pelt and flanks almost as shrunken as hers. One rear leg was wounded and dragging. The blunt snout turned, the nostrils twitched. Ratha ducked back. Then, as the creature turned once more to its meal, she peered past the ragged spongy ends of the fallen timber. At last something she could catch.

She gathered herself, bunched and sprang over the log. She landed short, slipped in the mud, leaped again and landed on her prey with her front paws.

Her tail swung wildly to keep her balance as the animal squirmed beneath her pads. She felt herself toppling, struck one forepaw out to catch herself and felt her prey slip out from beneath the other. Furious, she lunged and snapped, but the creature, despite its injury, was far away from her, scooting across the flat toward the reeds. Ratha flung herself after it, howling in anguish. She chased the animal up and down through the high grass, desperation keeping her only a few tail-lengths behind. The marsh grass opened into a meadow of ferns and she was gaining on her quarry when a flurry of black and brown erupted from nowhere and something charged into her, knocking her aside from her prey. There was a shrill scream from the animal, a deep growl and then silence.

Ratha scrambled out of the clump of ferns and staggered to her feet. A young male of her own kind stood a short distance away, staring back at her. Her marsh-shrew, now lifeless, dangled from his jaws. He dropped it in among the ferns and began to play with it, glancing from time to time at Ratha. Driven by hunger, she moved closer. He lashed his tail, growled, picked the carcass up and pranced a short distance through the ferns. There he laid it down, ambled a few tail-lengths away and began grooming himself.

Ratha flattened and crawled through the ferns, freezing whenever he looked her way. His smell was oddly familiar, she realized, between the waves of hunger that were sweeping over her. She slunk forward again, raising her whiskers above the fronds. He turned, yawned in her face and ducked his head among the ferns. A loud crunch of teeth on bone told her he was eating her prey.

With an outraged scream, Ratha flung herself at him but exhaustion made her fall short. She pushed herself up on wobbly legs, fluffed her tail and spat. He flicked one ear and went on eating. Only half the carcass was left.

"Scavenger!" Ratha hissed. "Un-Named dung-eater! Flea-ridden chewer of bones! *Arrr,* you can't understand my words, bone-chewer, but you'll understand my teeth!"

The other gazed at her, a scrap of fur and flesh hanging from his jowls. It disappeared into his mouth in several swift bites and his lips drew back from his teeth as he chewed, revealing a broken lower fang. Ratha looked at his ears. One had a piece bitten out of it and the ragged edge bore the marks of teeth. Hers. It was the raider who had attacked Fessran's dapplebacks in Ratha's first encounter with the Un-Named raiders.

"The same words again, clan cat?" he said, looking straight at her. "Do they teach you no others?"

Ratha's nape bristled and she felt the fur rising all the

way down her spine to her tail. Her nostrils flared. She was unsure of whether to attack or retreat and did neither. She could only stare at the mangled carcass between his forepaws and swallow the warm saliva flooding her mouth.

He tore another strip from the prey. The smell from the glistening flesh brought Ratha forward. Saliva slipped between her teeth and ran over her lips into her fur.

"You are far from home ground, clan cat." He gulped the meat. "And far from the herdbeasts that keep you fed."

Ratha took another step forward. She could see the ends of her whiskers quivering. "I chased the marsh-shrew, broken-fanged one. Let me have what is left of it."

"Yes, you chased it," he agreed. His tone was light, but his eyes were wary. "You didn't catch it. I caught it."

"I caught it. My paws were on it before yours. I drew first blood."

"Is that a new clan law? I thought they had enough laws and leaders to bare their throats to." He grinned, exposing the jagged edge of his fang.

"Give me my prey!" Ratha howled and flung herself at him. Her trembling legs turned her lunge into a stumble.

He snatched up the remains of the prey and trotted beyond her reach. He sat down among the ferns and gave her a mocking look. "You are a bad hunter, clan cat. Only good hunters eat," he said between his teeth, lifting his head to let the rest of the carcass slide into his open gullet.

"Raider! Bone-chewer! I broke your fang and tore your ear. Come near me or steal my prey again and I will chew your tail off and stuff it down your gluttonous throat!"

He lolled his tongue out at her, turned, and, tail in the air, sauntered away.

Ratha went to where the shrew's carcass had lain, hoping to find a few neglected morsels. She found only moss, stained with blood and spittle. She bent her head and licked the green carpet, but only got the faintest taste. She closed her eyes and felt her belly twist in despair.

Only good hunters eat, she thought.

She lifted her head and bared her fangs. She shredded the moss with her claws.

She had lost her world and everything in it. The herder's knowledge that served her in the clan was worthless here. She had left her people far behind. Now, she realized, as she felt the grinding pain of hunger fade into a frightening numbness inside her, she must leave their ways behind as well.

I was raised to be a herder, part of her mind cried. *That life is gone. What else is there? Nothing,* the same part of her mind answered. *In choosing to leave the clan, you chose to die.*

Despair paralyzed Ratha. She wanted to sink down onto the moss and lie still forever. To become dry bones, scattered by the feet of those who would pass this way. Crumbling bones, crawling with insects.

Another part of her mind began speaking. She quieted the turmoil inside and listened. This part spoke in images and feelings rather than words. It told of scents followed along star-lit trails, of stalking and waiting in shadow, of branches breaking close by and the sudden fever at the smell of the prey. It told of a life far older than that of the clan, a life far deeper and, in a strange way, far wiser. The old part of her mind told Ratha she had that wisdom. She woke from the telling as she would from a dream and she trembled, for it was far stronger than the clan-taught knowledge. The way of the clan, she knew, went back many seasons and many lifetimes. She knew the names of those who led the clan, from the first ones all the way to Baire and Meoran. The way of the herder was old, but there was another way, ancient beyond memory. It went back to the time before the beginning. The way of the hunter.

Whiskers poked out of a burrow. A timorous nose followed. Earth and small stones tumbled as the occupant emerged and peered around. Hiding in a patch of weeds, Ratha tensed. She could see the black stripes along the animal's cheeks; the blunt snout. Delicate five-toed paws joined the whiskers in exploring the ground outside the burrow.

This hunt, Ratha thought, would be different. She knew hunger had robbed her of the speed and agility a hunter needed. She still had something that might make the difference if she used it properly: her cleverness. If she could outwit three-horns and Un-Named raiders, surely she could catch a shrew.

The marsh-shrew looked toward Ratha's hiding place, lifted its chin and showed long chisel teeth, as if it knew she was there.

The animal's forequarters were already out of the hole and the hindquarters soon followed. The striped shrew began wandering away from its burrow, stopping every few paces to raise its muzzle and sniff the air. Ratha's excitement grew with every step the animal took away from its den. She quivered and bunched herself together, treading softly with her forepaws, waiting until the shrew was far from the burrow. She jerked sharply, fighting the impulse to pounce. There was something else that had to be done first.

She remained still until the shrew reached a stand of marsh grass and began to gnaw on the tuberous roots. Ratha gave it one last glance, left her hiding place and crept, not toward the shrew, but toward the empty burrow. A mound of dried mud stood to one side of the entrance, a product of the shrew's excavations. With one swipe, she pushed the fill into the burrow and added a few pawfuls of surface mud. She pressed hard to pack it solid, then, with another glance over her shoulder, slunk back to her place in the rushes. As she settled in her nest, she purred softly to herself, pleased with her cleverness. This hunting business wasn't so hard if one gave it some thought, she decided.

The hard part was staying still until the shrew had finished its meal of roots, and even after it had left the marsh grass, it still wasn't ready to return to the den. Ratha watched, her impatience mixed with grudging admiration as her prey turned hunter, attacking and devouring flies and beetles. She saw the shrew leap at a dragonfly droning low over the marsh and when the little hunter fell back on the mud, she saw that it bore a broken jeweled body in its jaws. Her keen ears caught muffled snaps as the shrew bit off the insect's legs and then continuous frantic crunching until only the lacy wings were left, scattered on the mud beside the still-twitching legs.

The shrew sniffed among the remains, turned its head up and looked at the sky, as if wishing for more and, finally sated, waddled back toward its lair. Halfway there, it stopped and its careless amble turned into a wary creep. Hidden in the grass, Ratha shivered, trying to still the clamor in her brain. The promise of food had awakened her stomach and it growled its impatience at her. Spring now. Now. NOW!

Ratha's hind legs shot back, throwing her through the rushes. She stayed flat, hugging the ground. The shrew bolted for its den, launched itself at the entrance and bounced off the packed mud. It scurried back and forth, dodging her wildly slapping paws. She chased it away from the burrow, across the mudflat between the rushes, around a rotting log and back again. Reeds slapped her face as she dashed through them, trying to keep her prey in sight.

The shrew tried again for its burrow. It flung itself onto the packed earth and dug in a wild frenzy. By the time Ratha reached the den, the shrew had bored halfway in. She skidded to a stop; scooped the shrew out of its hole. It nipped her pad and she dropped it, squalling in pain. Squeaking shrilly, the animal reared up on its hind paws and showed its teeth. Ratha circled the shrew as it squealed and danced. She lifted one paw and slapped down hard, trying to squash the shrew into the mud. It bounced high into the air and shot off in a different direction. Ratha whirled and caught a glimpse of another tunnel opening in a mudbank beneath a tangle of swamp grass roots. The shrew was heading straight for it.

With a yowl of rage, Ratha scrambled after her prey. Despair gave her speed, but her shaky legs failed to stop her in time. The shrew reached the second tunnel before she did. She made one last snap at the vanishing hindquarters before she overshot and plowed headfirst into the bank.

The impact ground her teeth against gravel and filled her mouth and nose with mud.

Ratha recoiled, rearing back and clawing the air. The ooze clung inside her mouth, blocked her nose and she fell on her back, retching, trying to push the vile-tasting muck out with frantic thrusts of her tongue. Her maltreated stomach cramped and convulsed, sending its meager contents up her throat. She stretched her mouth wide, letting the bitter fluid stream over her tongue and through her nose, turning the ooze to sizzling froth that dripped from her jaws. Her stomach was empty, but the spasms continued, wrenching her belly and thrusting her hind legs out stiff until they quivered and cramped.

For a moment she thought she was going to heave her insides up onto the marsh mud, but the sickness soon subsided, leaving her a limp and panting heap of fur, drooling brown saliva.

She wished then that she could die and that the clan could know how she died. Meoran would howl until he farted if he knew that the proud bearer of the Red Tongue had choked on swamp mud trying to catch a wretched shrew! She squeezed her eyes shut and felt fluid run from them to join the stuff dribbling from her eyes and nose. The Red Tongue? Why think of that now? It was gone. Finding the fire once was a fluke. She would never find it again. This was the life she would have to lead, if she could.

Slowly Ratha rolled from her side onto her stomach and dragged herself through a clump of rushes to the shore on the other side. Her belly ached; her nose and throat burned. Her lips and tongue were raw. Her fangs had lost their usual smooth slickness against her tongue and felt etched and gritty.

Scum edged the bank and clung to the half-drowned rushes. A rainbow film on the water's surface shimmered in translucent colors. Ratha closed her eyes and put out her tongue to drink.

A paw slid under her neck, shoving her muzzle away from the water. Ratha gave a weak cry and pushed stupidly against it, feeling a strong foreleg against her jaw. She opened her eyes. At seeing her companion's tinted reflection, she cried again and turned her head away, hating the taste of bile in her mouth and hating the intruder for not letting her drink. Again she tried and again he thrust her back. She lay panting, her chin in the mud. He walked in front of her, flicking a ragged ear.

"Clan cat, doesn't your nose tell you this is bad water?"

"I'm thirsty. My mouth burns. Let me drink." Ratha whimpered.

"I know. I saw you being sick. You'll be much sicker if you drink here. There's a stream further up. You'll be able to find it."

"Bone-chewer, keep to your own trail! I'll decide for myself where to drink." She glared at him with all the hate she could muster. She narrowed her eyes, feeling them go to slits. "Why do you care if I get sick? You took my prey; you want me to starve. Go away." Ratha rolled away from him onto her side and curled into a ball. She heard his footsteps squelch on the marshy ground. They stopped. She cracked one eyelid, hoping the silence meant he was gone. No. He was still there, sitting a short distance away, watching her with yellow eyes. Yellow eyes, in a face that seemed strangely familiar, as if it echoed the face of another.

Ratha groaned and slid her chin across her forepaws, as she looked up at him. "Bone-chewer, why do you stay?"

"I'm full. I have nothing else to do. And you are interesting. I've never seen such a poor hunter in my life."

"Leave me alone!" Ratha snarled weakly. "Why should I hunt if you take everything I catch?"

"You flatter yourself, clan cat. You have yet to catch anything."

Ratha jerked her head up and glared at him again, wishing she had the strength left to tear him into small scraps. Her head shook with anger and weariness. "I caught *you*, raider. Let your ear and your broken fang remind you of that."

She let her head sink back to her forepaws. The weeds rustled and she felt feet pad beside her. She stiffened. "What are you going to do now, raider? Kill and eat me?"

From somewhere above her head came a low rumble that sounded more amused than threatening. "No. There's not enough flesh on you to be worth the killing." He cocked his head at her. His coat gleamed with red-gold highlights in the hazy afternoon sun. "Despite what you may have been told about the Un-Named, we do not eat our own kind."

Ratha hitched herself away from him, but his tail still brushed her ribs as he curled it across his feet. "You are not of my kind, bone-chewer," she growled.

"There are differences," he agreed. "I am not nearly as foolish. Now that we know each other, clan cat, shall I show you where the stream lies?"

Ratha only grunted and ignored him. Her thirst was

fading, along with everything else. All she wanted now was sleep. There was something still stirring in her mind, though, that would not leave her alone.

I fought the raider in the meadow but that's not why I know his smell and his face. It is as if I know him, and yet I don't. Why?

She opened one eye and peered past the brush of her tail at him. Her eyelid felt heavy. She let it fall shut, blotting him out. His smell grew stronger and teeth seized her ruff. Ratha's eyes flew open as he hauled her up off the mud, shoving her forepaws underneath her with one swipe of his foot. When he let her go, she sagged, her legs buckled and she flopped down.

He backed off and gave her a puzzled look, faintly tinged with sadness. "Are you of the clan so weak that you can only lie down and die when you meet hardship? I thought you had more spirit when you mauled me in the meadow."

"Fine words from one who stole my prey!" Ratha hissed bitterly. "Had I eaten, I could follow you."

He circled her, his tail twitching.

"Too late, bone-chewer," she said hoarsely.

"Lie with your whiskers in the mud, then, clan cat" he said scornfully, his own bristling. Ratha closed her eyes and buried her nose in her forepaws. When she opened them again he was gone. She listened to the wind threshing the swamp grass and the cries of birds high overhead.

Who is he? she wondered, but then, as she drifted off to sleep, decided that now it really didn't matter.

A smell woke her. Musky, rich, intoxicating, the odor filled her nose and her whole hungry being. It lured her back out of a sleep that was letting her slip closer and closer to death. She plunged her fangs into the furry body lying beside her. Not until she felt the warm flesh between her jaws did she realize she was awake. She sank her teeth in to their full depth but she was too weak to manage a shearing bite. She squeezed the meat between her jaws, sucking the salty juices. Her stomach jumped in astonishment and began to churn greedily.

Where the kill had come from, she didn't know and didn't care. It was here, it was hers, and to her hunger-sharpened senses, it was the best thing she had ever tasted. Once she gained enough strength to start eating in earnest, she started at the head and had devoured half of the carcass when a now-familiar smell and familiar step made her freeze.

She hunched over the prey. She began to eat rapidly, with both paws guarding the carcass, gulping chunks that still had fur attached. He sat down and watched her. She shot wary glances at him between bites.

"Eat slowly, clan cat, or it will do you no good."

Ratha's ears started to flatten, but they pricked up again as she thought of something.

The prey . . . she hadn't caught it. Had he? She stopped eating, turned the remains over with her paw and inspected it for the marks that might be left by a broken fang.

"Don't bother, clan cat. I caught it," he said.

Ratha raised her chin and eyed him. "Why?"

"For the same reason I pushed you away from that tainted water."

Ratha lowered her head and slowly finished her meal.

"The Un-Named do not give help without a reason. What is it you wish from me, raider?"

"The Un-Named do not speak either, according to the great wisdom of the clan," he replied with a grin, but the yellow in his eyes had turned slightly bitter. Ratha pushed herself up on her forepaws and stretched, feeling the fullness of her belly and the returning strength in her legs. The fur on her face felt stiff and tight, caked with filth and dried fluid. With mild dismay, she realized she was mud-spattered from nose to tail. She licked one paw and began to scrub at her muzzle. After several strokes she stopped, dissatisfied with the results.

"You, clan cat, are a mess." The young male stood up and arched his back, showing off sleek copper-gold fur. "I'll show you the stream. You'll never get all that mud off with your tongue." With a wave of his tail, he trotted off. Ratha heaved herself to her feet, growling irritably.

The stranger led the way along a narrow trail, marked with deer and dappleback prints, edged with moss and mushrooms. Gradually the marshy ground gave way to a drier track, leading them uphill to a brook emerging from a cleft in the grassy slope. Ratha went to the spring and lapped the upwelling water. It was cold and clear, and she dipped her chin in and drank until her teeth ached. Once her thirst was slaked, she let the water flow over her tongue, from one side of her jaw to the other, cooling and rinsing her mouth until the last taste of sickness was gone.

She waded downstream and crouched in the shallows, letting the bubbling current ruffle her fur backwards. With chattering teeth she leaped out of the brook, wriggled on the grass and shook herself dry, sending a small shower in her companion's direction. He sneezed and trotted uphill beyond range. There he sat, on the slope above the spring, something unreadable in his eyes.

Ratha turned her tail to him and walked away.

"Where do you go now, clan cat?" His voice came from behind her. She stopped, lowered her tail and looked back at him. It was nearly sunset and the slanting red light set fire to his coat as he glanced over his shoulder at the sinking sun. Ratha caught herself thinking that he was very beautiful and immediately squelched the idea.

"To hunt, raider. My belly is full now and I am strong."

"What do you know of hunting?" he asked scornfully. "You've never hunted anything except grasshoppers and wayward herdbeasts."

"I know how to stalk and pounce. I know how to wait until the prey has left its hole and then fill the hole with dirt. I almost got that shrew."

"No matter how good you were at stalking and pouncing, and no matter how clever you were, you would never have caught that shrew. And you won't catch any other animals either," he said.

Ratha dug her foreclaws into the ground. He was still waiting, still wearing that maddening grin that showed his broken fang. She wanted to knock out the other one. "All right, raider," she said, taking a breath, "tell me why I won't catch anything."

"You don't know your prey. That striped shrew. What do you know about it?" he asked.

"I know what it smells like. I know what its prints look like. I know where it hides and what it eats. Isn't that enough?"

"You didn't know the one thing that might have saved you from eating mud instead of shrew. That shrew has many holes and they are all connected."

Ratha eyed him suspiciously. "What would a shrew want with so many holes? It can't sleep in more than one at a time. I would only want one. Everyone at home has only a single den. Some have to share."

The stranger sighed. "You are thinking like the clan herder you are. To catch a shrew, you must think as the shrew does."

Ratha wrinkled her nose. "Shrews can't think, can they? Not as we do."

"Oh yes, they can. They can be quite clever, as you will learn."

"But they don't have names . . . or clans either," Ratha spluttered.

"Must all who are clever have names and clans?" he asked, looking at her intently.

Ratha felt uncomfortable under his stare. "No," she said at last. "You have neither clan nor name, but you are quite clever. And that shrew was also clever."

"Not all animals have tunnels," he said, continuing. "Many hide in other ways. What you know now may let you hunt marsh shrews, but you'll get pretty sick of them." Ratha flicked her tail irritably as he paused. "There's a lot you need to know," he said and added, as if to himself, "I almost think I should teach you."

"You?" Ratha backed away, her tail fluffed. "I'd rather go back to the clan than have you as a teacher!"

He stared at her intently. His eyes held hers. He walked up to her and thrust his muzzle into her face. She tried to break the intensity of his stare, but could not and sat down nervously on her tail. "You can't go back to them, clan cat," he said. She sensed, as she looked past her reflection into the yellow depths of his eyes, that he knew much more about her than one of the Un-Named should know.

"You can't go back," he said again, softly. "And you can't live here without my help. No other among the Un-Named will aid you." He withdrew his face and she pulled her tail out from underneath herself and glared at him defiantly.

"I can find another clan. They'll take me in."

"There are no clans among our kind."

Ratha started to spit back a reply, but she knew deep inside that he spoke truth. However far she might wander, she would never find another herding community such as the one she had left. It had never been a real hope and it died as soon as it arose.

"Why? Why will you do this for me?" she demanded, knowing that she had no choice but to take his help if he offered to give it.

"Because of what I am, I suppose."

"You?" Ratha's spirit came back. "You are a raider and a bone-chewer!"

He ducked his head and grinned ruefully. "I am indeed, clan cat. But you may find I am something more."

"Hah! If you are the only one of all the other bone-chewers who will help me, why did I meet you instead of one of the others?"

"You didn't find me," he said, yawning. "I found you."

"Found me?" Ratha's jaw dropped. "You were looking for me? Why would an Un-Named bone-chewer be looking for me?"

"Perhaps to teach you some manners, young one," he

snapped, giving her an irritated cuff. Ratha jumped away and shook her head. Her eyes narrowed.

"I don't think you are an Un-Named One. You are far too clever. You remind me of someone in the clan, although I can't remember who." Ratha felt the fur rise on her nape. "Did Meoran send you to find me and kill me?"

"If he had, the marsh birds would be picking at your dirty pelt. No, clan cat. I bear no name and I obey no one." He grinned again. "Except my stomach."

"That I can believe," she said sourly, letting her prickling fur soften. *He must be telling the truth,* she thought. *Meoran would never have anyone like him in the clan.*

"Time to hunt, clan cat," he said, turning his face toward her. "We'll start with marsh-shrews. Later I'll teach you how to catch bush-tails and diggers. Are you ready?"

"Yes . . ." she said, and her voice trailed off.

"Mmm?" He crooked his tail.

"What do I call you?"

"Don't call me anything. I don't have a name."

"I have to call you something if I'm going to talk to you. If you can call me 'clan cat,' I should be able to call you something," she said stubbornly.

He flicked an ear. "Very well."

She hesitated. "What do you want me to call you?"

"You want the name. You choose it."

"*Arrr,* it isn't really a name," Ratha haid doubtfully. "Only the clan can give someone a *real* name, such as mine."

He looked irritated. "All that means is that it was bestowed upon you by some fat whelp that everybody bares their throat to. For no good reason I can think of," he added scornfully.

Ratha began sorting through possibilities. None of the names of those in the clan fitted him at all. The only one that even came close was one she had invented. The more she thought about it, the more she liked it. And there was nothing wrong with it. *After all,* she thought, *it isn't a real name.*

She saw him peer into her face and knew he had caught the glint in her eye. "I've got one," she said.

He drew back his whiskers. "I should have known better. Very well, clan cat. What am I to be called?"

"Bonechewer!"

"Arrr," he grumbled. "I suppose it suits me. Very well then. Follow me to the marsh and I'll see if I can make you into a hunter."

Ratha followed him, cheered by her minor revenge. Bonechewer. It really wasn't bad.

That evening he and Ratha caught more striped shrews and she managed to trap and kill one by herself. By nightfall, she was full and drowsy. She wanted a den where she could sleep. Instead, Bonechewer took her to a moonlit glade beneath the slope where the spring ran and told her to hide amid the ferns.

"We aren't going to hunt," he said in response to her grumble that she was stuffed right down to her tail. "Just stay here with me and watch."

He crouched beside her and they watched as the glade began to stir. Ratha had run trails and herded animals by night, but she had never stopped to notice how the darkness brought so many small creatures out of their dens. Even though Ratha's hunger was sated, she quivered with excitement and felt Bonechewer's paw descend on her to keep her from wreaking havoc among the night denizens of the meadow.

Tiny feet pattered back and forth through the underbrush, rustling last season's brittle leaves. Bonechewer listened and told her what creatures made which sounds. Some of them she knew, from her nights of guarding clan herds. Most, however, she didn't and had difficulty telling one animal's noises from those of another. Her ears were tuned to the calls of lost or straying herdbeasts or to the sounds of raiders lying in wait in the brush.

She started when a little blacksnake emerged from its hole almost between her forepaws and slithered away, its scales edged with silver. She watched it crawl through the grass and onto a rock still warm with the day's heat. As the blacksnake coiled itself with a soft scrape of scales, an animal with dingy gray fur, a pointed nose and a long bare tail ambled by the base of the rock. The blacksnake raised its head, tongue darting and scanned the bare-tail as it went by. The snake sank down again, loosening its coils. Ratha wrinkled her nose at the bare-tail's rank odor and agreed with the blacksnake that there were better meals to be had. A second bare-tail followed the first, the tail arched over its back. Several gray bundles dangled upside down by their own small tails wrapped around the larger one. The smelly bare-tail, Bonechewer said, often carried her young that way.

Bonechewer didn't take Ratha back to his den until sunrise and she slept until midday. Again they hunted marsh-shrews, and when both had killed and eaten their fill, he took Ratha to another place where she could hide and watch. They spent several evenings hidden together.

Each evening Bonechewer showed her the creatures that made up his hunter's world. He told her about their lives and habits and drilled her until she knew them. Not until she understood every quirk and characteristic of a prey animal did he let her hunt. She complained bitterly at first, for her instincts told her to pounce.

As she learned more, however, she complained less, for she began to see the wisdom in his method. Once she turned seriously to the task, she became so absorbed that it threatened to distract her from the business of filling her belly. Bonechewer varied things by showing her other hunters who shared his territory. One of Bonechewer's neighbors was the flightless bird that had attacked her on her first hunt. From afar, she watched it stride across the marshland, the furred carcass of its catch dangling from its hooked beak. That limp pelt could have easily been hers, she thought, shivering. When the great head lifted and the lizard eyes stared her way as if they knew exactly where she was hiding, Ratha broke cover and fled, ending the lesson for that day.

Once Bonechewer took her out of the marsh along the lakeshore and turned inland until they came to a small plateau dotted with trees and wildflowers.

There they saw a huge beast with the body, neck and head of an oversized dappleback. The creature's forelegs were longer than the rear legs, its back sloping down from shoulders to withers. Shaggy orange fur covered back and belly. Instead of hoofed toes, the feet bore sickle claws that forced the creature to walk with an awkward shuffle. Ratha hid among the flowers and watched the shambleclaw as it reared up to strip tender leaves from the trees or grub for roots with its claws.

It seemed to Ratha, as she followed Bonechewer on hunts and expeditions, that she was seeing every kind of animal there was. How narrow the herder's life seemed to her now as she began to relish the variety of forms and the variety of flavors. Bonechewer also taught her to fish in the lake and she found that the finny denizens of the water were as varied as creatures on land and sometimes even queerer. He showed her a fish with four eyes, two above and two below the surface of the water. He said it tasted dreadful, but was fun to watch on lazy summer afternoons as it shot down dragonflies with a stream of water and gobbled the drowning insects as they thrashed on the surface.

The only creature they had not seen was another of their own kind. Bonechewer prowled his territory alone except for her and they saw no other Un-Named hunters. To Ratha, accustomed to eating or working alongside many others, this solitary existence seemed strange and unsettling.

They were stalking meadow mice on the hillside below the spring when Ratha asked him why he never saw the other raiders.

"They don't come here," he answered, after finishing his kill.

"Why?"

"Why should they? They have their territories and I have mine. They stay on their ground and I stay on mine. I like it that way."

"If you like hunting alone," Ratha asked, puzzled, "why did you take me in?"

He grinned at her and she grinned back at the sight of the limp tail still hanging out of his mouth. He swallowed and the tail disappeared. "You're different," he said.

"I'm Named, if that's what you mean," Ratha answered tartly, not quite sure what she was getting into.

"*Ptahh!* That silly custom? It means nothing to me."

"If my name doesn't make me different, then what does?" Ratha demanded.

"You'll see, clan cat." He turned his head sharply and pointed with a paw. "There's a fat one over there." Ratha followed his gaze and saw the grass rippling. She wanted an answer to her question more than she wanted another mouse, but she sensed she wouldn't get it. At least not from him. She put away her annoyance and began to stalk, but she couldn't help wondering what he meant.

CHAPTER 8

SUMMER'S GOLDEN grass and lazy sun faded into wind and blowing leaves. The rushes beside the shore withered, turning brittle. Their crisp green odor turned dry and nutty. The mornings became cold and drizzly; the afternoons gray. Only once in a while did the sun seep through the clouds hanging above the lake. Everything smelled dank and rotten.

Ratha shed her summer coat and with it the last faint tracings of her spots. Her fur grew back thickly in gold and cream. She was pleased with her new beauty, but, to her dismay, it didn't last. The autumn rain turned all the trails to mud and she returned from hunting soggy and spattered from nose to tail. Bonechewer also shed his copper fur for a somber brown, which looked black in the rain.

The weather kept small creatures in their burrows. Both Ratha and Bonechewer worked hard to keep their bellies full. There were times when they returned empty to their den and could only lie and listen to each other's stomachs growl until hunger forced them to hunt again.

Ratha learned to eat lizards and earthworms and to chew on tubers she dug from the ground. She developed a taste for the noxious bare-tails, for they were often the only thing she could catch.

Autumn yielded to winter. The rain fell hard and often turned to sleet. Ratha and Bonechewer hunted by day and spent the bitter nights curled up with each other in a nest of leaves in a hollow pine. It got so cold that the one who slept closer to the entrance would wake shivering, his or her whiskers rimed with frost.

The morning was still and pale as Ratha poked her whiskers out of the den. She was alone, as Bonechewer had risen earlier to forage. She crawled out and shook herself. She felt itchy and irritable. There was a strange fragile feeling in the air, an uneasy lull between last night's storm and the mass of heavy clouds crawling down the ridge above the lake.

Better hunt now, she thought, knowing that she and Bonechewer would spend most of the short day huddled together in their den while the new storm lashed the lake to churning froth and flattened the rushes.

She circled the old pine until she picked up Bonechewer's scent. Soon she saw his tracks and followed them up along the lakeshore.

There she found him, up to his chest in muddy water. He was trying to drag something ashore. As Ratha came closer, she could see that his prize was the drowned carcass of a young deer. She waded in, despite the freezing water, and helped him haul it ashore.

"It hasn't been dead long," said Bonechewer, nosing the body. "For carrion, it is fresh. See? The eyes are still firm and clear."

"A three-horn fawn," Ratha said, noticing a bony swelling on the animal's nose that matched the two horn-buds on its head. She placed a paw on the fawn's ribs and rocked the carcass. It seemed oddly limp and the head rolled on the ground.

"Are you sure it's fresh?" she asked Bonechewer. "Put your paw on the back. Here, between the shoulders."

He did. "The back is broken," he said, cocking his head. "So is the neck. And here are the marks of teeth. This beast didn't drown. I think this is a kill."

"Who would throw their kill into the lake?"

Bonechewer twitched his tail. "Someone may have lost it in the storm last night. He may have been dragging it along the ledges that overhang the lake on the far side. We may find the hunter's body washed up further along the shore."

Ratha sat down and stared at the carcass. The prickly sensation she had been feeling all morning had soured her temper. "Bonechewer, I haven't seen any three-horns around the lake, or anywhere else here."

"I haven't either," he answered, shaking his pelt dry. "There aren't any. I've lived here long enough to know."

"Then where did this one come from?"

He grinned. "Perhaps Meoran sent you a gift."

"Bonechewer!" Ratha stamped, sending mud up her leg, spattering her chest. Again she stared at the carcass, feeling waves of heat wash over her. She was in no mood for mysteries. She should just eat and be done with it. Something kept her back. This animal had to belong to the clan herds. There was no other place it could have come from, for it was fat and well taken care of, not scrawny and wild.

Bonechewer yawned, "I don't care where it came from. It's fresh and both of us could use a good meal."

"Yarrr," Ratha agreed, although the sight of the slain clan animal disturbed her more than she would admit. She was sure Bonechewer was teasing, but she sensed truth behind his words, even if it was twisted. She glanced at her companion, who was already tearing at the fawn's belly. The sound of him eating and the smell of flesh in the damp air made her stomach cramp with hunger. She joined him and ate.

When Ratha thought she couldn't force another bite down her throat, she felt Bonechewer start and stiffen beside her. She wiped her muzzle on the inside of her fore-leg and stared over the barrel of the kill. In a patch of weeds several tail lengths away, sat two intruders, one gray, one spotted. Ratha bristled and started to growl.

"Sss, no!" Bonechewer commanded and her challenge

died into a puzzled whimper. She watched as he stepped, stiff-legged, in front of the carcass and faced the two.

These were the Un-Named, Ratha realized, her heart thudding in her chest. One was a half-grown cub and the other an elder, but they looked rough and wild. Their faces were wary, their eyes hunters' eyes. Their smell, drifting to her through the drizzle, was a scent she had never smelled before. The Un-Named had a strong odor, both sour and musky at once. It was laced with a mixture of prey blood-scents, some old, some fresh. It held the stale scent of age and the smell of mud carried far between weary pawpads. And along with the scents of the Un-Named and the creatures they hunted came the wild scents of unknown valleys, plains and forests where a hunter might roam in freedom or die miserably of starvation.

Ratha stared at the Un-Named Ones and saw that what their smell told her was also written in their eyes. Would such a life allow them to learn anything more than survival? She had been taught that the clanless ones knew nothing but the urge to fill their bellies. She knew better now. Bonechewer bore no name, yet he spoke as well as any in the clan. But she realized, as she glanced at him and then at the two Un-Named, he was as different from them as he was from those in the clan. She waited, watching Bonechewer. She saw his eyes narrow and his mouth open.

She waited for him to attack or to roar a challenge at the witless ones. He did neither. He spoke to the Un-Named cub as he would have spoken to her. "Do you travel alone with the gray, spotted-coat? Or do more follow?"

The strange cub got up and walked forward. The gray

female remained seated, following the cub with eyes that seemed strangely unfocused and diffuse. Ratha thought at first that the gray was blind, but she saw the grizzled head turn and the slitted pupils move as the cub walked past.

She sought the cub's gaze, thinking she would see the same dull stare. As his eyes met hers, she felt her fur rise. His gaze was as sharp and clear as Bonechewer's. Yet he was Un-Named. Would he speak?

He waited, holding Ratha's eyes as if he knew the question burning behind them. Then he turned to Bonechewer. "More follow, dweller-by-the-water. Hunting grows hard. We turn to other ways."

The sound of his voice sent another shock through Ratha. She let out her breath slowly. She had been as wrong about the Un-Named cub as she had been about Bonechewer. The clan knows nothing about the Un-Named, she thought. *Nothing*.

The spotted coat spoke again. "There will be many tracks across your ground before this season is done." The cub's gaze strayed to the gutted carcass. "Ho, dweller-by-the-water," he said. "The lake has brought you a good kill."

"A good kill. Are these the marks of your teeth on its neck, little spotted-coat?" Bonechewer asked.

"No, dweller-by-the-water."

"Then make your tracks across my ground and leave me alone."

The cub stepped forward, head lowered, tail stiff. "You have not been long among us if you have forgotten the wanderer's claim, dweller-by-the-water. The old one and I are far from home ground and we are hungry."

"I had not forgotten, spotted-coat." Bonechewer grinned, showing all of his fangs. "I hoped you were too young to know about it. Ah well. Come then, and bring the gray."

"Bonechewer!" Ratha's jaw dropped. "Why are you doing this? They have no right to the kill!"

Both the cub and the gray turned green eyes on her. "She speaks for you, dweller-by-the-water?" the cub asked Bonechewer, who had stepped quickly to Ratha's side.

"Ratha," Bonechewer hissed in her flattened ear, "if you want yourself in one piece, shut your jaws and let me speak to them."

"You fear them? A spotted-coat and a gray half your size? They have no right to this kill," Ratha spat back. "It was taken from clan herds. I'll fight for it even if you won't!"

"The clan? *Ptahh!* You would fight for them? Meoran would kill you if you returned to them. Fight to fill your own belly, if you must, but speak no more of the clan."

Ratha's ears drooped. "If we kept the deer, we wouldn't have to hunt tomorrow. They are only a spotted coat and a gray."

"A spotted coat and a gray, yesss, but others follow." Bonechewer's whiskers poked Ratha's cheek. "I don't want to fight all the Un-Named. Be still, I tell you, and let them eat." He shoved Ratha aside from the kill, opening the way for the two intruders. Hatred and outrage burned in her, and for a moment her fangs were bared against Bonechewer's coat.

"You know better than that, clan cat," he said very softly. "Your belly is full. Let them fill theirs."

Ratha's anger settled. She watched as the cub went and nudged the gray. He pointed to the carcass with one outstretched paw. The elder lifted her head, stared at the meat and licked her chops.

"Food," Ratha heard the cub say. "Come. Eat." The grizzled one peered past him to Ratha and Bonechewer. She whimpered, raised her hackles and showed her teeth, yellowed and worn. "No," the cub said, pawing her. "No fight. No hurt. Gray one can eat."

Bonechewer walked off a distance and sat down, his back turned. Ratha, however, stayed close, watching. Something about the gray female repelled yet fascinated her. The cub, slavering, trotted to the carcass and began ripping at the flank. The gray followed him and the two ate until their bellies were swollen.

At last, the two were finished. Ratha noticed, with dismay, that not much remained of the deer except the skull and shanks. The rest was eaten or scattered. The gray-coat coughed, shook off the rain pattering on her fur and swung around. Not knowing quite why she did so, Ratha set herself in front of the gray, blocking the old one's path.

"Old one, if you eat of our kill," Ratha said, "you must give us answers in return. Who are you? Where is your home ground? Where do you journey in such bad weather?"

The gray's answer was a swipe at her face. Ratha ducked.

"Save your words, muddy one," came the cub's voice from behind her. Ratha turned to see him licking his whiskers. "The old one can't speak. She barely understands what I say to her."

"Why?" Ratha demanded. "Has she lost her wits to age?"

"She never had any. That's the way she's always been." The cub yawned and stretched until his tail quivered.

Ratha backed away from the gray-coat. The rheumy eyes followed her and she felt imprisoned by their dull stare. Her stomach tightened with anger and revulsion. The cub lifted his brows at her.

"I'm sorry for her," Ratha stammered, wishing she had never come near the gray.

"Why be sorry?" the cub asked. "She doesn't care. She doesn't know anything else. She's a better hunter than most of the others. I like her because she doesn't talk."

Ratha opened her mouth again, but couldn't think of anything to say. Despite her words, she was feeling sorrier for herself than for the gray-coat. Again she had been wrong. The answer had seemed simple and easy to catch between her teeth. Now it wiggled loose like a marsh-shrew and escaped down a hole of contradictions. She felt upset and uncomfortable, as if she had been caught doing something shameful. But all she had done was to ask a few questions. No. It was those eyes that chilled her, those ancient eyes that should have been full of life's wisdom and instead were empty.

Thunder rumbled overhead and the rain sheeted down, stinging Ratha's skin beneath her coat. The cub and the gray looked at her one last time. She ducked her head to avoid the old one's gaze. The two jogged away through the weeds, lifting their feet high to avoid puddles. Ratha stood still, watching them disappear into the rain. She felt someone come up behind her. She gave a violent start before she realized it was Bonechewer.

"They bother you, don't they," he said.

"Not the cub. The gray . . . she doesn't have anything in her eyes, Bonechewer. I don't know how else to explain it."

"Your clan teaches that the Un-Named are witless," Bonechewer said, a harsh edge to his voice. "Why should you be upset to find that some of them are?"

"I thought Meoran was wrong . . ." Ratha faltered. "What I was taught; it was just words. I said them, I learned them; I even questioned them, but I never knew what those words meant. Not until I looked into the gray-coat's eyes and found nothing there."

Bonechewer heaved a sigh. "You thought you had caught the truth, didn't you. Again, you were wrong. Each time you try you will be wrong. The only truth is that the Un-Named are of many kinds. Some are like you and me. Some are like the gray-coat. Some are different from either. You will have to learn not to be bothered by what you see."

"And I will see more of them?" Ratha asked.

"Yes, you will."

"Does seeing ones like the gray-coat bother you?"

"It used to," Bonechewer said. "It doesn't any more." He paused. "I learned never to look too deeply into any-one's eyes."

"Except mine," Ratha said boldly, remembering his intense stare that seemed to pierce into her depths.

"True, clan cat," he admitted, wrinkling his nose. "I do make mistakes sometimes. Is there anything left on that deer?"

Ratha inspected the stripped carcass. The other two had devoured what she and Bonechewer had left of the viscera and the meat. Rain crawled along the bare white ribs and dripped through. The fawn's head and shanks still bore coarse fur. The rest had been torn off. The only part worth taking was the head. Ratha stared moodily at the carcass. She wanted to get rid of the deer, to forget they had found it.

"Do you want the head?" Bonechewer asked. He came up behind her and nudged her, making her flinch. His touch sent a wave of heat rushing through her body with a violence that made her gasp. The cold rushed in and she shivered hard. Unable to keep still, she began to pace back and forth. "No," she growled. "There isn't enough there to risk breaking a tooth cracking it."

"Then help me drag it back into the lake. I don't want these bones on my ground."

Ratha made an angry turn, lost her balance and toppled.

Bonechewer nosed her as she clambered to her feet. "You're hot."

"I've been running," she snapped, but inwardly she was alarmed. Had she caught a fever? She felt so hot and wild that she wanted to run up the hill and howl or plunge herself in the lake.

Bonechewer was still nosing her, digging his muzzle into her flank. Her irritation flared. "Stop sniffing at me as if I was a putrid kill!"

He ducked her swipe and backed off. She saw a hungry glow rise in his eyes. Yet he had eaten. What else did he want?

She sat down and scratched herself. Besides being hot, she was itchy. Had she caught some illness? If so, it was a strange one. She had never felt anything quite like this before.

Bonechewer began to tug at the carcass. Grudgingly Ratha joined him and helped him haul the remains through the rushes to the lakeside. Try as she would, she could not help bumping against him and each touch sent another heat shock through her, starting at her middle and rippling out in both directions to her head and tail.

Ratha and Bonechewer reached the shore and threw the carcass in. She watched it sink beneath the gray water until only the faintest glimmer of white bone showed on the bottom.

Her belly was full and she wanted to curl up in the den and sleep. She wanted time to think, to try and make sense of what she had learned. Perhaps, as Bonechewer had said, she would always be wrong. Perhaps there was no sense to be made of it.

Bonechewer brushed against her as he passed. His scent and his closeness drove the questions from her mind. She shook her head, trying to throw off the fuzziness that was creeping over her thoughts. She only made herself dizzy.

Bonechewer, far down the path, lifted his tail and waved the white spot at the end. Ratha lowered her head and trotted after him, leaving only the rain pattering on the lakeshore.

The next morning, Ratha woke, nestled in brittle leaves inside the ancient pine, once hollowed by fire. Age and weather had softened the sharp smell of charred timber. Resin seeped through the cracked wood and mixed its smell with the fragrance of the dry leaves.

Ratha blinked sleepily, rolled over and rested her chin on the bark sill at the entrance. She was still lightheaded, although the sensation wasn't as unpleasant as it had been.

She snuggled into the leaves and watched the winter sun rise. Last night's fever had fallen, leaving her comfortably warm and lazy.

Something worried at her mind, trying to catch her attention. She sensed that it was important or had been important. Odd that she couldn't remember what it was. She sighed, feeling the cold wind on her nose in contrast to the snug heat of her body.

Bonechewer lay curled up near her, feeling warm and smelling musky. The sunlight fell on his coat, turning it from shadowed brown to burnished copper. Ratha rolled over next to him and leaned over him, fascinated by the pattern of hair on his chest and foreleg. Each hair was gleaming and haloed; so perfectly placed in the pattern that flowed down his leg until it ended in a whorl on the back of his foot.

His smell hypnotized her; drew her closer. A wild dark scent, tinged with bitterness. A scent powerful enough to send shivers down her spine to the tip of her tail.

Bonechewer stirred as the sun warmed him. Ratha retreated, frightened by the motion and astonished at her feelings. He settled and his scent drew her back. One paw flexed, showing ivory claws, and he yawned, rubbing his cheek in the leaves. One eye opened. The one-eyed golden stare made Ratha feel confused and abashed. She ducked her head.

"Hmm," he said and yawned until the back of his tongue showed. "You're feeling better, aren't you."

Ratha gave him a puzzled stare.

"You spent half the night trying to push me out of the den. I suppose you don't remember."

He rolled over on his back, the motion sending waves

of his scent toward Ratha. They rocked her, sweeping over her and through her until she could barely stand. Bonechewer had never smelled quite like this before. Had his odor changed? No. It was her. Her nose, her eyes. Everything was so much stronger, so much more intense that she could scarcely bear it. What was wrong with her?

Bonechewer wiggled on his back, his paws open, his eyes inviting. It was too much. Ratha jumped out of the den and trotted away a short distance. The day was clear and the wind nippy. Overhead, the sky was cloudless and blue. Ratha fluffed her fur and began licking herself, letting the task calm her mind. She began to enjoy it much more than she ever had. The feeling of fur gliding beneath her tongue, the warmth and roughness of her tongue pressing the fur against her skin; all of these sensations kept her licking even though she had groomed herself thoroughly. It felt nice, especially on that itchy place at the base of her tail.

She was suddenly aware that another tongue had joined hers, licking the nape of her neck while she was grooming her belly. She snapped her head up, catching Bonechewer beneath the chin. He shook his head ruefully and backed away, leaving her swimming in his scent. She tucked her tail between her legs and scuttled away. She crouched, watching him from a distance. He cocked his head and grinned at her, then took several steps toward her.

Ratha felt her lips slide back from her teeth.

"Stay away," she growled.

"All right," he said good-naturedly. "You're not ready yet. Are you hungry?"

"Go stalk your own kill," she snapped. "I can feed

myself." The comfortable lazy feeling was gone. She felt prickly and hot. Bonechewer turned tail and sauntered off.

Wrathfully yet regretfully, she watched him go.

Ratha didn't feel hungry, but she knew she should eat. She trotted back and forth until she found a likely looking hole and settled down beside it, waiting for the occupant to emerge. But she could not keep still. She itched and prickled and burned until she could no longer stand it. She gave up after several tries and scratched herself furiously. She began licking, dragging her tongue over her chest and belly. That was good, but it still wasn't enough. She flopped on her back and began rolling back and forth in the grass. That still wasn't enough. She lay and pedaled her rear paws in sheer frustration. *I want something and I don't know what it is. How can I want it if I don't know what it is?*

She stopped wriggling. Bonechewer was back, two lizards dangling from his jaws. He dropped one, went away and began eating the other. Ratha scrambled to her feet and shook off the dirt and pine needles clinging to her coat. She didn't want to be caught acting like a cub. Soon the urge to roll and rub overwhelmed her embarrassment. She flung herself on her back and writhed and wriggled until she thought her coat would be worn off.

A shadow blocked the sky and something hit her face. The something was limp, scaly and smelled delicious. Ratha's hunger came back in a rush and she seized the lizard Bonechewer had dropped on her face. She devoured the prey, savoring every bite and crunch of bone until the morsel was gone. She looked up, licking her whiskers.

Bonechewer's eyes seemed to glow amber in his dark

face. He nosed her and this time she did not leap away. He began licking her and, although she shivered, she stayed put, sensing that his tongue was the answer to all her itches and prickles. He was warm, and his scent so rich. . . .

A strange cry bubbled up inside her throat, wild and plaintive. Ratha could scarcely believe that this was her own voice. She lay with her head and chest against the ground, her heart threatening to burst her ribs. Teeth seized her ruff. She cried out again and again, unable to stop calling, even though the sound of her own voice frightened her. She felt his belly fur against her back and she felt him shift, slowly, repositioning his feet. His scent washed over her, taking her, spinning her until the hunger, the fright and the astonishment all blended together. She rubbed her head against the ground, calling until her voice was raw.

His weight bore her down and she felt his paws press into her back, alternating in a deliberate rhythm. He loosened his grip on her ruff and seized her further back, between the shoulders. His tail swept hers aside. Ratha arched her back to meet him, and a new note came into her call. His voice joined hers and they were together, stiff and trembling.

With a violent motion, he pulled away. The sudden pain was so sharp and deep Ratha screamed and flung herself around to face her tormentor. Her claws dragged through his fur and the skin beneath, opening a bright wound on his shoulder. He staggered back, and Ratha could see from his eyes that he had not expected such a vicious assault. She lunged at him again. He fled, not out of sight, but beyond her reach, crouching beneath a bush and watching her, measuring her. . . . She turned away from those glowing amber eyes and began to smooth her coat. She licked angrily, trying to wash away the traces of his odor that remained on her, but his smell kept wafting to her from where he crouched, still watching. She flattened her ears and snarled.

"Come near me again, raider and I'll tear you into pieces too small to be worth eating!"

"I imagine you would," Bonechewer replied, keeping his distance. "I'll wait. You'll feel differently about me in a little while."

Ratha turned her back on him, stalked back to the hollow tree and climbed inside. She was still sore and throbbing, but she felt much more like herself again. She resolved to have nothing more to do with him. She curled up and went to sleep.

To her dismay, she woke up as hot and itchy as she had the first time. This time she stayed inside the tree, licking herself, rolling on her back, wondering again what was the matter with her.

"You smell good, clan cat," came Bonechewer's voice from just outside. "Shall I come in?"

Ratha stuck her paw out, bared her claws, swiped back and forth several times, hoping his nose would get in the way.

She waited, listening. Nothing. He had gone. Good, she thought vehemently.

Her frustration, however, remained and grew until she could hardly endure it. She thrashed around, sending up a storm of dry leaves and needles inside the hollow tree. At last she collapsed in a disgruntled heap, letting the leaves settle on her. She lolled her head out the entrance. What am I going to do, she wondered. Am I always going to feel like this? I won't be able to hunt. I'll starve to death.

Ratha let her head sag, closing her eyes against the midday sun. She felt someone's breath against her face and then a tongue, tentatively licking her cheek. Bonechewer again. She grunted, letting her head sag further. The tongue stopped.

"Are you going to claw me again?" his voice said in her ear.

Ratha growled, but she knew there was no menace in her voice. He knew too. The tongue laved her ear and went under her jaw. Defeated, she let herself slide back inside the tree. His tongue followed her. She felt him step inside and lie down beside her.

They mated several more times that day and the next. Each time Ratha's memory of the pain that came at the end of their coupling made her vow she would never join with him again, but the fever of her heat drove her to him. Her appetite was magnified and she devoured the morsels he brought her with savage bites. The self she had once known seemed very remote and far away. Would this feeling pass or would she be forever enslaved to her body's demands?

Bonechewer tried to comfort her in the intervals between matings. Some of his harshness and indifference seemed to fall away, revealing a gentler nature than Ratha had thought him capable of.

The sun rose and set several times before her fever finally began to cool. Bonechewer's smell became pleasant rather than intoxicating. Her senses lost their heightened sensitivity. Other thoughts crept back into her mind as the urgency of mating faded. Her mind became clear enough to think about the future and survival. For those few days, she thought, it had been as though the future no longer existed, so strongly did her needs focus her mind on each moment as it passed.

Although Ratha rejoiced in the return of stability to her body and mind, there was a lingering regret. The few days of her heat, detached as they were from the rest of her life, had brought her new sensations, new thoughts and new feelings. Now that she had experienced it once, she knew what to expect if and when it came again. There might come a time, she thought, when she would welcome the changes in her body; she would willingly enter the waking dream that swung her between madness and delight.

Ratha thought at first that she would be exactly as she was before her heat. Some of her new feelings lingered, however, telling her that not everything was the same. Certain places on her belly remained tender. Deep in her loins was a heaviness that did not change whether she ate much or little.

During the next few days Ratha hunted with Bonechewer. They saw no more of the Un-Named. She thought less and less about them, although the encounter with the gray-coat returned to her mind. As days passed and no other intruders appeared, Ratha decided that the strange cub and the gray had indeed been traveling alone. When she said as much to Bonechewer he drew back his whiskers, took her out in the downpour and showed her tracks filling up with muddy water. The marks were neither hers nor Bonechewer's.

Ratha stared at the tracks, then at Bonechewer.

"Why don't I challenge them, clan cat? Is that what you are asking with your eyes?"

"There are too many of them, you said . . ." Ratha answered cautiously.

He grunted and said, "This is the only way the wanderers can go. On one side of my ground lies the lake. On the other lie the mountains. They must cross my ground. I can't stop them. I do not want to." He circled the tracks and then began to paw mud over them. "I make sure that as they pass, they catch no sight of me."

"Why?" Ratha asked. "Do you fear them?"

He patted the mud down. "No. But I don't want to share my prey with everyone that passes, as I did the cub and gray-coat."

"The wanderer's claim," Ratha remembered. "Is that a law among the Un-Named?"

"As close as we come to a law, I suppose." Bonechewer sounded annoyed. "But we have work enough to fill our own bellies so I let the strangers hunt for themselves." He turned away, flicking his tail. Beneath the sharp tang of irritation in his scent, Ratha detected a trace of worry.

He turned away to hunt. Ratha gazed at the smeared pawprints. She dipped her muzzle and smelled the edge of one track, but the rain had washed its scent away. She lifted her head and jogged after Bonechewer.

The next day Ratha returned to the same spot and saw fresh tracks. Bonechewer did not come with her and she decided to say nothing to him about it. He knew and, it seemed, he didn't partcularly care. Ratha began leaving the den earlier, hoping she might see the ones who made the tracks. Once she hid before sunrise and caught a glimpse of shadows moving far away in the misty drizzle.

Where were the travelers coming from, she wondered, and where were they going? Why would Bonechewer retreat each day to the far reaches of his territory and not venture near the trail? Part of it, she knew, was selfishness, but his odor and his manner suggested something more.

Once or twice, Ratha, hunting mice on the hillside, saw him stop on the trail the Un-Named Ones had taken. He looked down the path after their tracks and there was a longing in his eyes as if he wanted to join them on their journey. Then, as Ratha watched, his expression changed to disgust. He rubbed out the remaining pawmarks and leaped away through the bushes.

She noticed that his prowling was not random. Each day he spent in a certain section of his territory, inspecting it, marking it and making sure everything was as it should be before. . . .

Before he leaves, Ratha thought to herself and felt cold and lonely as she shadowed him in the early morning drizzle. He had said nothing to her about such a journey, yet he appeared to be making preparations, catching more than he could eat and storing the rest in the crotch of a tree or under a flat stone. Often he would break away from these activities, as if he did them against his will, but if Ratha watched long enough, she would see him renew his efforts. She should go, she thought miserably. She had learned enough from him that she might survive the rest of the winter if she worked hard. He seemed caught up in some inner struggle that she could not understand, yet she sensed that it involved her in some way, as well as the Un-Named she had seen on the trail. The deer carcass they had fished from the lake was part of it too. She had a few of the pieces, but not enough to fit together.

She slunk through the wet grass and peered between the stems. She caught a glimpse of a rain-slick copper coat.

There he was. Checking the trail as he usually did. Should she follow? He never found anything except pawmarks. Why should she waste her time?

She lifted her head and saw birds wheeling and dipping beneath the gray mass of clouds. A breeze tickled her whiskers, bringing with it the smell of the marshlands and the hills. She sensed, as she stood still and let the wind ruffle her fur, that this might be the last day she spent here.

Bonechewer had come out into the opening and was pacing toward the trail. Ratha saw him stop and stare up the path. The curve of a hill cut off her view, but she knew from Bonechewer's reaction that he had seen more than pawmarks. She scampered down the hill, keeping herself hidden. She made a wide circuit behind Bonechewer and followed him, creeping low on her belly, scuttling from one weed patch to the next until she was quite close to Bonechewer.

As she approached the trail, she saw that it wasn't empty. There were three of the Un-Named there. She dropped down behind a rise and hid, stretching out in the long grass, her chin resting on the top of the knoll. Now she could see and hear everything.

She watched Bonechewer approach the three on the trail. Two were tawny, the other black. The tawny ones were heavy and each bore a ruff. Their scent, drifting to Ratha through the damp air, told her they were males. They had the same eyes as the witless gray female and Ratha knew they wouldn't speak. The two males crouched and curled their tails across their feet. The black sat upright, green eyes luminous in a narrow ebony face. The eyes fixed on Bonechewer.

Ratha crawled further over the crest of the knoll, feeling her heart thump against the ground. Would the black one speak or be as dumb as the two others?

The black rose onto all four feet as the copper-coat approached.

"I wondered when you would come, nightling," Ratha heard Bonechewer say.

"The gathering place calls, dweller-by-the-water," the stranger replied. The black's odor and voice were female. "I and my companions are the last."

"They who gather will wait for you," Bonechewer said.

The black came a few steps down the trail, keeping her eyes on him. "We need you, dweller-by-the-water. Few among us have your gifts."

The green eyes were intense, half pleading, half-threatening. Ratha saw Bonechewer's hackles rise.

"That I know, nightling. How I will use them is for me to decide."

The black lowered her whiskers and walked down the trail past Bonechewer. The two tawny males followed her. She paused and looked over one silken shoulder at Bonechewer. "I could make use of their teeth, dweller-by-the-water."

Ratha tensed, gathering herself for a possible charge up the hill to Bonechewer's aid.

"You could, nightling," Bonechewer answered pleasantly, but Ratha saw the muscles bunch beneath his fur.

"No, dweller-by-the-water," the black said, showing the pointed tips of her fangs. "I am not so foolish as that. You are right, the decision is yours to make. If we are your people, then come. If not, then return to those of the clan from which you came and leave this territory to the Un-Named."

Ratha crept closer. If the black was right, Bonechewer was not one of the Un-Named. Clan-born? Could he be? That might explain many things.

The black waved her tail and trotted down the path, followed by her two companions. Bonechewer stared at the ground until their footsteps faded. Only then did he raise his head. He swung his muzzle back and forth, flicking his tail. Then he turned and gazed downhill to where Ratha was hiding.

"Clever, clan cat," he said loudly, "but the wind has shifted and I can smell you."

Disgruntled, Ratha trotted uphill to the path. As she approached, he laid his ears back until he looked as if he didn't have any.

"So, dweller-by-the-water," she said mockingly, staying beyond reach of his claws, "do you take the trail with your people? And will you raid those who were also your people?"

"*Yarr.* So you know my little secret," he said, slightly taken aback. "No matter. You would have found out fairly soon. One wouldn't know it from your hunting ability, but you are quite clever. Too clever, I think."

She eyed him. "You bear no love for the Un-Named. That I know from watching you rub out their tracks."

"I have no love of growing thin, either. The weather is already harsh and growing worse. Were I to stay here alone, my land would barely feed me. It will not feed the two of us. You are eating more every day, clan cat." He looked pointedly at her belly. Her pregnancy was becoming noticeable even as her appetite was growing more voracious.

"Then we go," Ratha said, taking a step down the trail.

Bonechewer's whiskers twitched and he looked uncomfortable. "The journey will not be easy and there will be things you won't like."

"Do I have a choice? If I am to bear your cubs, I must eat. As for the things I won't like, I'll deal with them as they come. When I think about what I've lived through, I know I can survive anything."

At least, I hope I can, she thought as she jogged along the trail beside Bonechewer.

Despite Bonechewer's warning, Ratha found the journey to be pleasant at first. The hills were open, clothed only in waving grasses, and the trail rose and dipped among them. Every once in a while the sun escaped the clouds and made the rain-washed earth seem bright and new.

When night came, or when the day grew cold and the rain turned to sleet, Ratha would crouch with Bonechewer in a burrow or beneath a bush until they could resume their journey.

At first, the two of them were the only ones on the trail, but soon they saw and passed others, including the black and her companions. Bonechewer traveled fast, and Ratha had to push herself to keep up with him. He caught most of what they ate, for he could flush prey from the weeds along the trail and bring the animal down before Ratha had gone very far ahead of him. Sometimes the two shared what they caught with the Un-Named Ones they passed. When their bellies and jaws were empty, their fellow travelers would share with them.

As the days passed like the ground underfoot, Ratha noticed more of the Un-Named emerging from the underbrush or from side trails to join. The path, once dotted with individuals moving far apart, became a river of furry pelts stretching away in both directions. Bonechewer could no longer hunt beside the trail, for the prey animals had either been killed or frightened away by the travelers who preceded him.

While he was gone on hunting excursions, Ratha sometimes sat by the side of the path and watched as the Un-Named went by. Grizzled patriarchs, scruffy half-growns, females shepherding cubs, fight-scarred males, all of the kinds she had seen in the clan and others besides. Some were strong while others were half-starved and barely able to totter along at the rear. Some were sleek and as well-groomed as Ratha had seen in the clan. Others were rough, tattered and mangy.

But there was no way to tell, before she looked in each pair of eyes, whether or not the mind behind them had the spark of intelligence. In some it barely flickered, while in others it burned and lit their whole being from the inside out. The gift often showed itself in those in whom Ratha least expected to find it, and, perversely, was absent from those she assumed would have it. Shaggy, sullen hunters, who at first glance seemed capable only of brutality would surprise her by the depth of their gaze. Elders, whose gray fur betokened wisdom, startled her out of her assumptions when she saw the emptiness behind their faces.

Why? The question beat in her mind as her paws beat the trail. Why some and not others?

She also noticed that most eyes were dull; that ones such as she and Bonechewer had were rarities among the Un-Named. Few could understand speech and fewer still could speak at all, let alone with any sophistication.

Why? Why among these folk was the gift so rare? It was not so in the clan.

Ratha thought about these questions, but she could get no answers that satisfied her. Only her own study of the Un-Named would tell her, she decided. Somehow she sensed that the answer would come soon and part of it might come from her own self, although how she did not know. The thought, instead of reassuring her, made her feel uneasy. She said nothing of this to Bonechewer. She knew he wasn't interested in either the questions or the answers.

The path grew steeper, the trail windy and narrow as the hills became mountains. It rained continuously and all the travelers acquired the same color, the dull brown of mud. Each day, Ratha woke chilled and sodden to plod along in the line, staring at the trail or at the curtain of rain in front of her whiskers. Bonechewer was quiet, almost sullen, showing little of his former energy.

Something began to bother Ratha, and at first she could not tell what it was. It was a feeling of familiarity, as though this country was not entirely new to her. The smells, the way the wind blew, the shape of the leaves and the rocks on the path told Ratha that she had passed through these mountains once before. Not on the same trail; she knew that. Perhaps not even across the same spur that the group was crossing now. Her memory could only provide her with vague images, for she had run most of the way, driven by rage and terror and the terrible pain of betrayal.

She found herself trembling as she put each foot in front of the other and she left the trail and stood aside, watching the others pass, blurred shadows behind the rain. She stood there, telling herself that it happened long ago and not to her. The Ratha that slogged along this muddy trail with the ragged Un-Named could scarcely be the Ratha who had brandished the Red Tongue before the clan. That part of her life was gone now and she cursed the things that woke her memory.

"Are you tired, Ratha?" a voice said. Bonechewer had left the line to join her by the side of the trail. She looked up, trying to hide her misery, but she was sure Bonechewer caught it, for there was a flicker in his eyes and for a moment he looked guilty.

"Come," Bonechewer said gruffly, glancing back toward the trail. "I don't want to be the last to get there."

"How far?" Ratha asked.

"Less than a day's travel. We should be there by sunset."

Ratha wiped her pads on the grass and shook out the mud between them. There was no sense in doing so, for she knew she would pick up more as soon as she stepped back on the path. She intended it to annoy Bonechewer, and it did, for he drew back his whiskers and plunged into the stream, leaving her alone by the side of the trail.

The rest of the day she walked by herself, despite the others jostling around her. The rain slackened and then stopped. The clouds lightened and a little sunlight filtered through, edging the wet grass with silver. The drops clinging to her whiskers caught the light and startled her with their sparkle. She shook her head and tossed them all away.

The grass became scrubby and then sparse as Ratha climbed the mountain along with the others. The sun fell low, sending shadows among the peaks, and she knew that the Un-Named and she were almost at the end of their journey.

The line now was long and straggling. Some of the travelers Ratha had seen at the beginning were no longer in their places, having fallen out by the side. They reached the top of the ridge and wound along its spine as the clouds turned from gray to rose and gold.

Ratha saw an outcropping of rock rising from the flank of the hill. As she and the others at the end of the line approached, the river of the Un-Named ended, breaking up into streamlets that poured around and over the great mass of stone. This was the gathering place.

The sun flared over the edge of the rock, blinding her for an instant. Dazed and weary, she let the flow carry her to the base, and she washed up against it, caught in her own little eddy, while the others surged by her.

"Sss, up here," came Bonechewer's voice from above her. Ratha stretched her neck back and saw the outline of his head against the dusk. Ratha gathered herself and leaped up to the ledge where he was sitting.

"Look," he said and Ratha did. Up and down the steep rock face, eyes glowed and damp pelts gleamed faintly in the sun's last light. Bonechewer rose and walked along the ledge, Ratha followed, placing her feet carefully, for the stone was weathered and broken. Pieces skittered out from under her pads and went clattering down the rock face until their echo died. The ledge led into a cleft and then they were through to the other side. Here the stone had split and fallen apart in several sections, creating a sheltered hollow where many more of the Un-Named were gathered. Out of the stiff wind that blew on the rock face, Ratha was warmer. She followed Bonechewer as he picked his way over talus and fallen boulders, giving greeting to the Un-Named perched on top of them or clustered around them. No one spoke to Ratha, although she felt their eyes follow her as she moved among them.

"Bone—" Ratha started. His tail slapped her across the muzzle before she could say his name. Hurt and outraged, Ratha snapped at the tail and caught a mouthful of fur before he whisked it away.

"Why did you—" she demanded, but he cut her off before she could finish.

"To keep you from making a fool of yourself and of me as well," he said softly. "There is no use of names here. Do not forget."

"How am I to speak to you if I can't use your name?" Ratha asked, feeling bewildered.

"Call me dweller-by-the-water, as they do. Or, better still, be quiet and listen."

"Yarrr." Ratha flattened her ears but she knew he was right. He had stopped calling her "clan cat" as well. Although the nickname had begun as an insult, he used it now in an affectionate sense. To have this stripped from her left her feeling empty and desolate, as if she were becoming one of those who had nothing behind their eyes. She hung her head and swallowed hard.

"What is the matter, young one?" The voice was not Bonechewer's, although he still stood nearby. Ratha looked up into a pair of glowing green eyes in a face so black it seemed to her that the eyes floated by themselves in the dark.

"She is just tired, nightling," Bonechewer said before Ratha could gather her wits to speak.

"I haven't seen or smelled her before," the black remarked, "yet she is too old to be of the last litters. Did she come with you, dweller-by-the-water?"

"She joined me on the trail," Bonechewer said shortly. Ratha sensed a certain tension between him and the black one.

"We meet at the same place, among the stones-with-fangs."

"I will be there, nightling."

"Good." The black turned and snarled at the two dull-eyed shadows standing behind her. "Away, cubs! I have no need of you until sunrise." With guttural growls, the two males lowered their heads and padded away.

"Why do you keep them, nightling?" Bonechewer asked. "You are worthy of better companions."

"If I wanted companions, I would choose others. The witless ones obey me and that is all I ask."

"All you ask, nightling?" Bonechewer said.

The black opened her eyes all the way, revealing their full depth. "There are certain things that wit or lack of wit does not affect, dweller-by-the-water. And you seem to have made a similar choice, for I have not heard your little female speak."

"I can speak," Ratha spluttered, sending a burning glance at Bonechewer.

The other yawned and arched her back. "Ah. Perhaps, then, he will bring you to council."

"I think not, nightling."

"Very well, dweller-by-the-water," the black said and trotted away.

"Your little female!" Ratha spat in disgust and pawed in the dirt as if she were burying dung. "If there are many like her among the Un-Named, I want nothing more to do with them. Where are you going?" she asked, for she felt Bonechewer start to move away from her.

"To the stones-with-fangs."

"Are you taking me?"

"No. You stay here. Curl up and sleep. You won't get much sleep later."

"Sleep! How can I—" Ratha stopped. He was already gone, his shadow disappearing among the rocks.

She lashed her tail and dug her claws into the gravel.

What was this gathering for? What was this council the black spoke of and why hadn't Bonechewer taken her? Was he afraid she would embarrass him by speaking his name? Ratha snorted. He was just being silly. Who other than she and he would know that "Bonechewer" was even a name? There had to be another reason.

She sniffed the ground. Bonechewer's track was still fresh. She could follow him to the place he spoke of, the stones-with-fangs. Perhaps she could hide and attend the meeting in secret. Perhaps she would even get a chance to maul that slinky black before she could summon her body-guards. Now *that* was an appealing idea.

CHAPTER 9

RATHA PEERED between rows of jagged stones that rose from the cavern floor. Those who had come to meet were settling, and she watched them form a circle under the phosphorescent light that shone from the roof of the cave. Bonechewer sat next to two huge gray hunters, the odd blue-green glow turning his copper coat inky and his eyes emerald. Beside him on the other side sat the black. A grizzled elder who limped on three legs, a silver-coat, and a young male barely out of his spots made up the rest of the gathering.

They spoke quietly among themselves for a while and Ratha could hear nothing but water dripping from overhead into puddles on the floor. A particularly cold drop landed on her and she jumped, shivering. Then she huddled and fluffed her fur, trying to keep warm. It was like being in the mouth of a huge beast, she thought, looking up at the stone fangs that also hung down from the ceiling. Perhaps this was the maw of some great unknown animal who lay buried in the mountain. Ratha imagined the jaws closing, the spikes overhead driving down to mesh with those rising from the floor.

No, she thought, trying to still her racing heart. Even if this is the mouth of a great beast, the jaws will never move again. *It has died,* she thought. *I am in the mouth of a dead, cold beast.*

The voices grew louder, drawing Ratha's attention back to the Un-Named in their circle. Now she could hear what they were saying. She crept forward on her belly, laying her nose between two of the stone teeth.

One of the gray hunters was talking to the black.

"For you and your people, it is easy to wait," the shaggy speaker was grumbling. "My people have come far and empty bellies have no patience. How am I to answer them?"

"In the language you have always used, gray hunter," the black said, laying her tail across her delicate feet. "Claws and, if needed, teeth." She looked at him through slitted eyes. "Do you doubt your strength?"

"It is talk I doubt. Let there be less of it. I and my people came to kill, not talk. When does the hunt begin?"

"When *all* are here, gray one," interrupted the grizzled male in a scratchy voice.

"Don't misunderstand me, gray hunter," the black said, opening her green eyes wide. Her voice took on a silky tone. "I do understand your difficulty. I, at least, can talk to the ones I lead and many of them will listen to reason."

"Enough!" snapped the grizzled cripple. "We have come here to plan, not to quarrel." He turned to Bonechewer. "I see you decided to come after all, dweller-by-the-water. Your absence last season cost us, as you well know."

"I will do what I can," Bonechewer said.

Ratha was starting to get stiff and drops of water were soaking her ruff, but she dared not move. She had heard enough to whet her curiosity, not enough to answer her questions, although she sensed she was getting close.

"I am curious, dweller-by-the-water, why you came this

time." Scratchy-voice was speaking again. Ratha pricked her ears to catch Bonechewer's answer.

"Old one, I hoped that you would listen to me, even though you have heard my words before."

The gray hunter jumped to his feet. "Don't listen to him! He would keep us hungry and save the herds of the hated ones. He is not one of us. He is clan-born filth!"

"Gray one, when you have finished howling and are ready to listen," Bonechewer said, his voice acid, "I will tell you why I think as I do."

The big silver-coat glared at Bonechewer and then around the circle, seeking support. Many of the eyes on Bonechewer were hostile.

"You gray idiot! Do you think I care anything for those who cast me out, who would have slain me as a cub?"

He lunged at the silver-coat as he spoke and the other shrank away. Bonechewer stood, letting his fur flatten as he turned to the others.

"Take from the herds, yes. Let the hated ones work for you. I say nothing against that. But I hear voices that speak of turning this into a vengeance hunt, of slaughtering the herds and those who keep them." He stopped and gazed around the cavern. "You will be pulling the fur from your own tails if you do that. The clan keeps us alive. Not many of you great hunters will admit that, but it is raiding and scavenging that feeds us during this season."

"*Ptahh!* We should kill the hated ones and take their ground. Game is richer there than in our territories. That will keep us. Spare them?" The silver-coat curled his lip, showing heavy fangs. "No!"

Ratha could see from the circle of eyes that Bonechewer had little sympathy in the group.

The only one who didn't look openly hostile was the black female, but the sight of her only disgusted Ratha.

He's right, she thought frantically as Bonechewer returned to his place. *He's right. Why won't they listen?*

"Very well," Bonechewer said. "I see that few of you share my concern. I can say no more. If you wish to keep me on this council, I will serve as you ask. Let me say only that I have warned you."

There was silence, broken by the echoes of water dripping in the recesses of the cavern. The group began talking among themselves again in low voices and Ratha could no longer hear what they said. She didn't care. She had heard enough.

She eased herself up, shaking as much from fear as from cold. Her legs, stiff and numb, moved awkwardly. As she turned, she kicked a piece of broken stone. It clicked as it bounced and the echo reverberated across the cavern.

Ratha froze. She glanced back at the group. All of them were on their feet, ears pricked, hackles raised. She gave a soft moan of despair. They would find her, tear her, and fling her remains down the rockface.

"Wait, all of you," she heard Bonechewer's voice say. "Stay here. I know who that is."

Ratha gave a start and felt her stomach sink even further. She could not bear to let him find her. She turned tail and fled out of the cavern, across a flooded gallery and into the tunnel she had come in by. In the tunnel she paused for a moment, the pulsebeat in her throat almost choking her. She heard the sound of splashing and leaped into a gallop. He was after her. What he would do when he caught her, she didn't know.

Now she was running in total darkness, trusting only her whiskers to keep her away from the rock walls.

"Ratha!" Bonechewer's voice came from behind her, hollow and hissing. "Ratha!"

Cold fresh air tickled her nose, and as she ran, she breathed great gulps of it. She was almost out, she thought, scrabbling up a graveled incline. She thrust her head out and glanced around. No one was here. She was free! Soon she would be racing down the mountainside, leaving the Un-Named far behind. She would go back to the clan and warn them. Someone there would listen even if Meoran didn't. Her excitement almost choked her. At last, at last, she would be going home.

She was barely out of the hole when she felt jaws clamp on her tail. Something jerked her back, snapping her head and knocking the wind out of her. She struggled, but Bonechewer kept a tight grip on her tail. She pulled until it was raw, then collapsed in a heap, worn out and terrified.

She felt the jaws loosen and peered along her flank. Bonechewer's eyes glowed back at her. She shut hers tight again, waiting for his teeth.

"Sit up, Ratha." He cuffed her, but the blow was mild. She only went into a tighter huddle. "I'm not going to hurt you. Sit up and listen."

Gradually Ratha uncurled and looked up at him doubtfully.

Bonechewer grinned; not a friendly expression. The moonlight gleamed on his teeth, and Ratha remembered how, long ago, she had fought him in the meadow.

"You're no danger to us, despite your heroics," he said. "Go and warn the clan. What good will it do them? How many of the clan are there? How many of the Un-Named? Think about that for a while."

Ratha sat, feeling the cold seep back inside her. "They would be ready to fight," she said, but her words sounded uncertain, even to herself.

"Do you think that would make any difference?" Bonechewer leaned over her. "The marsh-shrew is ready to fight, but it is I who eat the marsh-shrew. Your warning might prolong the fight a little and cause a few more of the Un-Named to die, but it won't make any difference."

"No . . ." Ratha faltered, feeling despair creeping back along with the cold.

"You can't change it, Ratha. I can't either. You heard me try."

Ratha got up, feeling the night wind cut through her. The stars overhead were hard, with a steely glitter. "The clan has lived with Un-Named raids," she said in a low voice, turning her back on the wind and Bonechewer. "They will survive. They always have."

He walked around and faced her. "You must have heard enough in the cavern to know the Un-Named will no longer kill just for food."

"Why?" Ratha asked, and hated the pleading sound of her voice. "Why have things changed?"

"I don't know. Perhaps because Meoran grazes his flocks on territory once held by the Un-Named. Perhaps because the winter has been hard and hunger listens readily to hate. Or because there are so many of us now that our land can no longer feed us."

Ratha shut her eyes, but blocking out sight could not block out truth. His voice went on.

"I saw this starting to happen the season before last," he

said. "That is why I stayed away. I nearly starved, but I knew that without me, they would fail in their plan to kill the herders and take the beasts. They did fail." Bonechewer paused. "Do you remember how frequent and fierce the raids were that season? There were quite a few of the Un-Named who sought to destroy the clan. Now, most of them agree with the silver-coat."

Ratha looked at him scornfully. "They failed because you didn't come with them? Hah! One more set of teeth wouldn't have helped them."

"One more mind would have. I am clan-born, Ratha. I lived long enough among our people to know how they think and what they will do. The raiders needed that knowledge."

Our people, Ratha thought, staring at Bonechewer. *He calls them our people . . .*

She whirled on Bonechewer, her misery turning her savage. "Why do you care?" she hissed.

"I don't." His gaze was cool. "I have no love for the clan. To me, they exist to feed us and that alone is my reason. If they die, we die. That is the truth, but the other Un-Named are too stupid to see it." His eyes narrowed. "*You* are the one who cares, Ratha. Too bad Meoran threw away his one chance when he drove you out."

"What do you mean?" Ratha demanded.

"I'll let you find the answer to that."

Ratha flattened her ears and bowed her head. Her heart jumped as she heard cries far up the slope. *They're looking for us, she thought.* Bonechewer touched her, making her flinch. "Ratha," he said and she turned fierce eyes on him. "The clan won't survive. Nothing you can do will change that, so stop thinking about it. You will survive."

"How? By turning raider and helping to slay herdfolk I once knew?"

Bonechewer waited for Ratha to calm herself before he went on. "You can't afford to think about them, Ratha. Think only of yourself. Life with the Un-Named is not pleasant, but you keep your belly full."

Bonechewer's voice was in her ear again, soft and relentless. "The clan drove you out, as they drove me. They would have killed you. Do you remember? Were those faces any less savage than the Un-Named Ones around you?"

Ratha listened. His words brought the memories back and fanned them until they burned in her mind as the torch had in her mouth. She stood before the clan again, seeing the hate in their eyes. One voice rose from the pack to betray her and she shuddered. That one voice . . . Thakur.

She ground her teeth together, feeling her rage grow. The memory of Thakur's face as he hung from Meoran's jaws would never leave her mind. If Meoran had only killed him then. . . . All in the clan deserved to die and Thakur most of all.

A growl bubbled in her throat.

"Ah, you do remember," said Bonechewer.

She narrowed her eyes at him. "Where will I go now?"

"Wherever you please. If you come with me, I will hide you for the night."

"What about the council? Didn't you tell them you knew who was hiding in the cavern?"

"I'll tell them something they'll believe. You let me worry about that."

"When I come back, I will go to the council," Ratha said. "They need those who can speak and think. Perhaps I too will be a leader."

"A leader? You? *Ptahh!* You crept among them and listened to what you should not have heard. If you go before them, I will tell them it was you who hid among the stones-with-fangs."

Ratha waited, glaring at him. He was right; he had the power to turn the council against her. It would not be difficult, for she was a stranger among the Un-Named.

"You may hunt with us," Bonechewer said, "but not as a leader. You will be among the lowest of the Un-Named. You will not speak of the clan. You will not speak at all so that you keep from revealing who you are and where you come from. Only then will you be safe."

"Shall I also rub mud on my face to dull my eyes?" Ratha cried bitterly. "Or make myself believe I am one of the witless ones I walk among?"

Bonechewer looked at her steadily. "Your belly will be full. That is all I promised you."

Ratha followed him up the slope, her steps heavy, her throat burning. She remembered again the she-cub who had brandished the Red Tongue before the clan. She wished to the depths of her being that she had her creature once again. The soft mist around her turned all things gray and formless, mocking her memory of the bright flame. She would never find her creature again. Ratha hung her head and walked on.

CHAPTER 10

As THE SUN set many days later, the forest sent shadows creeping across the meadow. The shapes of trees elongated into talons, reaching out toward the herd and its guardians huddled together at the center.

Ratha lay hidden, along with others of the Un-Named. From the forest they watched and waited for night. The sun's glow faded over the treetops and the light filtering through became weak and pale. Soon would come the order to attack.

She shifted, trying to move away from the bony flank that pressed too close to hers. She wrinkled her nose at the sour smell of dirty fur and decaying teeth. She glared at the gray-coat. The old mouth grinned, an ugly grin, lacking mirth or understanding. When the Un-Named left the gathering rock the gray had attached herself to Ratha, abandoning the young cub who had been her trail companion. No threats or cuffs could discourage her.

The aged one's rheumy eyes glowed dimly with pleasure each time Ratha repressed a shudder or withdrew from her touch.

The sight and smell of her makes me miserable, Ratha thought. *She knows it and she delights in it.*

She turned away from the malicious old eyes and watched the herders prowling around their animals, but she could not ignore the gray, whose presence hung about her, turning the air stagnant and choking.

It isn't age or dirt or rotting teeth that sickens me so, Ratha thought. *There were aged, dirty ones in the clan. Old and smelly as they were, the wisdom in their eyes made me respect them. There is no wisdom in hers, and she has lived her life with this terrible emptiness. She knows only enough to taunt me for my fear of it.*

In the meadow, a three-horn bawled. Ratha watched the clan herdfolk draw into a tighter circle about their animals. They knew the raid was coming.

Leaves brushed her nose as she peered out of the thicket. She was afraid to let her gaze linger on any one form for fear it would become someone she knew.

I am one of the Un-Named, she told herself fiercely. *I am enemy.*

But she could not help thinking about Fessran and Thakur . . . although it was not easy to think about him. She didn't want to think about Bonechewer either. She had come with him as companion and equal. Now he was with the elite of the council while she was left among the lowest of the Un-Named, forbidden to reveal she was anything more than they. It was bitter meat for her, and it was worse to know her own foolishness had placed her here. She ground her teeth together, remembering those gold eyes and the mocking broken-fanged grin.

It would be easier to hate him, she thought, had she not heard the words he spoke in the council. What he said then was wise and right. And he believed it. He had thrown himself at the silver-coat because he believed it.

Maybe it is better to be like the Un-Named, she thought bitterly. *Not to think, not to remember . . . would make it easier.*

A hoarse scream cut through the dusk; the signal to

attack. A young cub leader leaped out of the thicket. Ratha ran after him, followed by two dun-colored males and the ancient gray. Another fawn-colored female streaked by Ratha as the cub leader shouted things that were lost in the pounding of feet and the wild cries that came from every throat. Ratha found herself howling along with them and the savage joy of the pack swept her with it.

The Un-Named spilled from the forest into the meadow, rising like a great wave against the herders, who stood together in a tight determined circle about their beasts. Yet the raiders did not become an amorphous mass; instead they held together in their groups and struck at the weak points in the clan's defenses.

Another pack led by a young silver-coat raced past Ratha's group and clashed with the herders. It broke apart into individual fights. Out of the corner of her eye, Ratha saw old Srass rear up to meet the young silver-coat. The two went down in a writhing, slashing blur. The cub led his group through the herders' broken line toward the three-horns, now unguarded. The animals wheeled and began to stampede acros the meadow. Ratha could hear the herders shrieking orders back and forth to each other as the three-horns split apart from the dapplebacks and thundered across the grass. Both raiders and herders went down beneath those trampling feet, and the torn earth was stained with blood. Ratha, wild with the intoxication of the chase, launched herself after the biggest stag she could see. He was on the outside edge of the herd, galloping easily, his horns held high.

She forgot the Named, the clan or anything except the magnificent animal. It would take all her skill to bring this one down. This kill would show she was indeed a hunter. She sped after the three-horn stag. She dived in among the pounding legs, dodging, turning, barely escaping flashing hooves and tossing horns. She reached her quarry and cut him out of the herd, leaping up to nip at his flanks and withers. An ecstatic bound carried her right onto his back and she rode him for several wild seconds, her claws digging deep into the coarse fur. He bucked, throwing her off, but she landed running and the chase began again.

She ran the three-horn as she had never run any of the herdbeasts when she had served the clan. She ran him, reveling in her strength and her skill as a hunter and herder. She turned and twisted, countering every lunge and thrust, dancing around him, leading him in circles until at last, eyes rolling and exhausted, the stag began to slow and Ratha closed in for the kill.

She did not realize her skill had given her away until an angry cry rose from behind her.

"She is clan!" the voice bellowed. "A clan herder kills with the raiders! Tear her tail off! Trample her guts into the ground!"

Ratha looked back to see Srass chasing her, bleeding from the wounds the silver-coat had given him. She was young and still unwounded, but Srass's rage lent him speed. Suddenly he was beside her flank and then at her shoulder. She heard his heavy panting and felt his breath behind her ears. Frightened now, she tried to pull ahead, but before she could gain any distance, his teeth locked in her ruff and the two rolled over and over in the grass.

Ratha flailed and kicked, gouging Srass's belly as he snapped at her throat. She ripped off the rest of one ragged ear. He clawed her chest and gashed the inside of her foreleg. Then, abruptly, the fight ended. Ratha tumbled free. She leaped to her feet, completely bewildered. She shook her head and stared.

Srass was struggling beneath the two dun-colored raiders and the old gray. The silver-coat seized the old herder's nape in his jaws. Srass tried to wrench free, but the four together overpowered him and at last he ceased fighting. He lifted his chin and bared his throat in submission. Ratha thought then that they would let him go, for he was thoroughly beaten. The silver-coat loosened his grip only to seize Srass again at the back of his head behind the ears. The old herder stiffened and fear dulled his eyes.

"Take the herdbeasts," Ratha said. "Leave him. He isn't worth the killing." Her voice died in her throat as she saw that none of the four had moved away from Srass.

"He bared his throat to you. He will not fight again. Leave him!" Ratha said.

"I came to taste clan blood," snarled the silver-coat between his teeth.

With a malicious glance at Ratha, the old gray seized the flesh of Srass's flank and tore it open. The duns, both mute, showed their teeth at Ratha. They were going to kill, she thought with growing horror. Srass had bared his throat. All knew that sign, even the Un-Named. It was a law older than any other, and rarely disobeyed.

Ratha saw the muscles bunch in the silver's cheeks.

"At least do him the honor of tearing out his throat!" she shrieked at them.

The silver-coat gave her one brief glance. His jaws sheared shut. Srass screamed and Ratha heard the hollow crunch of bone. The herder's body convulsed, the spasming muscles pulling his limbs in ways they were not meant to go. The scream continued from Srass's open mouth even after his head had been crushed. With a last shudder, the body fell limp and the terror-filled eyes went blank.

The silver-coat opened his jaws and Srass fell to the ground with a heavy thud. Blood seeped from his ruined head and neck.

"Is this how you kill?" Ratha faced the silver-coat. "You slay those of the clan as you kill prey. *Ptahh!*"

"To us they are prey," the silver answered, licking his red-stained jaws. He narrowed his eyes at Ratha. "I heard this one cry out that you, female, are also of the clan even though you run with the Un-Named." He left Srass and took a step toward her. "Your head would be easier to crush. Perhaps your feet had better take it away before my jaws open again."

She spat, whirled around and galloped away from them. The night rang with howls and shrieks and the bawling of terrified animals. As she ran, Ratha could see the shapes of raiders dragging slain dapplebacks toward the trees. The moon had risen and the flattened grass showed black stains where the raiders had made their kills.

The sounds of fighting grew and faded as the battle raged back and forth across the meadow. The herders were losing, their circle shrinking as they bunched together to protect the remaining three-horns and dapplebacks.

Ratha stopped and licked the wound on her foreleg. It was starting to crust and stiffen, making her limp. She closed her eyes, seeing again Srass's face as he died. He had been killed like a herdbeast and his eyes had rolled like a herdbeast's when the silver-coat's teeth crushed his skull. Ratha shuddered. None of the Named had died such a death until now. It seemed as though all of the laws that governed her kind, Un-Named or clan, were breaking. If one whose throat was bared could be killed like a herd-beast, then there were no laws and nothing made sense any more.

She knew that whatever was happening to her people, she was a part of it; however much she feared and hated the changes, she was helping to bring them about. Srass had died because he spotted a herder among the raiders. He had not come close enough to see her face or smell her odor, but he saw how she had run the three-horn and cut him out from the herd. Her skill and her recklessness betrayed her. Her mouth felt as bloody as the silver-coat's, as if it had been her teeth that crushed the old herder's skull.

No, she thought, trying to give herself some small comfort. *Srass's skull would have been too thick for my jaws.* But she knew as she ran that she shared equally with the Un-Named in his death.

Again she stopped. The fighting was now distant. All she could see were raiders dragging thrashing animals across the grass, leaving black stains between their paw-prints. They were still working in packs, as they had in the initial assault. One group looked familiar, and Ratha recognized the two dun-coats and the gray who had helped to kill Srass. The gray's jaws were dark with blood. The old one raised her ugly head and stared at Ratha. The pack leader dropped the neck of the dappleback he was dragging. Ratha was suddenly afraid he might be the silver-coat, but she saw the face of the young cub who had been leading the group when the raid started. He stared at her over the body of his prey. He bounded over the animal and, before Ratha could react, clawed her across the face.

"The council is not pleased with me for failing to keep my pack together. I pass their displeasure on to you." She fell back, shaking her head. Warm wetness seeped from the new cut on her muzzle and dripped onto her lower lip into her mouth. She was so relieved he wasn't the silver-coat that the blow only startled her. She got up tasting the metallic tang of her own blood.

"There are more beasts to drag away," the pack leader snarled. "The gray lags. Help her to carry her prey. Then you are to return with the others and bring the remaining kills." He looked hard at Ratha. "If you leave the pack again, you will be killed."

She lowered her head and walked toward the watery green eyes glinting in the dark above the indistinct bulk of the herdbeast. The gray's smell washed over her again, surrounding her and making her feel even more of a prisoner. The old female growled and seized the beast's neck. Ratha took the hock and followed the pull of her companion.

The packs dumped the kills in a moonlit clearing and were sent back to retrieve more. The rest of the night Ratha spent hauling the Un-Named kills from the meadow to the clearing deep in the forest. By the time the first sunlight filtered through the trees, Ratha's teeth were aching, her neck was stiff and her pads sore. She grew to hate the taste of coarse oily fur and the limp weight of the kill in her jaws. She resented having to drag beasts that others had slain.

It was midmorning when the pack carried the last of the carcasses into the clearing. Ratha pried her teeth loose from a dappleback's neck and let the horse's head drop. She staggered into the shade beneath a gnarled pine and collapsed. To her disgust, the gray female came and sat beside her, but she was too tired to drive the old one away. With her head on her paws, smelling the pungent needles that littered the earth beneath the tree, Ratha watched the raiders gather to feast on their prizes. Some had already come and had begun eating when the first carcasses were dragged in. Now the rest, ravenous and still savage from the battle, swarmed over the kills, spitting and squabbling with each other over who was to get the choicest pieces. She smelled the rich flesh as the carcasses were torn open and the entrails eaten. The odor only disgusted her and destroyed what little appetite she had. After hauling the dead creatures all night, smelling and tasting them, she could hardly bear the idea of eating from them. She thought with longing of the stringy marsh-shrews she had caught on Bonechewer's land.

A new group appeared among the gorging raiders and pushed aside a scruffy pack from a dappleback mare. These were the council leaders and the planners, Ratha realized, as she glanced at them, recognizing the black female and the old cripple she had seen in the cavern beneath the gathering rock. Among them, she saw Bonechewer.

The Un-Named council leaders began to eat. Ratha saw the black place a paw on the mare's flank and ribs. The black's shoulders hunched as she dived into the dappleback's belly. All the others attacked the carcass with equal relish except for Bonechewer. He hung back until the crippled one had finished, then took his place. He ate then, but Ratha could see from his eyes that he had as little appetite as she. She remembered his words to the council in the cavern, and she knew he was disgusted by the reckless slaughter. The Un-Named could ill-afford waste, he had said, even in the midst of plenty.

She raised her head from her paws, hoping to catch his eye. Her heart beat in her throat, her feelings a violent mix of hope and anger. Once or twice he lifted his muzzle, still chewing, as if he sensed someone was watching. Each time Ratha longed to call out, but caution stilled her. And then he did raise his chin and stared at her over the mare's flank. She leaped to her feet, panting in her excitement, but he looked away, as if ashamed. For a moment, she stood still. Then slowly she lay down again and rested her chin on her paws, staring at the dried needles tumbled together on the ground. When she looked up again, Bonechewer was gone.

For many days, the Un-Named stayed in the clearing, lazing in the pale winter sun and gorging themselves on their kills. Ratha, along with others of her pack, were posted as sentries to guard against attacks by the clan herders. None ever came, telling her that the clan was too weakened and dispirited to try for revenge.

She ate little and tried to stay far from the sounds of feasting. She felt odd sensations in her belly, vague aches, heaviness and strange rippling motions, as if something was moving inside her. She was also enlarged and her teats were tender. At first the feelings were mild and she hardly noticed. As the Un-Named alternately raided and feasted and the days grew colder, her pregnancy became obvious, earning her questioning looks from the others. This was not the season to bear cubs. If the Un-Named females were like the clan, they would mate in early spring and have their young in summer. She had done everything wrong, she thought miserably, as she stood in the rain watching for an attack that never came. She couldn't even bear cubs at the right time of year. They would be born too soon, before she could get away from the Un-Named. And even if she did, hunting in winter would be poor. She would starve and her cubs would die.

Ratha took no part in the raids following the first one. She, along with the gray-coat, was held back to drag away beasts that others had killed. She spent many nights wrestling carcasses through the undergrowth, collapsing at dawn to watch the raiders feast until they were bloated. After each raid she saw Bonechewer eating with the council leaders as before. She caught him giving her anxious glances but this time it was she who turned away.

One rainy morning between raids, she stood guard near the edge of the meadow where the fighting had been. Her partner hissed, taking her mind from her troubles. Ratha tensed, driving her claws into the spongy ground. Had the clan reclaimed enough strength to attack? The gray lurched to her feet, growling as the bushes rustled several tail-lengths away. Her ears went back, making her look uglier than ever.

"Ho, ancient one," came a voice from behind the bushes. "Still your noise. You know my smell." A coppery head poked through, framed by wet leaves. It disappeared for a moment, then Bonechewer pushed his way through the undergrowth, carrying meat in his mouth.

"Not for you," he said through his teeth as he pushed the slavering gray-coat aside. She whined and showed her teeth, but under his gaze, she backed off.

"There you are," Bonechewer said, and without further words, he laid the meat down in front of Ratha. She stared at it dully, then at him.

"Eat. You need it. That young fool of a pack leader is letting you starve."

She said nothing. She sniffed the aroma of the meat. It was fresh, taken from the latest kill. She still could not eat.

"Ratha," he said, growing exasperated. "I bring you something better than the rotten leavings you pick from old bones, yet you eat nothing and stare at me like that witless gray-coat. Have you forgotten how to speak?"

For a moment, she stared at him, able to answer only with her eyes. She had not spoken for so long that the words came slowly. His words shocked her and her own awkwardness frightened her. She fought down panic; the fear that she, in pretending to be mute and stupid, had actually become so. It lasted only an instant; then the words came.

"You said I was to be among the lowest of the Un-Named," she said, her voice hoarse from disuse.

"Even the lowest should have enough to eat," Bonechewer answered. He nudged her. "Every rib shows. If you get any thinner, you'll lose the cubs."

Ratha flattened her ears. "So that is why you watch me and bring me meat. You care nothing for me; only for what I carry in my belly. *Ptahh!*"

"Does it matter why I am here?" Bonechewer snarled back. "I could leave you to your pack leader's mercies; think about that."

Ratha kicked mud on the meat and walked away. "Give it to the gray-coat."

"I saved your ragged pelt, and believe me, it has cost

me to do even that. Few on the council listen to me now, and the foolish killing goes on. I can do nothing about it, just as I can do nothing for you except bring you extra food." Bonechewer pawed the meat. "Yes, I care about the cubs," he said, his eyes seeming to glow even in daylight. "But I want you just as much. The others want you killed, and if you do anything that brings you to their attention, you will not live long and I may not either."

Ratha lowered her muzzle and nosed the slab of flesh. As she took a first bite, she felt him gently licking her ears. Startled, she jumped back and stared at him in astonishment.

"All right," he said. "Eat. I'll leave you alone."

Ratha devoured half of the meat, all her stomach could hold. As she ate, she could hear the gray-coat whining softly.

"If I eat it all, I'll be sick," she said to Bonechewer. "Take some to the gray. She works as hard as I do."

"I thought you didn't like her."

"I don't," Ratha said, gaining back some of her spirit now that she had eaten. "I hate her, especially the look in her eyes. But you said that even the lowest should have enough to eat."

Bonechewer grinned at her and, with a toss of his head, threw the rest of the morsel to the old gray. She caught it in midair and began demolishing it in noisy gulps.

"I will come back," Bonechewer said, as he turned to go. "I'll bring you food as often as I can. I wish I had come sooner; I hate to see you so thin."

Ratha did not expect him to keep his word, but a day later, he appeared through the bushes with another piece of meat. This too, she shared with the gray, and the old one's eyes widened in astonishment. Every few days he came, bringing something he had taken from the freshest kill. Ratha began to anticipate his visits, not only for the food, but for the conversation. To all the others, she remained dumb. They thought her witless and she encouraged them to think so, hoping to dull certain memories of her performance in the meadow during the first raid.

As the weather grew harsher, the Un-Named began to raid once more. Ratha expected to have no part of the fighting. Again, she and the others of her pack were made to carry the spoils from the meadow. Her job was easier this time, for the slain beasts were few and small. Her only contact with the fighting was through Bonechewer, when he brought her food. She also hungered for news of the clan and that, too, Bonechewer brought, although none of it was cheerful.

He told her that plans were being made for a final raid in which the Un-Named would drive the clan from their dens, slaughter them and take their land. Ratha listened in silence. There was nothing she could do to change the fate of her people. She could only look out for herself and try to survive along with her cubs. She sought refuge in the old anger. Why should she mourn for those who had made her renegade and outcast because they did not understand the new power she had brought them? Whatever death Meoran died he would have earned. The only ones who tried to defend her, she remembered, had been Thakur and Fessran. And even Thakur had turned betrayer. *I will mourn for none of them except Fessran,* she thought bitterly.

That evening, she watched the packs assemble for the last attack on the clan. Her group was among them, since all were needed to fight and none to drag away kills. The only carcasses this time would be those of the enemy. Even so, Ratha was held back from the fighting, along with others too old, too young or otherwise unsuitable. Her pregnancy did not make her awkward, and she suspected the real reason was distrust.

She lay with her chin on her paws, glancing from time to time at the guards who had been assigned to keep watch on her and her companions. The night was quiet except for a breeze rustling the dry leaves and a last lonely cricket chirping. Once in a while, faraway shrieks and cries broke the stillness, and Ratha lifted her head. She thought of Srass's death in the first raid and shivered. That scene would be repeated again and again before dawn. The cries died out and she could hear only the wind and the cricket.

I hope Fessran escaped, she thought.

Toward dawn, she heard the raiders returning. They came, roaring their victory, and broke through the forest with a great crashing of branches. Many were wounded and some missing. Ratha lay and watched the Un-Named strut past in the dawn light. The clan, she guessed, had fought hard in its final battle.

An argument started between several of the pack leaders. Ratha ignored it at first, letting their angry words blend into the rest of the noise. Then she realized what the disputants were arguing about and she swivelled her ears to listen.

"What does it matter that a few of them still live?" asked the youngster who had led Ratha's pack. "We have their dens and their herds."

They walked beyond Ratha's hearing, still snarling at

each other. She went a few steps after them and nearly bumped into Bonechewer.

"*Yarrr!* Watch yourself. I hurt enough already," he growled, dodging awkwardly to avoid her. He limped away, fresh blood oozing from his flank. His face was a nest of scratches. Both ears were torn.

"It is over," he said flatly, looking at Ratha. He glanced at the boisterous raiders milling about. "They go to the dens. Come with me."

The path they took across the meadow was overgrown. The bodies on both sides looked half-eaten. Some were not only slain: they looked half-eaten and the insects had not been there long enough to consume them. Ratha remembered the gray-coat stripping flesh from Srass's flank even before he was dead. Numb as she was, she shuddered and shut her eyes, following Bonechewer by the sound of his footsteps and the grass brushing past his legs. The smell, however, she couldn't shut out, and it was with her all the way along the path until they reached the clan dens.

Bodies had lain there too, for there were sticky stains at the entrances to many of the lairs. Ratha could see the trails in the mud where the remains had been dragged away. Had one of them been Fessran or Thakur? Or perhaps her father, Yaran, or her mother Narir? From each den came faint familiar odors, and for a moment, she was a cub again, romping by the lairs, seeing the faces framed in the entrances. One face showed a touch of annoyance for being wakened by her noise. Another's eyes were indulgent, knowing she was only a cub and would learn soon enough. The memory left Ratha and she stared into the abandoned dens, empty except for the faint smell of those who had lived there.

Bonechewer walked back to her and together they wandered among the lairs, neither one saying anything. They watched the other Un-Named ones crawling in and out of the dens, claiming them, enlarging them and starting to dig new ones nearby. The clan's territory was now theirs, and here they would stay for the rest of the winter. New faces grinned from entrance holes, and one new owner called out to Ratha and Bonechewer, "Find one for yourselves! These are fine lairs indeed; too fine to belong to clan filth." The big silver-coat had taken possession of Meoran's den. The lair Ratha knew as Fessran's was now occupied by the young pack leader. She followed Bonechewer until he stopped at a small den in an earthen bank. He ducked and crawled inside. Ratha started to follow, then stopped. The smell wafting back to her was Bonechewer's, yet it wasn't. She sniffed the sill and sides of the hole, and she knew suddenly who the den had belonged to. Bonechewer, by accident or design, had found Thakur's den. Bonechewer's smell was oddly similar to the odor lingering on the sides of the lair.

Ratha backed away as if the smell had stung her nose. Her memories of Thakur were still too fresh, and the smell of him made them stronger.

"It isn't large," came Bonechewer's voice from inside, but it will hold the two of us. Come in and see."

"No, I don't like it," Ratha snapped. "Find another."

Bonechewer gave her a puzzled glance and crawled out of the den.

He led her to other dens, but each time she found a familiar smell and a face came up in her memory. However much she tried to wipe it away with hatred, the image persisted and seemed to haunt the cool earthen walls. She could escape it only by retreating outside into the sunshine. Only there could she stop trembling.

When Ratha had calmed herself, she wandered among the lairs, looking for Bonechewer. She spotted him standing near a den that lay apart from the rest. This lair had been deserted long before the coming of the Un-Named. Ratha remembered it being empty from her early cubhood.

She watched Bonechewer sniff the ruined entrance. He reached up and pawed more dirt down. The roof of the old den collapsed.

Ratha moved closer. What could he want with an old clan den? No one ever used it or went near it. Even cubs at play stayed away from it, not only because it was dark and crumbling, but because, the older cubs said, someone had been killed there. They claimed that the ground still smelled of old blood.

As Ratha thought about the abandoned lair, she remembered that she had once seen someone there, and with a shock, she recalled who it was.

Thakur. I saw Thakur there.

She dropped into the grass and crept downwind, trying not to disturb Bonechewer. He gazed at the old den with an expression Ratha had seen on another face, a face whose eyes were green instead of amber.

Then everything fell together and Ratha nearly jumped out of the grass. Now she knew. Reshara had birthed twin males, alike except for eye color.

Seek out old memories and bury them, Ratha thought as Bonechewer pawed more dirt into the lair. Is that the place where Reshara had her cubs?

She scuttled away so that Bonechewer would not see her. She stood up and shook the grass from her fur. Should she ask him? No. She had the truth now. Whether he would accept it or deny it made no difference.

Her pack leader found her and tried to put her in a lair with the gray and the two dun-coats, but Ratha escaped him and clambered up a tree. She sat up in the crotch, watching those down below and decided she would rather sleep out in the open or in this tree than in the dens that had once belonged to her people.

Despite harassment and threats from the others, Ratha stayed in her tree, only coming down to eat or serve as a sentry, guarding the Un-Named settlement from attacks by any of the previous owners who had survived. Some of the clan had survived, but who they were and where they were, she had no idea.

The weather grew colder. The rain turned to sleet and frost covered the ground, turning the soil hard. One morning Ratha woke in her tree with a carpet of snow on her back. Below her, everything was a soft, unbroken white. She climbed down from her tree. Nearby was a three-horn carcass that had been almost stripped. She found it and uncovered it, eating the frozen rags of meat still remaining on the bones. She thought longingly of the entrails and haunch meat the Un-Named leaders had dragged into their dens. Perhaps Bonechewer would bring her something today.

She found the old gray who always stood sentry with her. She had grown used to the ancient one with her wordless muttering and malicious eyes. She knew too that the gray served only to guard her, for the old one would be nearly useless in an attack.

Once she had resented it bitterly; now she thought no more about it and even welcomed her companion's company, dull and surly as it was. She watched the old female mark a tree, then went and left her own mark beside it. It was almost a ritual they performed before starting each watch. The gray then took up a position several tail-lengths from Ratha and turned her face outward. Ratha did the same.

Morning passed and then midday. The crisp winter breeze brought no new smells and the forest was muffled and silent. Shadows began creeping across the snow crust. Ratha decided Bonechewer was not going to come that day. She swallowed and ate some snow to ease the tight burning feeling in her throat. He hadn't come for several days. Perhaps he had grown tired of her, her prickliness and her swelling belly. Perhaps he had picked someone else whose coat wasn't rough and dull and whose temper was less unpredictable.

She told herself fiercely that her burning throat was hunger rather than hurt. She was dipping her muzzle into the snow again when she heard the gray snarl. The snarl turned into a whine and there was a soft thump.

Ratha turned. The gray-coat crouched, chewing on a chunk of flesh that spread red stains on the crystalline snow. Behind the gray, Bonechewer stood. Ratha waited for her morsel, but nothing appeared and Bonechewer's jaws were empty. Pangs of disappointment cramped her stomach.

"Do I get nothing this time?" she asked.

"I have more meat for you," he answered. "First, come with me. I want to show you something."

"I can't. I have to stand guard. And the old one will raise a fuss if I leave my place. My pack leader—"

"Will answer to me for the way he has treated you." Bonechewer showed his teeth as he spoke. "And as for the old gray, she will think of nothing but her meat. Come." He bounded away.

With a cautious glance toward her partner, Ratha padded after him. She saw that his pawprints were stained with tiny flecks of brown and red. She frowned and tried to catch up with him to ask why. She broke into a canter, showering snow over the bushes. Again she frowned, wrinkling her brows. He hadn't been that far ahead, had he? His prints led over a white-covered rise and down the other side. On top of a little cliff, they ended and Ratha could see no other tracks. For a moment, she felt panic. Had he tricked her? Had he enticed her away from her guard duty only to leave her? If she was found away from her post, she would be fair game for anyone, for they would assume she was escaping.

"Bonechewer!" she called, her voice sharp and raw with fear.

"In here," came his muffled reply from somewhere beneath her feet. She craned her neck over the bank and saw the top of his head and his ears above the snow. He twisted his head around and grinned at her.

"Where are you?" she demanded, wondering if he had buried himself in the snow just to tease her.

His head disappeared again. Ratha leaned over the bank, walking her forepaws down the steep slope. She was afraid to jump into the hollow beneath, fearing jagged rocks or stumps might be concealed under the snow. Without warning, her forepaws slipped and she plunged into an unexpected hole in the bank. She lost her footing completely, flipped and came down hard on her back. She lay in the snow, her head spinning, all four paws waving in the air. Bonechewer's face appeared upside down, framed between her own front paws. "What are you trying to do? Cave it in?"

Ratha gazed up at him. "Cave what in?"

"The den."

She rolled over slowly, shedding snow from her pelt. "Den? Is that what you wanted to show me?" She peered past him at the bank. Now she could see the low entrance and the dirt tracked onto the snow. "I don't want any of those clan dens. I told you that." She heaved herself to her feet.

"This isn't a clan lair," he answered.

"I don't believe you. It's too big for any other creature. Who dug it if the clan didn't?"

"I did," said Bonechewer.

"When?"

"I finished last night, before the snowfall. Just in time."

"The ground is too hard for digging," Ratha protested. Bonechewer gave her an exasperated look and turned over a front paw. The pad was torn and ragged; the toes raw and muddy. Ratha remembered the red and brown stains in his tracks. She walked past him and sniffed the hole. It smelled of freshly dug earth.

"You dug it," she admitted grudgingly. "Why?"

"Why do you think?" he snapped.

"For your cubs."

"*Yarrr!* They won't be born here. You're not that big yet. No. We'll be back on my land when they come."

"Then why did you dig it?"

"Because I know you don't freeze in that tree because you want to. The smells in those other lairs raise old memories you would rather keep buried. I know, Ratha," he said, his voice and his eyes growing soft. "I could not sleep in Reshara's den either."

She eyed him, wondering whether this was a challenge to reveal what she knew or an offer to let her share more of his life.

"You didn't see your lair-father die," she said slowly.

Bonechewer showed his teeth as he answered, "You grow bold, clan cat. Thakur must have told you, for it was he who saw Meoran's work." His eyes narrowed. "My brother herded his animals but let his tongue run free, it seems."

Ratha felt the fur rise on her nape. "You would speak that way of him? *Ptahh!* I know the Un-Named do not honor those they slay, but I thought you were different."

She thought he would strike her, but instead he licked a paw and said. "He is not slain. I did not see him among the clan dead."

Ratha's hope leaped ahead of her anger. "You didn't? Could he have escaped?"

"I'm sure he escaped, but searching for him would be useless," he added as Ratha started to open her mouth again. "If I know my brother, he will be far away by now."

She stared down at the trampled snow around her feet. Far away, she thought. Perhaps it is best. I will think no more of Thakur.

She peered into the new den Bonechewer had dug for her, but she did not go in. She dipped her muzzle and gently nipped the top of his forepaw.

"What are you doing now?" he demanded.

"Lift your foot."

He grunted and presented his paw to her, balancing on three legs. She began to lick the sore pads, cleaning mud from between his toes and from beneath his claws. The claws were blunted and dull, telling her that the soil had not yielded easily. No wonder he had been gone for several days! Once the paw was clean, she gave it several soothing licks and asked for the other.

After she finished, she crawled into the lair, turned around in the friendly darkness several times and lay with her forepaws hanging out the entrance.

"It is small, but well dug," she said critically. She could see he was waiting for more of a reaction. When she said nothing else, his whiskers drooped slightly in disappointment.

She wiggled on her belly and lolled her tongue out at him. "I like it. I couldn't have dug a better one."

"Good!" His whiskers sprang back to their usual exuberant bristle. "I dug it far enough away from the others so no one will try to take it. And if they are so stupid as to try, they will answer to me."

"Did you mean what you said about the cubs being born on your ground?" Ratha asked, growing serious again.

"Yes. As soon as the weather lets us travel, we'll go. I have had enough of the Un-Named and seen enough of their foolishness. They no longer need me, nor I them. I will run with them no more. You and I, Ratha, will run together."

He went with her back to her sentry post. There, they saw the old gray asleep in the snow, her chin on her paws.

"She'll wake soon. I should go, Ratha," he said, looking

into her eyes. "This has been hard for you, strong as you are. I am sorry for the part I played. Things won't get easier; not very soon. But I promise you that when this season ends, we will leave this place and never return." Ratha looked around at the white-covered landscape.

"Snowfall has just started." She sighed. "It will seem like a long time. At least I don't have to sleep in a tree."

"I know. The days may seem endless. When things get difficult, think of spring. And me," he added, with a glint of mischief in his eyes.

She watched him trot away over the snow. The gray-coat was starting to wake up, but despite that, Ratha was happy.

CHAPTER 11

SPRING WAS slower in coming to the heights than to the lowlands. As Ratha and Bonechewer wound their way out of the hills, the sparse grass and scrub bush gave way to new growth, green and springy underfoot. They did not take the old trail, still rutted and worn by the passage of the Un-Named. As if in unspoken agreement, neither one ventured toward it, preferring to find their own way across the endless meadow that covered the hills.

Bonechewer walked ahead of Ratha, keeping his pace slow. The long scar on his flank was only starting to fade. Clan fangs had driven deep, and he would limp for the rest of his life. Ratha followed his waving tail through the grass, feeling the new life moving inside her. She was so big now that even the low grass tips brushed her underneath and her graceful walk had become awkward, her swollen belly swinging from side to side at each step.

As she and Bonechewer left the hills and came onto the plain, tiny flowers appeared among the grasses, sending their scents up into the warm spring wind.

Ratha lifted her head and watched a bird drift in lazy circles overhead. The grief was still there in the back of her throat and the memories in the back of her mind. The clan was no more, broken and scattered by the attack of the Un-Named. She, and perhaps some other ragged band of survivors, were all that was left of those who had once followed the herder's way. Many others had left their blood where the three-horns and dapplebacks had once grazed. The Un-Named, too, had paid. Ratha remembered how the vultures circled and the picked bones grew gray and moldy.

The sun warmed her back, reminding her that those times were past. The unborn cubs moved again, and she felt little kicks inside, as if the young ones were impatient to be born.

Bonechewer stopped and came back, "Are you tired?" he asked.

"No, hungry."

Bonechewer grunted. "Those cubs eat more than you do. They'll be strong and healthy."

"I can hunt for a few more days," Ratha said, as Bonechewer took the weight off his injured leg.

"Hunt? You can't even crouch," he said, but his tone was gentle rather than mocking. "No, even with my bad leg the marsh-shrews will know me. You may get sick of marsh-shrews, but I swear there will be plenty of them."

"I will eat marsh-shrews," Ratha said as he nuzzled her bulging flank.

"*Yarrr!*" Bonechewer shook his head and winced. "He kicked me! Hard enough to make my nose sting. Is that any way to treat your lair-father?" He glared at Ratha's belly in mock anger.

"*She* kicked you." Ratha grinned. "That one's going to be a female."

"I'm glad they're not inside *me*," Bonechewer said vehemently.

"They'll be out soon." Ratha began walking.

"How soon?" Bonechewer looked alarmed.

"I don't know. They'll tell me. Come on, Three-Legs," she said, strutting ahead. "We still have a long way to go."

They saw several more sunsets before they reached the marsh where Bonechewer's territory lay. He was glad to be home, and he trotted all over it, from the lakeshore to the hillside meadow where the spring ran. Ratha tagged after him, eager for the tang of the marshland and the glitter of the morning sun on the lake. She even followed him into the water when he plunged in to wash dust from his coat. She bobbed and rolled like a sap-heavy log while Bonechewer chased fish. By sheer exuberance rather than skill, he managed to catch one. He swam back to her, holding his shiny prize aloft in his jaws. They paddled their way back to shore and feasted on the catch.

The next task was to dig a new den for the cubs. Ratha chose a site on the hillside near the spring where dirt was soft and the digging went fast. They took turns at hunting and digging and soon the excavation was finished. Ratha inspected it, cleared out the remaining loose dirt, stamped down the rest and began to line the den with dry grass, pine needles and tufts of her own fur pulled from her belly. Bonechewer helped her, trying to find the softest leaves and the most fragrant grasses with which to make the nest.

They were making their last trip with grass in their mouths when Ratha felt a sharp cramp begin high in her belly and ripple down both sides of her flank. She had felt such pangs before, but they were mild and soon ceased. This time it grew until it became painful. She moaned and dropped her mouthful of grass.

Bonechewer waited with her until the spasm had passed. Ratha leaned against him, feeling his strength and his warmth. The pain frightened her and she was grateful for his presence. Once the cramp ceased, she was able to walk on. Before they reached the den, it happened again and the contraction was stronger. Ratha felt something break deep inside and a gush of fluid which wet the fur beneath her tail.

"They're telling me," she gasped, her head low.

She felt Bonechewer seize her nape and pull her up. She staggered with him to the den. He pushed her inside, settled her on her bed and stood back, looking anxiously at her.

Ratha ground her teeth together as the next spasm

seized her. She thrust back with her hind legs and pushed against the wall of the den. Again the pain went away, leaving her panting and shivering. She looked for Bone-chewer, but he had gone.

Panic washed through Ratha as she shifted restlessly from side to side. The nest, so carefully dug and lined, seemed terribly uncomfortable, and the dark, rather than being cozy, made her feel as though she were suffocating.

I didn't know it would be like this, she thought, laying her head on the earthen floor and feeling the frantic pulse in her throat. *I thought mothers just went to sleep for a while, and when they woke, the cubs were there.*

The teats on her belly began to itch and she rolled on her side and licked them. She felt a surge beneath her tongue as another contraction started and traveled in waves along her flank. She gave a muffled cry and strained, pushing her rear paws against the den wall again. The pushing helped.

Her rapid panting was making her throat dry. She thought about going to the stream for a drink, but as she raised herself on her front paws, something seemed to twist inside her, grinding through her guts. She squeezed her eyes shut, flopped on her side and shoved her feet against the earthen wall.

Again, fear shot through her. How long would it take? Was it happening as it should? She didn't know. She was alone with her body and the strange and awesome thing that was happening to her.

She let the fear free and it hovered around her, a cold mist that chilled her no matter how deep she burrowed into the leaves or how hard she shivered. It took hold and raged through her body, making her muscles work against each other, driving her heartbeat up until she was panting with exhaustion and turning each contraction into a crushing pain. Ratha whimpered and rubbed her cheek in the dirt. She couldn't go any farther this way. If she let the fear possess her, she would die of terror, the cubs still unborn.

Every female since the first has gone through this, she thought furiously. *If they can, I can. The clan couldn't kill me; neither could the Un-Named. I am a herder of three-horns, the bearer of the Red Tongue and I am going to have these cubs.*

"Do you hear me, litterlings?" she growled at her belly. "If you give me any more trouble, I'll nip your wretched little tails when you come out!"

Ratha was startled to feel an answering kick from inside her. She grinned to herself. That one had to be the little female; the one that had kicked Bonechewer. The contractions began again and the fear rose, but Ratha fought it away.

"All right, little marsh-shrew," she said as she braced herself against the wall. "You're . . . coming . . . out!"

She grunted, strained until she thought she would burst and felt the cub slip backwards. She drew a breath and pushed against the wall until she thought she would make the den cave in. The pain gave way to exhilaration as she felt the cub inch downward through her. There was pressure between her loins and below her tail. One more push, she thought, feeling the skin bulge and stretch beneath her tail. The cub was coming headfirst, butting its way out into the world. Ratha's heart raced as she curled herself backwards to look. Something tore, something slipped and there was a wet wiggling body in the leaves beside her.

Ratha bent her head and began to wash the cub, licking fast and hard. The tiny creature squealed as she tumbled it back and forth with her tongue. Tiny claws raked her chin and the tiny tail lashed her nose. The odor of birth clung to it, warm, rich and dark; her own scent from deep inside her body. The cub had its own smell too, a smell that told Ratha that she had been right; her firstborn was the little female. She licked until her daughter was dry and fluffy and then swept the cub to a full teat. There was a tentative nuzzle and then the little mouth took the nipple and began to suck.

Ratha ate the afterbirth and lay back, waiting for the contractions that would bring the next cub. They did not come for a while and during this time she dozed, grateful for the interlude. Another cramp woke her. This time she was ready and the second cub was soon nursing beside the first. The third slid out with hardly any effort at all. The last seemed reluctant to enter the world and, after some struggling, came out tail first. Ratha licked and massaged him as she had all the others. Soon the little female and her three brothers were lying in a row, suckling and kneading her belly.

Worn and weary, but content, she stretched as she lay on her side.

A shadow blocked the sunlight at the mouth of the den. She raised her head. Bonechewer's scent drifted into the den. It was no longer the odor of her mate and her companion, but the scent of the male, sharp and threatening. Ratha's hackles rose.

"Ratha?" Bonechewer called. She could see his eyes glowing at the entrance to the den.

To her those eyes seemed savage and hungry. Her cubs, she thought, starting to growl. He was coming to kill and eat her cubs. She got up, shaking herself free of the clinging mouths and claws. Even as she rose to defend her litter, she was startled by her sudden rage. She knew Bonechewer only wanted to see his cubs, not to kill them. Her feelings were no longer just hers, but those of all lair-mothers before her. She trembled as the image of a dead cub dangling from bloodstained jaws seized her mind and would not let go.

"Ratha?" The voice was louder; the eyes closer.

"Stay out!" she hissed.

"I want to see them," Bonechewer said, shouldering his way in. "What's the matter with you?"

Ratha bared her teeth. "Get out!" She clawed at him. He flinched and backed away. He looked so lost and bewildered that Ratha wanted to go and soothe him. Yet she couldn't leave her cubs, and if he came toward her again she knew the ancient rage would force her to attack him.

"I'm not ready," she said, trying to take the harshness out of her voice.

"I want to see them," he said again.

Ratha swallowed. "Bonechewer . . ." she said trying to see him as her mate rather than a marauding male. Behind her the cubs squealed their impatience. She circled them nervously and lay down again.

Bonechewer retreated, but she could still see his face at the entrance to the den.

"Are you hungry, Ratha?" he asked softly. "Shall I hunt for you?"

"Yes," Ratha said gratefully. "When you come back, perhaps you can see them."

She heard him pad away and laid her chin in the leaves, remembering the hurt and misery in his eyes. There was no way she could explain it to him. A fear with no reason . . . once there had been a reason. Never had a clan male attacked and eaten his young. Perhaps it still happened among the Un-Named. Ratha felt the cubs clambering over her belly, hunting for milk. They butted their heads against her, their cries shrill and demanding. She gathered them together with her forepaws and gave them her teats. How strong they were already, she thought. What fierce hunters they would be when they grew!

Again she lay back and was drifting into sleep when another idea struck her. Hunting was not the only thing she could teach her cubs. *The clan is no more,* she thought, lifting her head and opening her eyes in the darkness. *But the way of the herder has not been lost, for I remember what I was taught and I can teach that way. Did Thakur not say that I could have been the best herder in the clan?*

The memory brought pain as well as pride. She nosed the cubs. She and her children could capture beasts from the forest as clan ancestors had and graze them here on the lowland meadows. As the cubs nursed, she dreamed of founding a new clan to take the place of the old. She could also teach the Un-Named as well, so that they could keep herds of their own and no longer live by raiding. Ratha listened to the soft sucking sounds and began to purr herself. She had seen too many old things die and been a part of the dying. Was change always deaths and endings? Her memory, in a bitter voice, seemed to agree, but another voice, softer but stronger, answered no. That voice was the breathing of her young beside her.

A beginning, she thought, feeling hope rise. Perhaps this time . . . a beginning.

Ratha nursed her dream along with her cubs and both flourished and grew. She tried to speak of her idea to Bonechewer, but he was more interested in his young themselves than as founding members of a future clan. Once she allowed him near the cubs, he proved to be an affectionate father as well as a determined provider. At first he approached them carefully and tenderly, dispelling Ratha's lingering fear. Soon the litter was crawling all over their father as well as their mother. They butted their heads into his belly, sucked on his fur and wrestled with his tail.

Once the cubs' eyes opened. Ratha could leave them while she went to hunt. Bonechewer stayed in the den with his children while Ratha ran across the marshland, stretching the cramp out of her legs and refreshing herself with the feel of sun and wind. On these expeditions, she planned how she would teach the youngsters how to herd. First, she would find a lone dappleback, perhaps too old or injured to stay with the herd. She would show the cubs how to take care of the little horse; how to keep it from straying; how to graze and water it. Then, perhaps, a dappleback mare with young. Those could be the start of a small herd. Such clever cubs as hers, she thought proudly, would learn the art in no time. They would far surpass their mother and then, when they had cubs of their own. . . .

Each day, Ratha watched the cubs, eager for signs of

their abilities. She was especially attentive to her first-born, a sturdy little female whose aggressiveness toward any moving object within a tail-length of her, including prickly ones, had earned her the name of Thistle-chaser. Bonechewer had bestowed the name upon his rambunctious daughter after repeatedly pulling out the spines that invariably embedded themselves in that tender little nose.

"She doesn't seem to learn," Ratha growled, watching Bonechewer soothe the crying cub.

"She will," he answered, letting his daughter wriggle free and flicking his tail beyond her reach. Defeated, Thistle-chaser scampered off to join her brothers.

Ratha watched the cubs stalk each other and leap into the air after low-flying insects. They were strong, fierce and quick. From the first day they had ventured outside the maternal lair, they had practiced the motions of stalking and pouncing. They seemed to be born hunters. Ratha felt dismay creep in beneath the feeling of pride. Hunting was important, but there were other things equally so, and those things the cubs seemed to ignore. Ratha pushed the uncomfortable feeling away. *They're young yet. Give them time.* Her inner voice echoed Bonechewer's words. *You can't make them grow any faster.* Ratha sighed. What should she expect? She didn't know. She could only draw upon the memories of her own cubhood. Even those, hazy as they were, seemed at variance with what she saw in her children.

When did I become aware of the world? she often wondered. When did I start to speak? I talk to Thistle-chaser and the others, but not one of them has answered, or has even tried to repeat the sounds I make.

Bonechewer could only counsel patience. "Ratha, you're

too impatient. You're looking for things that aren't there yet," he said, looking at her worried face.

Ratha gazed at Thistle-chaser, cuddling up to her father, licking her nose after another encounter with her namesake. "How old were you when you began to speak?" she asked Bonechewer.

"Older than she is, I'm sure."

"Don't you remember?"

"No." He nuzzled his daughter and looked up at Ratha. "You'll lose her soon enough, Ratha. Enjoy her as she is now."

He is right, she thought, but she couldn't rid herself of the nagging doubt. Ratha watched the two, almost envious of their happiness. Bonechewer didn't care what Thistle-chaser would do or be. He was content to play with her, cuddle her and make no demands on her until she was older.

Ratha tried to be patient, but her dream made her anxious. Each day, as spring yielded to summer, she looked for signs that the cubs would do more than hunt. She was cheered when Thistle-chaser and the others began to imitate her words and gestures. The first flush of pride faded when Ratha realized that the cubs had no idea what they were doing or that the sounds they made could bring anything more than praise. Ratha was now sure that the cubs' development was lagging and the knowledge festered like a tick in her skin. To her the summer wind was cold and the gold sunshine pale.

One evening Ratha and Bonechewer went to sit on the crest of the hill above the den. Bonechewer dozed between the long shadows in the last warmth from the setting sun. Ratha lay beside him and tried to sleep, but her misery kept her awake. Far down the hill she could hear lusty yowls as the cubs chased each other through the marsh grass. A piercing howl rose above the clamor. It wavered and broke into a forlorn wail. Bonechewer woke and shook his head sleepily. "I'll go," he said as Ratha started to heave herself to her feet. "She's probably pounced on another thorn ball."

"Leave her." Ratha stared at the ground between her paws. An insect crawled up onto a swaying grass blade and clung there waving its antennae. The carapace flashed and shimmered in the rosy sunlight. There was a soft rushing sound; grass brushing past legs.

Ratha snapped her head up. "I said, leave her!"

Puzzled, Bonechewer sat down, curling his tail over his feet. The light turned his fur to burnished copper, which caught highlights as his muscles rippled beneath his coat. Shadow hid the scar on his flank. He looked almost as he had when Ratha had first seen him, but now, seeing his beauty only brought bitterness into her throat.

Thistle-chaser too is beautiful, Ratha thought. Her coat will turn copper when the spots fade . . . and her eyes are green like mine. Large bright green eyes . . . and nothing behind them.

"Ratha," Bonechewer said.

"No! Maybe the pain will teach her to think before she jumps. Nothing else will."

He came back and nuzzled Ratha, but she would not be comforted. The wailing continued far down the hill and there was rage as well as pain in Thistle-chaser's cry.

"I'll get her. Wait here."

Ratha drove her foreclaws into the soil and watched him go. Soon he was back, the cub dangling from his mouth. Ratha could see the strain in his neck muscles; Thistle-chaser was getting too heavy to carry by the scruff. He draped her across his forepaws and turned her pads up one by one until he found the thorn and worked it loose with his teeth. The cub lay on her back, cradled between her father's paws. She rolled her head back and stared at Ratha. Ratha looked back, trying to find something of herself in those eyes, but what was there reminded her more of the eyes of the Un-Named.

Despair washed over her as she realized the full truth. The cubs she had birthed, tended and tried so hard to teach shared nothing of hers except the form of her body. Behind the pert little faces and mischievous eyes lay only the hunter's instincts.

Ratha ground her teeth together. It was so obvious as to be painful. Couldn't Bonechewer see?

Her mate had his nose buried in Thistle-chaser's belly. Four paws flailed around his muzzle as the body wriggled. "*Arr*, you're a wild one, cub!" he crooned, nuzzling and teasing his daughter. "You'll be as rude as your mother when you start to talk."

Ratha suspected his words were meant for her rather than Thistle-chaser. Bonechewer peeked up at her from between Thistle-chaser's paws, pretending to flinch under the expected cuff. His manner wilted slightly when he met Ratha's eyes.

"Stop lying to yourself and to me." Ratha's voice came from a strange place inside her, cold and remote. "She'll never talk." She shot out a paw, caught the back of Thistle-chaser's head and turned the cub's face to Bonechewer. For a moment he looked into the beautiful empty eyes. Then he squeezed his own eyes shut and laid his head against Thistle-chaser. Ratha withdrew her paw. She had seen enough.

Gently he soothed the cub, who had begun to whimper. "I was trying to make myself believe . . ." he said, not looking at Ratha.

"Why?" Ratha asked, barely able to speak through the misery burning her throat. "Why do our cubs have no light in their eyes? Why won't their tongues form words? The birth was hard. Did I injure them? Or was it something in me that is not there?" She walked back and forth in front of Bonechewer. Thistle-chaser lay between her father's paws, looking bewildered.

"No," Bonechewer said at last. "You are clanborn, Ratha. Had you mated with a male of your own kind, your cubs would have the light in their eyes."

"But you are of my kind," she faltered.

"Your cubs' eyes tell me that I am not."

"What does it matter that Reshara took an Un-Named male? You eyes are as bright as any in the clan and you have more wit than they. Why would our cubs lack what you have?"

"Such a thing does not make sense," Bonechewer admitted, looking down at Thistle-chaser. "Even so, I feared that it might be true. I did not listen to my fear."

Ratha stood stiff-legged, trying to understand what he had told her. Then her rage broke.

"You knew? You knew our cubs might be like this?" she cried. "Did you sire other witless ones as well?"

He cringed, burying his muzzle in Thistle-chaser's flank. "You were different . . . the other female was Un-Named."

Ratha felt her eyes go to slits. "Well, you have your cubs. I only wish they had been born dead!"

She flung back her head and screamed at the sky. Her dream was shattered. The one she had begun to love she could now only hate with a deep, burning bitterness like the Red Tongue in her belly.

"Ratha!"

She flung herself at him, slashing with teeth and claws. "Why? Why did you do this to me?"

Bonechewer dodged her attack, trying to shield Thistle-chaser and defend himself without hurting Ratha.

She raked his face, shrieking at him, "Why didn't you kill me in the raid that night? Give me some kindness now. Tear my throat out and leave me for the insects!"

Thistle-chaser scampered around Bonechewer's legs, delighted with this new game.

"Fight, Un-Named One!" Ratha howled as he backed away from her. His retreat only fed her rage. Hate and bitterness poured into her, filling her until that was all she knew. She struck at Bonechewer again and again, ripping his shoulder and laying his cheek open to the bone. He cowered in the dusk, dripping blood in his tracks. Ratha could hear the breath hissing in his throat. Thistle-chaser stumbled and rolled out from between her father's legs. Ratha pounced on the cub, biting hard and deep. Thistle-chaser shrieked, red welling onto the spotted fur beneath Ratha's nose.

A blow knocked her loose from the cub and sent her sprawling down the hillside. Bonechewer was on top of her, eyes blazing, fangs driving toward her throat.

Then he was gone and she was alone with the coming night and her pounding heart. Still dizzy with rage, she leaped up. She shut away the horrified part of her that recoiled at the taste of Thistle-chaser's blood in her mouth. As if from a great distance, she saw Bonechewer licking the wounded cub. She waited as he sensed her and turned around.

"Kill me," she said very softly. "I want no more of life."

His eyes were two coals from the fire of the setting sun, but he stood where he was. Ratha looked past him to Thistle-chaser.

"Why don't you leave them to starve and mate with someone else," she taunted. "Perhaps the next time . . ."

A sharp cuff flung her head to one side. She felt a muscle tear in her neck.

"Enough, Ratha." Bonechewer panted.

Ratha took one step toward him, her eyes on Thistle-chaser. The wounded cub cowered, shaking, ugly black stains spreading across her shoulder and chest. Again a part of Ratha's mind recoiled from the sight, but she forced that part away.

"Don't try," Bonechewer said. "You won't earn your death that way."

Ratha curled her lips back from her fangs as she watched Thistle-chaser.

"Do you really want her? She's witless!" Her voice was thick with scorn.

"I want her. And the others," Bonechewer said quietly. "You are right. They will never know themselves as you and I do. They will never share our gift of words. But they are mine and I will keep them, for I will have no others." He lowered his head. "I will not mate again, Ratha."

Her whiskers drooped as her rage fell, allowing her to

see the terror in Thistle-chaser's eyes. She sought her anger and used it to blur her sight. Soon enough, she knew, she would see all too clearly.

The cries of the other cubs drifted up the hill beneath the violet sky. The night wind touched Ratha's fur. Thistle-chaser's brothers were still at play. She turned to go downhill but Bonechewer blocked her way. "Stay away from them. I'm warning you."

He raised one paw, claws extended. "I won't kill you, but if you come near my cubs, you will leave blinded and limping."

Ratha drew back, trembling. Now she had truly lost everything. Bonechewer would never accept her again, and there would only be fear and hatred in Thistle-chaser's eyes. There was no returning along the trail she had chosen to take.

Again she fanned her anger into a blazing flame, burning away all regret or remorse.

"Take the cubs, Un-Named One," she snarled. "Feed them well so they do not slay you and gorge themselves on your carcass. I go."

She turned and trotted away, taking the path along the crest of the little hill above the marsh. The damp night wind brought her the many smells she had come to know. Never would she run here again.

She stopped and listened. Bonechewer was following her, making sure she was leaving his territory. Her anger failed her and despair seeped in. How she wanted to go to him, bury her head in his flank and beg his forgiveness, saying she would learn to love the cubs as they were, not as she wanted them to be.

He stopped at the edge of his territory. She ran on, leaving him behind. Her paws beat the ground as she galloped, filling her mind with the rhythm.

Now she was outcast to the Un-Named as well as the clan. All fangs would be bared against her wherever she went, for she would be known as a killer and a renegade. She ran, not looking or caring where she was going.

Behind her in the night a voice rose. Ratha tried to shut her ears to it, but the voice continued and grew louder. She stopped at a stream to drink and rinse the metallic taste of blood from her mouth. She ran on until at last Bonechewer's farewell faded and died, leaving her alone with the night as her only companion.

CHAPTER 12

FOR THE rest of the summer Ratha wandered, drifting across the land as if she were a leaf blown by a fitful wind. She often stood atop a sharp cliff, wondering whether to throw herself down, or lay in the dark of a cave, wishing starvation would take her quickly. But she always turned away from the cliff or dragged herself out of the cave to hunt. Something forced her to survive almost against her will.

Ratha lived each day, trying not to think about the past

or the future. Her eyes were always fixed on her prey or searching for those who would prey on her. When she looked at her reflection in the ponds and streams where she drank, she could barely answer the gaze of that thin face looking at her from beneath the water. Her belly twisted when she saw how the bitterness showed like the fresh scars not yet hidden beneath new fur. One who saw her in the days when Thakur called her yearling would never know her now, she thought. She walked with her head low and her fur was dull and rough.

She meant her wandering to be aimless, but she knew she was drifting back toward clan land. Something was calling her home, and she answered, even though she knew there was no home. Only gray bones remained in the meadow where the three-horns used to run and old dens filled with moldy leaves.

Why she was drawn to the old clan holdings she didn't know. There would be nothing waiting for her at the end of this trail. She often fought the pull, turning onto a new path each time her feet carried her toward the old. Many times before she had been able to leave worn trails behind and run on fresh paths, but this time she had no will or wish to challenge the new. She felt used up and worn out; as if the wounds Bonechewer had given her would never stop bleeding. Each day she cursed her body for living when the pain inside made her want to lie down and never rise again. The taste of Thistle-chaser's blood clung inside her mouth no matter how much water she drank trying to rinse it away.

At last, on a hot day in midsummer, Ratha stood on a stream bank, looking across. The meadow beyond spread far in every direction, the grass high and thick. Charred spikes that had once been trees stood against the sky, their trunks washed with waving grass, the space between blackened branches empty of leaves. Insects droned about Ratha's ears as she stood with the sun on her back, wondering whether to cross.

She turned and walked along the shaded stream bank, the mud cool beneath her feet. She emerged into an open patch and narrowed her eyes at the glitter of the sun on the water. A slight thinning of the grass on the far bank was all that marked the trail that had run across the stream and the meadow. Soon it would be entirely hidden.

Ratha remembered how she had run that trail, Fessran panting at her side as the clan-pack howled behind her. Those howls still seemed to echo through the hot, still air. Her ears trembled. She started, swiveling her ears forward. It hadn't all been memory. She had heard something, although it was faint and far away. She lifted her head and listened again, wondering if the sun on her head was making her dizzy. She looked across the meadow. No one was there, yet it seemed that the sound had come from that direction. Not howls of rage, but the echo of a high ringing cry she had heard before. She plunged into the tall grass and trotted toward the sound.

It was much further than she thought. The grass, uncropped, grew higher than she could raise her nose with all four feet on the ground. She seemed to run forever in a lush green cage whose walls moved with her as she ran. Stalks whipped her flanks and broke beneath her feet.

She froze, one paw lifted, yet the swishing sound of grass brushing past legs continued briefly and stopped. Ratha sniffed, trying to catch a scent, but she could only smell the sugary juices of the crushed grass. Hair bristled on her nape. She waited. No one appeared. The air was quiet. The cry she heard before came again, muffled by the hot, still air. It was the imperious call of a dappleback stallion gathering his flock of mares. Dappleback! Ratha's stomach rumbled. If she killed a mare, she could gorge herself, drag the rest up a tree and not have to hunt again for days. She bounded on through the grass, the ripe seed-heads lashing her back.

She slowed to a trot. Again she froze and the other sound that was not the stallion's cry continued on for an instant. Ratha sat up on her hind legs, peering back over the grass. There. A circle of stalks behind her was still waving. Ratha dropped down again, whirled and faced the green curtain behind her. Again, no one appeared.

Disgruntled, she made her way forward again, no longer trotting but gliding quietly between the stems, leaving as little evidence of her passage as possible.

Her tracker was staying downwind of her so the slight breeze that fanned her face bore none of the intruder's scent. The odor of dappleback was growing rich in her nostrils, making her wild with hunger. She could see them now, their backs brown and sweat-slicked above the wild wheat. Once she had tended and guarded such a herd. Now she was the raider and there was no one to defend this herd except the little stallion. Ratha crept close to the dapple-backs, crouched in the grass and picked out her quarry. An older mare, shaggy and ridgebacked. The little horse moved stiffly and lagged behind the others.

Ratha crawled, her belly to the ground, until she was sure that one short dash would bring down the prey. There was no sign of her shadower. Perhaps the intruder had gone or had never been there at all, an illusion made by capricious breezes playing through the grass.

Ratha gathered herself, tensed and sprang. A sharp yowl tore through the air behind her, almost before her paws left the ground. Nostrils flaring, the dapplebacks threw back their heads, wheeled and scattered. Ratha lost her prey in the confusion of bodies racing past her. She broke off her charge and veered away, retreating in the direction she had come.

She bounded high and saw the grass rippling as someone streaked toward her. The sunlight flashed on a dark copper coat and Ratha's throat went tight with fear. Had Bonechewer tracked her here? Had Thistle-chaser died of her wounds and her father come to take revenge? Ratha clamped her teeth together and dove through the grass, ignoring the knife-edged leaves that lashed her face.

However fast she ran or however she dodged and turned, her pursuer was there before her, cutting off her escape. She used all the tricks she knew from her days of herding three-horns, yet she couldn't shake this pursuer. Even Bonechewer wasn't as quick or agile. Every time she turned, she heard the grass break and caught a glimpse of gleaming copper. Bewildered and dizzy, she stood still, hunching her shoulders. This time he was coming. As soon as he appeared, she would leap and sink her fangs into his throat. . . .

The grass parted. Ratha sprang, tried to stop herself and tumbled. She scrambled to her feet, her tail creeping between her legs.

The face before her was Bonechewer's but the eyes were green, not yellow. Both fangs stood intact in his lower jaw. As he lowered his head to peer at her, she saw the puckered scars on his neck. She remembered how Meoran had seized him and thrust him forward against the fury of the Red Tongue. The memory reflected back at her from his eyes with a quality of uncertainty, as if he could not yet believe who she was.

"I was ready to track and slay a raider," Thakur said. "Instead I find you."

Ratha waited.

"And I have found a raider." Thakur's voice became hard. "You didn't come here just to watch the herd. Do you run with the Un-Named ones who still prey on my beasts? Were you among those I chased away last night?"

"I came to kill," Ratha answered, "but I run with no one except myself."

"My teeth seek a raider's throat," Thakur growled, lashing his tail against the grass. "Our animals are few and scrawny, yet still the Un-Named Ones prey. I would rip you open and hang you from a tree to tell them to seek other hunting grounds."

Ratha drew back her whiskers and gave him a bitter grin. "You would better please Meoran rather than the Un-Named if you hung my pelt from a tree. It would be more useful there than where it is now."

"Run, then," Thakur snarled at her. "I will do Meoran no service." He paused. "You look too much like her, yet you cannot be. You have the eyes of a hunter, not of the cub I taught."

"Then, if I am not Ratha, kill me," she said, looking at him steadily.

Thakur flattened his ears and bared his teeth as he approached. She smelled the sweat on his coat and his breath, heavy and acrid. He stopped, panting. He hung his head.

"Thakur, I am Ratha," she said.

"Then you know where I got these wounds on my neck," he said between his teeth. "They took too long to heal. There is another wound, not made by Meoran's fangs."

Ratha glared back at him. "Whose voice lifted above the clan yowling that night? Whose voice told them that my creature could be killed? Had you not spoken, Thakur, the clan would have listened to me, not Meoran!"

"I told you then it was not hatred that made me speak."

"Why?" Ratha cried, searching his eyes.

"I saw too many throats bared to the Red Tongue," Thakur said softly.

"And was that worse than throats bared to Meoran?" Ratha demanded.

"Meoran may be stupid and cruel, but he is of our kind. His power is the power of teeth and claws and that we understand even as we fear it. The Red Tongue's power we fear because we do not understand it. It is a fear that makes the strongest among us into crying cubs. Except for you, Ratha."

He stared at her long and hard.

"You thought I would use the Red Tongue's power to rule the clan? No! I wanted only to share my creature, to teach my people how to use it and care for it. Meoran was blind not to see."

"He was not blind," Thakur answered. "He saw what I saw, throats bared to the one who carried the Red Tongue. You would have ruled whether or not you chose."

Ratha's ears drooped in dismay as Thakur continued. "I did not want that for my people, or for you either."

"So that is why you spoke," Ratha said.

"It was not the Red Tongue's touch on my fur that I feared the most, Ratha. Meoran thinks that is why I spoke, but the truth is what I have told you. Do you believe me?"

Ratha looked down at her toes. "Does it matter whether or not I believe you? The Red Tongue is gone and the people we once called ours have been slain by the Un-Named."

"Not all of them," Thakur said. "The beasts I guard are not only mine."

Ratha's eyes widened. "The clan still lives? Where? How many?"

"Fewer than I have claws on all my feet. As to where, I can't tell you yet."

Ratha looked up at him, long-dead hopes starting to rise again.

"Yearling," Thakur said softly, startling her by using the old name, "I know you have run a long and bitter trail. I also know I helped set you on it. I am not sorry for what happened, for I had no other choice, but I wish I was not the cause of the pain I see behind your eyes."

Before she could speak again, the sharp yowl of a herder's call sounded over the meadow. Thakur sat up on his hind legs and peered through the grass.

"Cherfan's helping me," he said as he dropped down. "He's wondering where I am."

"Cherfan?" Ratha asked. "The greedy one who always ate before I did? He survived?"

Thakur looked amused. "You would remember that.

He became a good herder, although he was late in learning. He fought beside me in the raids and he has fathered the two new cubs we have in our little group." He paused, watching Ratha's face darken. "What is it, yearling?"

She glanced at him, aware she had betrayed herself. "Something I will tell you later. Go now, if you don't want Cherfan to find me."

"Wait here," Thakur said. A moment later he was gone, leaving only swaying grass to mark where he had been.

Ratha waited. Far above her a bird looped and dipped. Insects chirped monotonously and droned back and forth overhead, making her feel sleepy. The light slanted between the grass stems and a late afternoon breeze rustled the leaves. A worried little voice inside Ratha's head kept asking her why she trusted Thakur. He could easily bring Meoran or a hate-filled pack that would fall upon her and tear her to pieces. Or he could circle behind her and attack her through the grass curtain, she thought, feeling very vulnerable. *He trusts me to wait for him and not run away, even though I could. I think he is asking me what I choose.*

She lifted her muzzle, hearing him coming through the grass. He poked his head out, saw her and looked pleased. "Good, you stayed. I told Cherfan I chased the raider away. He's looking after the dapplebacks. I told him I was going to make sure the raider is gone." He grinned at her. "Is the raider gone, Ratha?"

She looked back at him, feeling very empty. "I could give you a better answer if I could fill my belly."

"There will be meat tonight," Thakur said. "Not much, for our kills have to last many days."

Ratha sat up. "The raider isn't gone," she teased, feeling some of her old spirit coming back. "The raider is Thakur.

It will be good to eat from Meoran's herd. Bring me a good piece, Thakur. Steal the liver if no one else has eaten it. I'll wait for you by the stream."

"No, yearling. What you want, you may take yourself. I want you to come back with me."

"Come back to the clan?" Ratha was aghast. "If Meoran is there, he'll rip me in half!"

"He is there, but I have reason to believe he will keep his claws sheathed. *If* you keep your mouth shut," Thakur added meaningfully and continued, "You speak of us as the clan, but we are only the remains of it; scarcely enough to fill a well-dug lair. The Un-Named took many lives, Ratha."

She swallowed. She was not yet ready to tell him that she had been there and watched her people die.

"Every one that remains is precious to us," Thakur said. "Meoran knows that now."

Ratha only wrinkled her nose. Thakur saw it and said, "You will find him much changed. Even I, who bear the scars of his teeth on my neck, can say that about him. It was he who saved those of us who did survive."

"It was he whose stupidity gave you to the jaws of the Un-Named," Ratha spat back.

"Yes. That too, he knows," said Thakur. "It is bitter meat to him."

"And you still keep him as leader? *Ptah!*"

"What has died is dead, Ratha. He is strong. We need his strength. We need yours as well. Come back to us."

She looked at him, seeing in his eyes what he had not been able to say. *It has been lonely without you, Ratha. Come back . . . come back to me.*

She lowered her head, seeing too much of Bonechewer

in the face before her. Could she put the bitterness behind? Here, again, was a new trail before her, one she never hoped she'd find. She thought she had nothing left to give anyone, but now. . . .

"You say there are new cubs," she said slowly. "How old are they?"

"Old enough to train as herders, but I haven't had time to teach them."

He looked at Ratha and she could see the hope rising in his face.

"It will be hard for me to see cubs again, knowing they are someone else's."

As Ratha watched him, she knew she had betrayed herself. Before she finished speaking, she wished that she could bite off her treacherous tongue and be mute for the rest of her days.

Thakur spoke. "I am wrong to call you 'yearling.' I see that you have grown older. You have been gone from us long enough to have birthed a family."

"To have birthed them and lost them."

He looked at her keenly. "I see that you have ended a trail. One too painful to set foot upon even in memory. I will not ask what happened."

"When I can, I'll tell you, Thakur," she said, and she was thankful it had been he who found her in the meadow. "If I help you with the herding, will you have enough time to teach?"

His eyes brightened. He raised his head and yowled at the sky. "*Arrowoo!*"

"Thakur! You'll bring the others!"

"I don't care. Now they can see you."

Ratha swallowed again. His happiness was starting to

infect her, and she wanted to let it in, but she was still afraid.

"Are you sure Meoran will listen?" she asked.

"If he has any wits at all, he will," Thakur said. "Just don't say anything to anger him."

He turned and pranced away through the grass, his tail high. Ratha followed.

Ratha climbed over water-smoothed stone, the sound of the stream below beating in her ears. Or perhaps it was her own heartbeat she heard, seeming to echo back and forth between the rocks. She looked up at the cliff face overhead, painted in streaks by the sun's last rays. In seasons past, when she was a cub, the stream had run much higher, undercutting the cliff, sculpturing and polishing the rock that now lay far above its banks.

Thakur's tail disappeared around a worn boulder and she hurried to catch up. She could smell the odor of a well-aged kill.

She emerged to find him standing on a sloping gray table of rock looking up into a water-carved cavern. There were shapes in the cave, and they stirred as she approached behind Thakur. Eyes fixed on her. The meat smell came from the rear of the cavern. At the front, a husky dun-colored male stood over a fragile-looking female and her two spotted cubs. The dun coat came forward as the female nudged the cubs further into the cavern.

"Hold, Thakur," he said. "Who is that one with you?"

As he finished, Ratha caught a flurry of motion inside the cavern. A face appeared between two seated forms. The dazed eyes grew wide with joy and the ears pricked up. It was Fessran. Ratha saw her give a wary glance to one side, calm herself and begin sidling toward the entrance.

"Come smell her and tell me yourself, Cherfan," Thakur answered, nosing Ratha ahead of him. She approached Cherfan. Another movement brought her eyes back to the cavern and the large gray-coat standing beneath the center of the arch. Ratha froze. Cherfan looked back over his shoulder.

"I can tell you who she is," said a harsh voice, and amber eyes were fixed on Ratha. "Cherfan, stay back." The dun coat obeyed and retreated. Meoran turned to Thakur. "You know I have little patience with you these days, herder, yet you dare to push me further. Where did you find her and why do you bring her?" He sat, waiting for Thakur's answer.

"I found her in the high grass of the meadow. I thought she was a raider stalking our dapplebacks."

"Then do with her what is done to raiders," Meoran snapped.

"Wait, Meoran," Thakur's voice was stronger and louder, rising above the muted roar of the stream below.

"Hear me. She has not returned to us as an enemy even though you stripped her of her name and made her outcast. She wants to join again with her people."

Meoran curled back his lips, showing fangs like tusks.

"She wants to come back. Accept her. We of the Named are so few that to cast one aside is foolish. Once you would not have listened to words such as these, but I know you have changed."

"So it is your new knowledge of me that makes you bring her drooling to my den." Meoran sneered. "I would use that knowledge in a wiser way, herder."

Ratha swallowed and tried to hide her hunger. Thakur's front claws scraped on stone.

"I hear your words, Thakur," Meoran answered at last. "The wisdom I have learned from the Un-Named makes me admit what you say is true. Every one of our people we can gather in will help us to survive."

"Then may we accept her?" Thakur's eyes were bright, eager. He leaned forward.

"Hold, herder," Meoran growled, narrowing his eyes to amber slits. "There are more things to say."

Thakur lowered his muzzle, slightly abashed.

"You, Ratha, stand before me."

Slowly Ratha walked toward Meoran. The gray-coat seemed as massive as the stone he sat on. Cherfan and his mate came and stood beside him. More survivors from the broken clan peered out fom behind him. They were sons and daughters of clanfolk Ratha had known. Here was a young male with the crooked tail of Srass, the grizzled herder. Of the older clan members, the only one that remained was Meoran. He sat upright beside Cherfan, towering over the young father.

Thakur had told her on the trail that Meoran's rule was no less harsh than before, yet the harshness now was of necessity, not the petty tyranny it had been. His errors had cost him all of his sons and nearly all of his people; knowledge was imprinted as deeply on him as the gashes that Un-Named claws had made across his face. Cherfan looked at him as a son might look at a father and Ratha sensed he had earned that devotion.

The amber slits opened suddenly. "I do not forget the night when a cub carried the Red Tongue among us. And I see by your eyes that you have not forgotten either."

"It is gone, Meoran," Ratha answered. "It perished in the creek. By my foolishness."

"And not by the claws of the herder Fessran, as I was told." Meoran turned his head. Ratha followed his gaze to Fessran, crouching nervously in the shadow near the inside cavern wall. Meoran eyed her and yawned, showing the back of his tongue and all his teeth. "Sit up, herder, and don't cower like a cub. Ratha's tracks betrayed her. After I spared you I went back and saw where she slid and fell into the stream."

Fessran shot Ratha a fierce glance that stabbed her with joy and fear.

Meoran grinned. "Did it amuse you to think you fooled me? I spared you, Fessran, because I needed you. With the Red Tongue gone and the she-cub driven out, you were no threat to me. So you lived." He turned to Ratha. "So you wish to return. To be a herder once again. To eat at the clan kill and obey clan law."

"Yes, Meoran." Ratha looked down at her paws.

"You ask me to forget the night you and your creature shamed me before my people. That is asking much."

Ratha lifted her head and stared into the glowing orange eyes as she had stared into the heart of the Red Tongue. "Most of those who remember that night are dead now," she said softly. Everyone was still, listening. "There is no shame left in dead memories, Meoran. Now it is only between you and me."

"Ratha, be careful!" hissed Thakur behind her.

"Quiet, herder!" Meoran roared, startling everyone. In the rear of the cavern, a cub began to wail. "You come to me asking to share my meat and my den, yet you speak to me as an equal," Meoran said to Ratha.

"What I ask is to serve again as a herder and work for my meat." She felt her whiskers bristling. "I will obey clan law."

"Obeying clan law means obeying me," Meoran said in his deep voice. "That you must do without question."

"I will obey." Ratha clamped her teeth together, feeling her hatred build again.

"Look at me as you speak and let me see what your words really mean."

Ratha brought her gaze up to his.

The orange eyes semed to blaze out and devour her. She fought back, quietly, deep inside, hoping he couldn't see.

After a long moment, he looked away.

"You will obey me in words, perhaps, and in deeds, but not in heart. Every time I look at you, I will see challenge in your eyes."

"No!" Ratha cried miserably, knowing he saw what she could not hide. She would never forget that he too had bowed his great head before the power of the Red Tongue.

"Listen, you who were once of the clan," he said to those assembled around him. "I will hear other words. Shall she come back among us?"

"Shall we invite a tick into our fur? Or maggots into our meat," cried the young male with Srass's tail and ears.

"Yet, she is young and strong and could bear cubs," Cherfan argued, turning to Meoran. Mutterings grew and spread. Ratha listened and heard with dismay that most were against her. Fessran got up from her crouch against the wall and came toward Ratha. Her joy at seeing Ratha again was so obvious she could not hide it, and it was no further risk of Meoran's wrath to run to Ratha's side and welcome her openly.

Fessran sat close beside her and she felt her warmth and her fast breathing.

"Meoran!" Thakur cried. "Hate begets hate. Let old trails be covered with grass. If you turn her away, you will regret it. I need another herder. Cherfan's cubs need a teacher. The Un-Named are enemy enough. Why make another?"

Meoran raised his paw and pointed at Ratha. "The hate is not mine. She chooses the trail she will run. Look at her!"

Ratha stood, quivering, trying to quench the rage boiling inside her, trying to be the humble herder she was asking him to believe she was. She knew that the voice that had so often lied for once spoke truth.

It was something in her, something that burned deeper than the Red Tongue. It was something she did not want, for it betrayed all her wishes; all her hopes to be united once more with her people.

"Meoran is right," she said in a low voice. "I have chosen the path I run. He has not made me outcast, it is I who have made myself." She raised her head. "I say it in words now so that it will not be said in blood tomorrow. Take care of your people, Meoran."

She turned, choking on her last few words, and the hunger that twisted her belly. For a moment she saw the pain in the faces of her two friends; then she was beyond them and running down the stone slab. She heard Fessran leap up and run after her and she redoubled her speed. She heard panting just behind her and a voice. "Ratha, if you don't stop, I'm going to pull you down like a dappleback!"

Ratha slowed, jogged to a stop.

"Go back, Fessran. He needs all of you," she said.

"He's wrong!" Fessran cried, her face wild with agony. "We need you. For what he has done, I swear I'll seek his blood!"

"No!" Ratha hissed. "He's right, Fessran. Didn't you listen? Your people can only survive if they stay together, under one leader. The Red Tongue has tainted me, made me want something I was never meant for and should never have. You are still free of the taint, Fessran. Go back to Meoran, obey him and your people will live."

"Ratha!"

"Go back, Fessran," she said softly, touching the other with a paw. "And tell Thakur he is forgiven."

Then, before Fessran could speak again, Ratha bounded down the trail, leaving her friend behind. Darkness closed about her, seeming even to block out the stars overhead, and as she ran she felt as though she were plunging down the maw of some hideous thing that had risen up to swallow her.

CHAPTER 13

RATHA FLED to the edge of clan ground. There, by the stream bank amid the trees, she dug a den and lived by herself. Often, as she hunted shrews and bare-tails, she heard the sound of fighting in the meadow and the shrill cries of herders and raiders. She would turn her back on the noise and hunt elsewhere, for she hated both sides equally.

She thought that all the clan would shun her, for her friends would face Meoran's wrath if they came to search for her. That Thakur or Fessran might find their way to her den was too dangerous a hope to allow herself. She thought often of leaving again and becoming a wanderer, without people or territory. There was much to see beyond clan ground and even beyond the land held by the Un-Named. Once she had climbed up a peak and seen a sparkling line of blue where the hazy sky met the land. Wild new smells in the wind blowing into her face made her long to journey that way.

Soon, she knew, she would be gone. There was nothing holding her to this place and its pain. She would run free across new plains and valleys; see beasts that even Bone-chewer had never showed her, and if she ran far and fast enough, she might even escape her memories.

One morning Ratha returned from a night's prowl to find someone waiting at her den. Thakur.

Ratha's throat tightened. She had been longing to see him, but now that he was here and looking into her eyes, there was nothing for her to say.

Thakur lowered his head and nudged something on the ground near his foot. His nose had a smudge of red as he lifted his muzzle. Ratha sniffed and almost drowned in her own saliva, for her hunt had been unsuccessful. He had brought half a liver, fresh enough so that it was still dripping. Ratha dared not ask how much it cost him to take it.

"Meoran will know," he said in response to her look. "I may pay for it later, but that is my choice, yearling."

Ratha ate rapidly, shearing the juicy flesh between her teeth.

"I cannot stay long. Cherfan has taken my place; he does that much for me," Thakur's voice said beside her. "I will come and see you when I can, for as long as you stay near clan ground."

Ratha eyed what was left of the liver, wondering whether to eat it all or save some for later. Something made her glance at Thakur. His eyes and his smell told her he was hungry. There was not much food for the clan these days, yet he shared what there was with her.

"My belly is full," she said, nosing him toward the meat. "Eat."

He snapped at the liver. She listened to him chew and tear the food. When he was finished, she said, "I won't stay past this season."

Thakur's whiskers drooped. "I know, yearling. There is nothing for you here. I was wondering when your paws would seek a new trail now that this one is done."

"This one is done," said Ratha softly. She lifted her eyes to his. "And you, Thakur. Do your paws seek a new trail?"

She could see him retreat before her hopefulness.

"No, yearling. I am where I must be. If you and I were the only ones left, I would run beside you. If there were more of us to herd dapplebacks and fight off raiders, then too I would come. For our people, for Cherfan's cubs, I must stay."

Ratha licked him gently, above the scars on his neck where Meoran had torn him. "I will be here a little longer. Go to the ones who need you. Will you bring Fessran the next time?"

She felt him stiffen and he looked at the ground. Ratha clamped her teeth together, angry at herself for being so stupid.

"She is bitter enough toward Meoran," Thakur said. "I am afraid for her. If she sees you again it may feed her anger."

"And you do not want her to take the same path as I did," Ratha finished for him.

"Yearling, it is bad enough that you must be apart from us."

"Then hide the way to my den and scuff out my tracks in the mud so she may not find them," Ratha said wryly. "And tell her when I go."

"I will."

Thakur lifted his tail and trotted away along the stream bank.

As summer passed into fall, Ratha stayed by herself, alone except for Thakur's visits. Each time he would bring something, and she was grateful even for small rancid scraps, for her catches would not always fill her belly. He would bring news of the clan and how they were faring against the Un-Named. At first Ratha grunted and turned away when he spoke of the others, but she began to listen. She was lonely, and her hatred could not keep her as isolated as she wished.

She knew that Thakur was worried. The Un-Named pressed the herdfolk hard. Many days and nights the clan spent fighting. She also knew that winter would make the raiders hungrier and fiercer. Ratha could see in Thakur's eyes a gnawing fear that his little group, the last of the Named, might not survive.

With fall came winds that lashed the pines and swirled dust and leaves into the air. It ruffled Ratha's coat as if it wanted to seize her and fling her into the sky with the dust and dried leaves. Its moan in her ear made her wild, and the tug at her fur made her want to run until her paws blistered and her breath tore her throat.

She stayed still, watching the clouds build over the mountains. Everything told her it was time to go, yet she stayed, held by an old memory and a forbidden hope.

Thakur continued his visits, glad that she was staying, although puzzled as to why. The news he brought was sometimes joyful and often sad. Another female in the clan had given birth late in the year and the cubs were healthy. But one of Cherfan's youngsters had died trying to help his father defend the herd.

Ratha listened and mourned with Thakur over the loss. But his voice turned into a drone in her ear and her gaze strayed up between the swaying branches to the sky. Why did she even dare to hope that the Red Tongue might return?

Ratha's last hunt had worn her out. She didn't hear the first few droplets pattering down or the thunder's faraway rumble. She slept, nestled deep in her den.

She woke to a flash of light so brilliant she saw it through closed eyes. The noise was more a shock than a sound. The earth seemed to shiver beneath her feet and she flung herself to the rear of the den. Another flash from outside turned the brown soil white and left spots dancing in front of her eyes. There came another sound, a loud cracking and splintering, the sound of a great tree falling.

Ratha crept to the den mouth and peered out. She saw orange flame dive to earth, riding the crown of the toppling giant. The burning tree crashed among its neighbors, setting their branches afire. Smoke boiled up, meeting the rain.

She peered down. The stream below her ran black and glistening.

Ratha crouched at the mouth of her den, her heartbeat rocking her. The fire's fury made her want to run, yet a deeper longing drew her toward it. The line of trees was soon a wall of flame. Ratha could see shadows bounding and leaping; other creatures fleeing the fire.

The Red Tongue, she thought, looking at it. *The Red Tongue has come again.*

She saw deer running, silhouetted against the flames. Small creatures scampered past her, almost between her legs, their fear of the wildfire so great, they took no notice of her. A small snake slithered by, the firelight jeweling its scales. The rain had stopped, and Ratha could hear the crackle and sputter of the fire.

She heard something else and jerked her head around in fright. Coming toward her along the stream bank was a slender shadow.

"Thakur?" Ratha whispered, but her voice stuck in her throat. The stranger's gait told her it wasn't Thakur. Ratha huddled at the entrance, her head low, her ears back. Who else had found her den?

The smoke-blurred form halted. "Ratha?" The voice was Fessran's.

For a moment Ratha was silent, remembering why Thakur had not brought Fessran to see her.

"Ratha!" The voice came again, husky, and trembling. "I followed Thakur the last time he came. I waited until tonight."

"Why did you come, herder?" Ratha heard her own voice say. Fessran was suddenly before her, blocking out the shadowed orange light, replacing it with two burning eyes.

She paced before Ratha, lashing her tail. "A cub has died," she said.

"Thakur told me Cherfan's son was killed by raiders," Ratha said, looking up.

"By Meoran's stupidity! To ask a cub that young to guard the herd, without training! Meoran said there was no time for training. *Ptahh!* I saw the young one pulled down. Meoran was too late to save him. Now Cherfan's son lies with maggots crawling across his bones." Fessran's voice was low and harsh. "All of us will die, one by one.

There is no hope for the Named as long as Meoran leads us." She turned and stared at the fire.

Ratha waited, knowing and dreading what Fessran would say next.

"Meoran's power is ended. You and the Red Tongue are all we have against the Un-Named," Fessran hissed. "Take up your creature, Ratha. I will follow you again."

"No. That trail is closed to me," Ratha answered, but she too could not help staring beyond Fessran into the wall of writhing flame. Waves of heat beat in her face.

"No trail is closed to you if you bear the Red Tongue," Fessran's voice hissed in her ear.

"Go back to your den, herder," Ratha said between her teeth. "Leave the Red Tongue to burn and die."

The other's eyes widened. "Are you afraid to take up your creature again?"

"It never was my creature. Do you understand? *It never was my creature.* Fessran!" she cried as the other spat and leaped away.

"I do not fear the Red Tongue!" Fessran's howl came back.

It is not the Red Tongue I fear. Ratha stared after Fessran.

The bounding figure grew smaller and blacker against the rippling orange flame, curling around the lower branches of the trees, flowing up them like a river into the night sky.

For an instant Ratha could only watch. Then she too was running, stretching her muscles in a half-mad attempt to catch her friend. Fessran plunged toward the fire like a falling stone.

The sound of the fire grew in Ratha's ears until it

was a continuous pounding roar. The wind whipped across her back, feeding the rising flame. A cracking, groaning sound made her look up. Another tree started its majestic fall, fire streaming from its crown. It toppled forward into the meadow, igniting the dried grass. It fell across Fessran's track and Ratha could no longer see her.

She galloped toward the fallen tree, getting as close as she could before the thick smoke drove her back. She retreated, racing along the burning length of the fallen pine. Smoke rolled over her in searing clouds, choking her. As she skirted the tip of the pine, another tree crashed down in front of her, spitting sparks into the grass.

Ratha reared up on her hind legs, trying to see across the fiery barrier. There, deep in the inferno, was a figure whose image shimmered in the waves of heat rising from the flames.

"Fessran!" Ratha screamed and thought she heard an answer. The two trees had fallen toward each other so that they lay with their tips together, their trunks still hidden in the fire that engulfed the trees still standing. The two blazing trunks formed a barrier that trapped Fessran inside. The only way in or out between the two crowns, whose interlocked branches formed a menacing lattice, would be to break them away in order to get through.

Ratha leaped into the air, trying to catch a glimpse of Fessran. She saw her friend on the other side of the barrier, crouching in a patch of grass that had not yet caught. Ratha could hear her coughing.

She flung herself at the maze of burning branches, using her rage to drive away her fear. She sank her teeth into bark, feeling hot resin sting her tongue. She bit through small branches and broke away large ones, ignoring the flames leaping around her. Her mouth was soon bleeding, her paws scorched and blistered, but she attacked the blazing mass again and again as if she had gone mad. Then, suddenly, with a final flurry, she broke through.

For a moment she stared in disbelief. Fessran was there, encircled by flames, yet she carried a burning branch in her mouth. She swung her torch at the fire, trying to drive it away.

Fool! thought Ratha. *The creature does not fear itself.*

"Fessran!" she called and the head bearing the torch came up. Fessran gathered herself and leaped toward Ratha. The fire licked at them from both sides, burning their fur and searing their skin.

"Fool! Mad one!" spat Ratha even before they were out of the flames. "Leave it here with the rest!"

Fessran only curled her lips back, showing Ratha her teeth clamped on the shaft of the branch. Ratha tried to swat it out of her mouth, but Fessran dodged and galloped away. She stood, looking back at Ratha. "Take one for yourself and run with me," she said between her teeth.

Ratha stared at her. The power of the Red Tongue was rising again. There was nothing Ratha could do now to stop it. The night would only end in death, for Meoran would know by now where Fessran had gone and on what errand.

As if in defeat, Ratha lowered her head. With eyes still on Fessran, she seized a flaming branch and broke it off at the base. Despite herself, her heart beat faster. To have her creature once again was a triumph, even though a bitter one. Fessran trotted away, her torch held high. Ratha followed.

CHAPTER 14

THE STORM moved on, leaving the trees burning. Ratha and Fessran stood together on the far side of the stream, sensing that water would check the wildfire's advance. Ratha stuck her torch into the soft mudbank. Fessran still held hers between her jaws. The crackle of their two torches echoed the groaning roar of the wildfire. A touch of gray showed beyond the sparks shooting into the sky.

Ratha gathered a pile of branches, for she knew the torches would soon burn low. Fessran snapped her head around as the wet grass seemed to move in the firelight. Ratha nudged her friend, feeling Fessran shiver. She felt curiously calm.

"Meoran will not come," Fessran hissed. "We will have to seek him out. I grow weary of waiting here and the Red Tongue in the trees burns too close."

"He will be here, herder," Ratha answered. "Once he knows you have come seeking me, he will be on your track."

"I wish him speed," Fessran snarled, her teeth clenched on the torch shaft.

The grass waved again and Ratha heard footsteps. Fessran lunged with the torch as a shadow streaked out of the grass. A scent, made alien by a blast of acrid fear-smell, washed back over Ratha.

"Thakur!" she cried as Fessran froze where she was

standing. Thakur crouched in the shadows, glaring at both of them.

"Put that torch down or I'll take it away from you," Ratha snarled at Fessran. "It would have made more sense to give the Red Tongue to a dappleback. Put it down!"

Fessran obeyed, driving the splintered branch end deep into the mud beside Ratha's. Thakur crept into the circle of torchlight, his head lifted, his belly close to the ground. His ears flattened and his teeth flashed as he spoke.

"I feared you would find your creature again," he said to Ratha. "Meoran comes and the clan is with him. When he heard the sky-fire strike and found Fessran gone, he knew." He stopped, panting. "Run, both of you! Throw down your torches and flee! You escaped him once, you can again. Run!"

"No, Thakur. He will not be turned away as easily as he was the last time. He will hunt us until he has our blood," Ratha said in a low voice.

Thakur almost threw himself at Ratha, his eyes shimmering with rage and agony. "How many will die in this madness? Shall this be the death of my people; the Named killing the Named? Have they earned such a death? If so, tell me how."

Ratha's belly twisted as she watched him.

"Enough, Thakur," Fessran interrupted. "You have no stomach for this. Run away so that at least one will survive as the last of the Named."

Thakur turned from Fessran to Ratha.

"Do as she bids you. Or pick up a torch and stand with us," Ratha said softly.

He cast a look back over his shoulder. "He comes; I

hear him now," Thakur moaned. His voice rose to a hiss. "For the sake of your people, throw the cursed thing down and run!"

Ratha's head turned at the sound of footsteps. Smoke hung beneath the trees, boiling along the ground. There were shadows behind the haze. Amber eyes stared out from a massive shape as gray as the rolling smoke. It became large and solid as Meoran approached.

"Wise words, Thakur Torn-Claw." Meoran thrust his massive head through the haze. One bite from those jaws could crush the skull of a three-horn stag, Ratha knew. He was not one to provoke lightly.

For an instant the three of them stood still facing Meoran and the clan. Then, with a sudden shriek of rage, Fessran snatched up her torch and flung herself at Meoran. He reared, hauling his gray bulk into the air. He struck out with slashing foreclaws as Cherfan and the other young males rushed from behind to guard his flanks. Fessran tumbled away, bleeding. Her torch fell and guttered out.

"So this is the power of the Red Tongue." He sneered and kicked the smoldering branch away from her groping forepaws.

"Meoran, wait!" cried Thakur. "You have destroyed Fessran's creature. There is no need to take her life. Let me talk to her."

Fessran lay on her side, her neck and chest red and ragged. She lifted her head and glared hate at Meoran.

"Talk will do nothing," Meoran snarled. "Her eyes are like the eyes of the other, the she-cub."

Ratha watched Fessran quivering on the ground. She raised her head and met the gray-coat's stare. "The she-cub speaks," she said quietly. "Leave Fessran. She is not the one you seek. I told you before; it is between you and me, Meoran."

The clan leader took one heavy step forward. "Stay back," Ratha heard him growl to Cherfan and the other young males who flanked him. "This one is my meat."

He took another step and then jerked his head back in astonishment. Thakur stood in front of him, blocking his way to Ratha.

"The Named do not bare fangs against the Named," she heard Thakur say. "Do you forget the old laws?"

"*I* make the laws for the clan, Thakur Torn-Claw. Move aside!" Meoran spat at Thakur and struck him in the face. He bowed his head and Ratha saw him lick blood from his nose.

"The Named do not bare fangs against the Named," he said again, so softly that Ratha could barely hear him.

"I don't bother with fangs for such as you. Claws do well enough." Again Meoran lashed out at Thakur, laying the other's cheek open to the bone. Ratha flinched as if she had been the one struck. Something inside her began beating against the walls of its prison. She wanted to shriek at Thakur to stand aside and let her face Meoran alone. She began to tremble, fighting her rage. She knew if Meoran struck Thakur again, that her rage would win.

The two stood apart, stiff-legged and bristling, Thakur still blocking Meoran's way. The wild thing beating inside Ratha's chest was as angry at Thakur as Meoran. What right had he to interfere? Had he not betrayed her the night the Red Tongue died? Meoran's power would have fallen then. And what did he think he was doing now?

Did he think that seeing him bleed would calm her? No! Blood would bring blood.

Meoran raised a paw. Thakur looked at him, his face blank, expressionless. The blow came, with all of Meoran's weight behind it. Thakur reeled and his head snapped around spraying red onto Ratha's coat. He sank down in front of the gray coat.

Fessran shrieked and the cry tore through Ratha. She wrenched her torch from the ground. Meoran was approaching Thakur slowly, almost leisurely, his jaws opening for the killing bite. Flame barred his way. Again he reared striking out with his forelegs to knock Ratha's torch from her jaws as he had Fessran's but Ratha was too quick. The brand scorched his chest and he skittered back, howling.

"Ratha, no!" cried a hoarse voice and she caught a blurred glimpse of Thakur staggering to his feet, his mouth open in pain as the gleaming blood ran from his eye and cheek, dripping along his jaw.

Ratha walked toward Meoran with the torch in her teeth. All those that had clustered around the clan leader melted away. And Meoran cowered, terrified, mouth gaping, sides heaving.

"Close your jaw or your tongue shall meet the Red Tongue," Ratha snarled. He gulped and shut his mouth.

"On your side and offer your throat," Ratha ordered lifting her head with the torch. "Look well, you of the clan. The Law of the Named is now the Law of the Red Tongue."

They crouched together, their bellies to the ground. Cherfan, his mate, Srass's young son and the others all stared helplessly at the scene before them.

In her pride, Ratha answered their gaze and took her eyes from Meoran.

He exploded up at her, fangs seeking her throat. With a violent twist of her head, she swung the torch in a vicious arc and drove it down into those gaping jaws. The impact almost jarred her teeth loose from the shaft. Then, with a strange tearing sound, it gave, throwing Ratha off-balance. The shaft was torn out of her mouth and she was knocked aside.

She had lost, she thought dizzily as she fought to keep her footing. She whirled, ready to meet Meoran in a final desperate attack with teeth and claws. For a moment, she stood, stupefied.

Meoran spun in a circle like a cub chasing its tail. He was a blur of gray with a dancing patch of orange. And he was screaming.

When he paused, exhausted and spent, Ratha could see him and her rage froze into horror. The shaft of the torch protruded from his mouth, jamming it open. The blackened end, streaked with red showed beneath his chin and the Red Tongue curled up around his lower jaw on both sides. With a shock, Ratha realized she had driven the jagged end of the firebrand through the bottom of his mouth. Blood and froth bubbled up around the shaft and sizzled in the flame.

Meoran cried again, a half-choked scream. He pawed at the hated thing, now so terribly embedded in his own flesh. The Red Tongue blazed up wrathfully and Meoran flung himself back and forth as it licked at his face, blistering his jowls.

From the corner of her eye, Ratha saw Thakur lurch through the swirling haze toward Meoran.

"The stream!" he cried. "It dies in water! Seek the stream."

Ratha stood frozen as Meoran staggered toward the creek. She did nothing to help or to hinder him. She no longer wished to be the one to decide how he would die.

Meoran shrieked and reeled back from the bank. Fessran leaped at him from the rushes, blood-spattered, vengeance-hunger hot in her eyes. She struck at the torch shaft penetrating his lower jaw, using the pain to drive him back from the water.

"Eat well, night creature," she crooned to the flame. "He is a feast worthy of your hunger. Dance on his bones, sear his entrails and make him sing as he dies!"

Each time Meoran tried to gain the stream, Fessran was before him, singing a soft song to the flame and striking at Meoran's face. The fur was black on his muzzle and ruff. The skin beneath was starting to swell.

Ratha leaped toward Fessran, but Thakur reached Fessran first. He caught her by the hindquarters and rolled away, dragging her with him. Meoran plunged past Ratha, the fire wreathing his head and neck. He did not reach the stream. He fell, writhing, into the grass. The wind whipped the Red Tongue.

Ratha saw Thakur approach, but the spreading fire drove him back. With a last spasm, Meoran's body became still and started burning.

Thakur stood before the gray-coat's pyre, Fessran's limp form at his feet. Ratha could see him shuddering.

He turned and walked to the pile of branches she had

gathered. He took one in his mouth and lit the end in the fire engulfing Meoran.

Ratha waited, trembling, as he approached her. She could see only one of his eyes and she feared the light there was the glow of madness. The fire was before her now, speaking with a savage voice. She stared into it. She would burn with Meoran.

"Ratha!" came Thakur's voice and she looked into the ravaged face. "Are you ready?"

"To die by the Red Tongue? Yes. It is right. I am glad you will do it." She lifted her chin, baring her throat. She closed her eyes.

"No! Not to die," Thakur hissed. "To live as you told us. By the Law of the Red Tongue."

Her eyes flew open. He was extending the torch shaft to her. "Take it, Giver of the New Law," he said between his teeth.

Ratha bowed her head. "May my teeth rot if I ever take it into my mouth again! Fling it away, Thakur. The way of the Red Tongue is madness."

"Madness it may be," said Thakur, "but it is also life. Look to your people, Giver of the New Law."

Ratha looked past him to the others of the Named who still crouched before her. She saw Cherfan huddling beside his mate, his eyes bright with terror. As Ratha's gaze met his, he lifted his throat and bared it to her. His mate, crouching beside him, did the same.

"No!" Ratha whispered. "I never wished to rule. Meoran!"

"He lies burning in the grass. He will soon be ash and bones. His law is ended. The New Law must rule."

"Then you or Fessran. . . ." Ratha faltered.

"They do not bare their throats to me or to Fessran," Thakur said. "Take the torch and lead your people."

Again Ratha searched the eyes of those crouching before her. More chins were lifted. More throats bared. There were still those with eyes that waited and doubted.

Slowly she opened her jaws and felt Thakur place the branch between her teeth. His grip loosened and she felt the weight in her mouth and saw the Red Tongue dancing before her face. She watched Thakur back away, half of his face crusted and swollen. He too crouched and lifted his chin. She looked to the clan and saw that all throats were bared. She still had a choice. She could fling down the torch and throw herself into Meoran's pyre. Or she could seek the trail that ran back to the mountains, abandoning her people to the ravages of the clanless ones.

The Red Tongue is madness. Thakur's words came back to her again. *It is also life.* He had left one thing unspoken. *Now it is the only life we have.*

She seized the branch, tasting the bitter bark. The wildfire still ate the trees and Meoran's pyre was spreading through the grass.

"This is my creature," Ratha said, holding the flame aloft. "It shall be yours as well. I will teach you to keep it and feed it, for it must never be allowed to die. You shall be called the Named no longer. Now you are the People of the Red Tongue.

She swung the torch around. "Follow me to the dens!" she cried. "Tonight we will give the raiders something new to taste. Do you hear me?"

The answer came back in a roar that deafened her. Her heart beating wildly, she sprang ahead, carrying the Red Tongue, and heard the sound of her people following.

CHAPTER 15

RATHA STARED into the depths of the fire, curling up from its nest of branches into the night sky. It burned loudly, crackling and spitting. The Red Tongue lived both by day and by night, but to Ratha it seemed strongest when it burned against the darkness. It was a creature of the night, yet it obeyed none of the laws of stealth and silence that governed other animals.

Her people gathered around the fire. She could see their green and yellow eyes through the shimmering air and the smoky haze. She took her gaze from the fire's heart, looking away into cool blackness. The Red Tongue's image still danced before her eyes in ghostly form and she shut them. She could not delay long. Her people were waiting. So were the Un-Named who hid in the forest beyond the meadow's edge.

Ratha seized a branch from the pile beside her. It was a good one, she thought, smelling the sharp tang of pitch. She thrust one end into the flame, pulled it out and watched the Red Tongue blossom around the end.

"Fessran," she said between her teeth. Fessran limped to her and took the torch.

"May the Red Tongue be strong tonight," she said before her jaws closed on the shaft.

"Guard the animals well, herder," Ratha answered when her jaws were free. "If my creature holds the Un-Named from our throats tonight, then you shall share the power I hold. I do not forget who fought with me when the Red Tongue's light first shone in the eyes of the clan."

Fessran dipped her torch and carried it away.

I would also have called you friend, for you have been to me like a lair-sister, Ratha thought. *But I dare not do more than acknowledge your loyalty.*

She said another name and lit another torch, watching as the next herder came forward from the circle. He took his brand and followed Fessran.

Again, Ratha plunged a branch into the Red Tongue and passed it to a pair of waiting jaws. One herder after another took their torches and trotted away to take up their station between the herdbeasts and the Un-Named. The orange stars of the firebrands shone up and down the meadow, sending dancing shadows across the grass into the trees. Screams broke from the forest, as if the firelight had reached in and clawed those hiding there. She had heard those screams before. They had risen from her own throat when she hid where the Un-Named were hiding now. But as each herder took his or her place, the cries changed. The screams of hate and triumph faltered as uncertainty crept in. The voices wavered, and Ratha could hear wrath fighting with fear. A new creature stalked the meadow this night and the Un-Named were afraid.

She thought of her old pack, of the young leader, the witless old gray and the others. They would be crouching together beneath the trees and turning to each other with eyes filled with bewilderment. What was this terrible blazing thing that chased the night away and stole the courage from the strongest among them? Where and why did it come? Only one among the Un-Named would know. Ratha stared beyond the fire, trying not to remember

Bonechewer. He might be out there along with the cubs she had birthed with him.

She bared her fangs as if Bonechewer were standing before her, wearing that mocking grin that showed his broken fang. She grabbed a branch, biting so hard that it cracked. She threw it aside, seized another and thrust it into the fire. When she turned, the face before her was Bonechewer's. She felt her tail flare into a brush and all the hairs along her back stiffened.

The eyes were green, not amber and the muzzle bore a long jagged wound, still swollen and crusted.

"Thakur," she said and let all her hairs lie flat. "Are you the last?"

He approached, his eyes puzzled and wary.

No wonder, she thought. *I must have looked ready to attack him.*

"All the others have taken their torches, Giver of the New Law," he said, but he did not open his mouth for the fire-brand as the others had.

"You may go without one if you wish," Ratha said. She placed the branch back in the fire. "It must hurt you to open your mouth."

"It will take much time to heal," said Thakur. "Meoran did not keep his claws clean."

"Once you feared my creature," Ratha said softly.

"I still fear it. I fear it more now than I ever did."

He looked steadily at Ratha, and there was something in his eyes and his smell that chilled her.

"I mocked you for your fear," she said. "I will not mock you again."

"I will take a torch," Thakur answered. "I will need it

when the raiders strike. But first, Giver of the New Law, I will show you your people."

She wrinkled her brows at him, dismayed and puzzled by his words. Now was the time to prepare for the attack that might break from the forest at any instant. It was not the time to follow Thakur about the meadow to see whatever he might have to show her. She was about to refuse and send him back to the herd when the thought came almost unbidden into her mind.

He is the wisest among us. I turned his wisdom away when I should have listened. Now, perhaps, it is too late, but I will listen this time.

She let the fire burn by itself and followed Thakur. He did not lead her directly to the nearest torchbearer. Instead he walked toward a flame flickering at the far end of the meadow. He approached from behind and downwind so that the torchbearer could neither see nor smell him. He was almost within reach of the herder's tail when the other leaped up and whirled around, swinging the firebrand. The flame roared and Thakur flattened in the grass. He rolled away, leaving Ratha facing the torchbearer. A paralyzing fear shot through her as she saw her own creature in the jaws of another. She who had tamed the Red Tongue could only cower before it in the instant before the torchbearer stopped his assault.

Beneath the fear was anger. Thakur had deliberately startled the young herder and then scuttled aside, letting her be the one to face the attack. He knew there would be no real danger once the torchbearer recognized her.

The young face was one she knew well; even too well. The torchbearer was the son of Srass, the old herder she had seen killed in the meadow. She remembered the old herder's face at the last moment of his life; as the gray-coat ripped flesh from his quivering flank and the silver's teeth crushed his skull. Pain and rage distorted the ugly muzzle but it was still Srass's face until he died. Now she looked at the herder who was Srass's son and saw nothing she knew. The red light that shone from the torchbearer's eyes came from a fire that burned within as well as without. It was a new kind of wildness and a new kind of savagry she had never seen in those who used only teeth and claws.

She would have whimpered and backed away, but pride and anger held her where she stood. The torchbearer lowered his brand and his face became again the face of Srass's son with all its lop-eared homeliness. But Ratha knew she would never be able to look at him again without remembering the change the fire had cast over him.

Is this how I looked when I stood before the clan with the Red Tongue in my jaws?

"Keep your guard, herder," she said at last. "We should not have startled you."

At the corner of her eye, she saw Thakur rise from his crouch and shake dry grass from his fur. Howls echoed across the meadow from the forest, and she saw the young herder turn to challenge the hidden enemy, the fire's glow leaping in his eyes.

"Come, Giver of the New Law," said a voice very near her. "I am still without a torch."

Ratha's fury rose and spilled over. "Thakur, I could feed you the Red Tongue as I did Meoran or have you gutted like a herdbeast!"

He looked back at her and the green of his eyes seemed to swallow her. "You could, Giver of the New Law. You may."

The reply enraged her further, but she could do nothing except fume and bristle. She knew she could not strike him. "Why do you show me this?" she burst out at last. "You know as well as I that we must keep the Red Tongue if we are to live."

"Look inside yourself for the answer," he said. He paused. "I see you are angry, so I know you have found it." He trotted back toward the fire she had left burning at the center of the meadow.

She ground her teeth together as if she were slicing meat. He knew as well as she that they could not turn aside from this new trail. What was he trying to do then?

One must know the path one runs even if the ground underfoot is not as one chooses, she thought and the answer almost came in Thakur's voice. Her ears flattened. She was not grateful. Sometimes it was easier to take a path not knowing what lay underfoot or ahead.

The cries from the forest rose in pitch and intensity. Soon the Un-Named would begin their attack. The hair rose on Ratha's neck, letting the cold of the night onto her skin. Would the Red Tongue save her people? They were still few and the Un-Named many. Only when morning came would she know, if she herself were still alive.

Another thought rose from beneath her anger and it too seemed to speak in Thakur's voice. Even if the Red Tongue saved her people, they would never be the same. Once they were the Named, under Baire and then Meoran. Now they would be what she called them, a new name given without realizing what it truly meant. The People of the Red Tongue. And now she had seen the first of her new breed and now she knew.

As she returned to her fire, she passed other herdfolk. She approached them openly, letting herself be seen and smelled. Perhaps what she had seen in the young herder's eyes was only anger at being startled. Perhaps it was only the brief intensity of fear that changed him and not the stamp of the Red Tongue. It was a new hope, but it did not live long enough to grow. Each of the torchbearers, even though unprovoked, held traces of the same look she had seen in the face of Srass's son. Violent and gentle alike were all transformed by the blazing power they held between their jaws.

This is what we are, Ratha thought as she went from one to the other. *This is what we are now.*

Thakur was standing beside the fire when she returned. She lit a branch for him and gave it to him without words, feeling as though she were kicking mud into a clear pool even though she must drink from it later. He lowered his brand and trotted away, becoming one more of the flickering orange dots scattered about the meadow.

Again the raider's cries swelled from the meadow. Ratha lifted her muzzle, her ears quivering. She saw the circle of herders about her tighten, bunching their beasts in the center. The torches swung outward.

She seized a branch of her own, lit it and left the fire to burn in its dirt clearing. As she reached the outer edge of the circle, the attack began.

She had hoped that the Red Tongue in the forest would have frightened the raiders away, but she knew that hate and hunger were as strong as fear. Her worries were confirmed when a scout reported that the Un-Named were circling around the areas that were still burning. He had spotted one group of the raiders making their way along a stream bank, making her suspect that there was at least one among the Un-Named who had some knowledge of the Red Tongue. She did not admit to herself that she knew who that one might be.

Shadows that had been as still as rocks or bushes against the trees crept swiftly into the meadow. They streamed from the forest, eyes and teeth glinting as they emerged into the open.

Ratha planted her torch and looked about her in all directions. There are too many, she thought, feeling her heartbeat shake her. *Even with the Red Tongue, we are too few.* The herders about her seemed to share her dismay, for she heard whimpers and saw bodies huddling together. And the raiders seemed to sense it too. They came faster, their hissing grew more vicious. And then they were no longer creeping but charging; black forms bore down on the herders from all sides. Ratha seized her torch again and thrust it outward with the rest. The attack gathered speed. The torchbearers waited.

Trembling, Ratha tried to peer beyond the circle of orange light. The raiders were still coming but the attack was faltering, its edges growing ragged as many of the Un-Named hesitated before the firelight. Ratha could hear individual voices rise above the yowling as the Un-Named leaders tried to drive their packs to fight. There was fear in those cries as well as rage. Fights began in the Un-Named ranks. Those who sought to flee the new power battled with those who forced them to attack. The mass of the enemy became a churning moonlit sea, turning in on itself.

It quieted. The howls of those who had fled faded into the forest. The torchbearer's brands shone into fewer eyes, but in those faces hate ruled over fear. The first attack had failed. The second was about to begin.

The herders faced the Un-Named across an open swath of meadow. With a howl that rose to a shriek, a shape flew from the Un-Named ranks. Firelight flashed on a silvery pelt and Ratha recognized the jaws that had crushed Srass's skull. The silvercoat drew the others after him and the Un-Named surged forward to meet the herders.

Torches fluttered and roared. Bared fangs were met with fire. The attackers reeled back howling from the touch of the flames and some carried the terrible creature away with them, smoldering as hot coals and ash in their fur ate into their flesh. Some went mad with fear and lay thrashing and frothing while their companions trampled them.

Ratha whirled to face the snarling silver. She dodged as he flung himself at her and dragged her torch across his face over his eye. The charred wood snapped, the end falling onto his foreleg. Blind and fear-crazed, the silver lurched away.

Ratha saw two other herders beating him across the back with their brands as he fled. She lost sight of him.

The branch in her mouth was now only glowing coals, creeping toward her whiskers. She dropped it and scuffed dirt on it. Other brands were also burning down or had broken against Un-Named ribs. She saw torchbearers slashing with fangs and claws and blood gleaming red in the firelight. She ducked a raider's strike and ran to the bonfire. She lit a new torch and passed it to a wounded herder who carried only a broken stub, too dazed to throw the useless thing away. His eyes brightened; he snatched the new light and plunged back into the fray. As she stood panting, Fessran came alongside.

"Giver of the New Law, let me carry new torches to the ones who need them," she said. "That is not your duty."

"It shall be yours, Fessran. You are now the keeper of the Red Tongue and its cubs. If it still burns when dawn comes, its tending shall be your honor and your duty."

Fessran passed her a lighted branch. "Go and drive the Un-Named back. The Red Tongue will eat their bodies when the sun rises."

Ratha charged back into the fighting, her roar spilling from between her teeth. She leaped at the nearest enemy, raking him and searing him. Cries of rage and triumph broke from the weary herders, and they flung themselves on the raiders with renewed fury.

The Un-Named began to fall back. Slowly they gave way. They fought only to save themselves, and no longer tried to break through the herder's circle to attack the milling herdbeasts. The mass of the enemy began to thin and Ratha saw more moonlit forms streak away into the trees.

She drove her torch into the ground beside a stiffening body and let out a mocking yowl. "They run!" she cried. "They are as cubs before the power of the Red Tongue. Let them taste it once again before the forest shelters them. To me, my people!"

The enemy's ranks wavered and broke. The herders bore down on them and many cried their death scream before they reached the forest.

And then, all at once, it was over and the night fell quiet except for the soft screams of the wounded and dying.

Ratha stood with the torch guttering in her mouth, staring across the emptied meadow. Her heart gradually stopped its pounding. She had won. After such a beating as they had taken tonight, the Un-Named would not come again. The little flock of herdbeasts would grow large and cubs would play in the high grass, well-fed and free of fear.

She plodded back across the meadow, her feet dragging from weariness. Now there was no need to run fast. When she reached the bonfire, Fessran took the burning stick from her jaws and returned it to the flames. Others followed in Ratha's wake and gave their brands back to Fessran. There was one more thing to be done and for that they needed their jaws free.

Among the Un-Named dead were the wounded, writhing in pain or trying to drag their shattered bodies from the meadow. Ratha watched her people walk among them. The herders vented their still-smoldering anger on the bleeding ones, clawing and slashing at them until they were torn lumps of flesh in which the breath trembled one last time and left. Ratha watched grimly. She had not given the order to mutilate the wounded, but she had not forbidden it either. She remembered how the raiders had eaten from Srass while he still lived. She watched, but took no part for the taste of blood mixed with the bitterness of charred bark was still thick in her mouth.

"Giver of the New Law," a voice said, and she looked up into Thakur's eyes. They were lit not by the firebrand, but by the faint glow of dawn over the forest.

"I am weary," she said crossly. "If you wish to show me more of the change in my people, you will wait until I have slept."

"It is not your people I wish to show you," Thakur answered.

Ratha's eyes narrowed. "One of the Un-Named?"

"One of the wounded raiders. He lives. He asks for you. He knows your name."

She felt a sudden chill in her belly. It spread along her back, down the insides of her legs. Only one among the raiders knew her by her name. She had thought he was far away and safe on his own land.

"Lead me to where he lies," she said roughly.

Thakur took her to the edge of the forest, to the long faint shadow of a small pine standing apart from the rest. The shadow grew darker and the grass lighter as the sky turned from violet to rose and then to gold. Two herders sat together, eyeing the wounded raider who lay beneath the pine. At her approach they uncurled their tails from about their feet and bared their fangs at the raider.

"No," Ratha said sharply. "There will be no killing until I command it."

She and Thakur approached the Un-Named one. A muscle jerked beneath the red-smeared copper pelt. Ratha heard a voice, hoarse and weak.

"Does she come, brother? I grow too weary to lift my head."

"She comes," Thakur answered and Ratha felt him nudge her ahead while he stayed behind. She stepped into the coolness beneath the trees. The raider's muzzle pulled back scorched and swollen lips in a mocking grin. There was the broken lower fang.

"Come here, Ratha," Bonechewer said, bloody froth dribbling from his mouth." "Let me see the one who now leads the clan. Ah, yes," he said as she neared him. "You have grown strong and fierce. You will be a better leader than Meoran. What a fool he was to drive you out! What a fool!"

Ratha nearly pounced on him. She jumped and landed with her forepaws almost touching his face. She glared down at him. "Why did you come? Why?"

"To see you," he answered, gazing up at her. "Perhaps to die at your fangs."

"Bonechewer, stop mocking me, or I swear by the Red Tongue, you will have your wish! You told me you would no longer run with the Un-Named. Did your land yield too little to feed you this season?"

"No." He coughed and his chest heaved. Ratha could see why the blood seeped from his mouth. The lower part of his chest was crushed and caved in. Blood welled there too and the flat, jagged end of a broken bone showed in the wound.

"I'm a mess, aren't I, clan cat? That's what I get for leading a pack of cowards. They fought me to escape the Red Tongue and when I went down, they trampled me." He grinned again, grimacing with pain. "Then your herders came along and played with me for a while. Not the death I would have chosen."

"Why did you come?" Ratha's voice grew soft and trembled, despite her wish to hate him.

"After I drove you away and the cubs left, there was nothing to hold me to my land. When the Un-Named came through again, I went with them."

"The cubs left?"

"Yes. You were right about them. I could not believe I fathered such a litter. I could scarcely keep them from each other's throats or from mine either. They are out there, the savage little killers."

"Did Thistle-chaser live?"

"Yes, she lives, half-mad as she is. You may see her in the packs if the Un-Named are foolish enough to venture here again." He coughed and shuddered. "I have seen you again, Ratha. That is all I dared ask for and all I wish."

"Is that all you want from me, Bonechewer?" she asked, trying to suppress the sudden grief that welled up inside her.

"If your fangs would help me toward the dark trail, I would not resent it," he answered. "Or if you cannot kill me, tell another to do it."

Ratha swallowed, barely able to speak. She looked toward Thakur. He rose and came toward Bonechewer. Her flank brushed his as the two passed.

"Away, herders!" she cried at the two still sitting and staring. "There is no need for you here." They whirled about and dashed away. She followed at a trot then slowed to a walk, watching her people dragging the Un-Named corpses into the dirt clearing where the fire burned. Fessran and the others who helped her were piling fuel on the flames, making them bright and hot, eager to consume the bodies. At the other end of the meadow, the dapplebacks grazed peacefully, showing no sign of the night's terrors. Ratha let her eyes rest on that scene and turned her back on the fire.

Grass rustled behind her and a familiar smell was with her. Not until Thakur was beside her did she turn her head.

"I held my brother's throat until he was still," he said softly.

"Did he say anything more?"

"Only that clan leaders are not forbidden to grieve."

Ratha's jaw dropped. "That arrogant mangy son of a scavenger! He thought I would cry for him? He thought . . . I would . . . cry . . . for. . . ." Her voice broke into a keening wail as her sorrow escaped at last. She stamped, lashed her tail and flung her head back and forth. All the rage, hate and sorrow she had felt and kept hidden now took her and shook her until she was left panting and exhausted. She stumbled to Thakur and laid her head against his chest. "I am even more a fool," she muttered, her sides still heaving. "A clan leader should not bawl like a cub."

"No one was watching," Thakur chided gently.

At last she lifted her head and gazed across the meadow. There the dapplebacks grazed, with the herders around them. Soon there would be three-horns and other kinds of beasts, for Thakur and others in the group were good at catching and taming them.

My people will survive, Ratha thought. *They have changed, even as I have, but they will survive. That is what matters.*

"I left my brother under the pine," Thakur said. "Is that what you wished?"

"It is. His bones shall lie there and those who pass shall honor them." Ratha drew a breath. "Once I hated him. Now there is nothing left to hate. He was my mate, Thakur, with everything that it meant. I will not soon forget him."

"Nor I, Ratha."

She turned to Thakur, to the green-eyed face that echoed the one whose amber eyes were closed in death. No. He was not Bonechewer, and he too evoked memories that, if anything, were more painful. She would take no mate until the raw memories were soothed and healed by time. But, she sensed, he would be a wise and comforting friend and would run beside her on the rough new trail that lay ahead of her and her people.

It would not be an easy path, and the dangers that lay there might be beyond her capability to face. Yet ragged and weary as she was, she lifted her muzzle in voiceless challenge to those things still unknown.

She was Ratha, she-cub, herder of three-horns, tamer of the Red Tongue and leader of her people.

Whatever came, she would meet it with all the strength and wit she could command. One thing she knew; as long as she and the Red Tongue lived, her people would survive.

Triumph overcame her weariness. She lifted her tail and trotted after Thakur as he walked across the meadow toward the rising sun.

You'll fall in love with these new

Laurel-Leaf

romances!

MODEL BEHAVIOR
by John McNamara

Shortly after the disappearance of his idol–a pretty teenage model who was in town on a commercial shoot–Dave Callahan begins to wonder: Why does the new girl at school look so familiar?

LOVE STORY: TAKE THREE
by Gloria Miklowitz

Now that Valerie's landed a part in a TV pilot, everyone treats her like a big success. But Valerie just wants to be a normal teenager, especially with her new boyfriend Tom, who's still in the dark about Valerie's career. Can Valerie fall in love with Tom and still keep her secret?

For a complete listing of these titles, plus many more, write to us at the address below and we will send you the Dell Readers Service Listing.